We Are of Dust

CLARE COOMBES

The Liverpool Publishing Company

First published in Great Britain in 2018 by The Liverpool Publishing
Company Ltd
Copyright © The Liverpool Publishing Company Ltd 2018
Cover design: Bodhi Design
Editing: Matthew McKeown

ISBN print: 978-1-9993005-0-0
ISBN eBook: 978-1-9993005-1-7

**The Liverpool Publishing Company is an imprint of
The Liverpool Editing Company Ltd**

BY THE SAME AUTHOR

Definitions

WE ARE OF DUST

Table of Contents

COVER

COPYRIGHT

BY THE SAME AUTHOR

DEDICATION AND POEM

CHAPTER ONE - The Girl and the Trip to the Camp

CHAPTER TWO - The Boy Learns a Lesson in Courage

CHAPTER THREE - The Girl and the Art of Lying

CHAPTER FOUR - The Boy and the Fire

CHAPTER FIVE - The Girl and the Glass

CHAPTER SIX - The Boy on the Balcony

CHAPTER SEVEN - The Girl goes Submarine

CHAPTER EIGHT - The Boy and the Final Dance

CHAPTER NINE - The Girl and the Boy on the Train

CHAPTER TEN - The Boy and the Girl on the Deck of the Ship

CHAPTER ELEVEN - The Girl tries to get off the Ship

CHAPTER TWELVE - The Boy and the Pact

CHAPTER THIRTEEN - The Girl takes a Gamble

CHAPTER FOURTEEN - The Boy is reunited with an Old Friend

CHAPTER FIFTEEN - The Girl is reunited with an Old Friend

CHAPTER SIXTEEN - The Boy hears talk of a Monster

CHAPTER SEVENTEEN - The Girl finds herself Hiding Again

CHAPTER EIGHTEEN - The Boy makes a Decision

CHAPTER NINETEEN- The Girl is given a Choice

CHAPTER TWENTY - The Boy and the Tortures of the Past

CHAPTER TWENTY-ONE - The Girl and the Weight of the Guilt

CHAPTER TWENTY-TWO - The Boy learns that Trust needs to be Earned

CHAPTER TWENTY-THREE - The Girl and the Red Lipstick

CHAPTER TWENTY-FOUR - The Boy and the Drawings

CHAPTER TWENTY-FIVE - The Girl and the Hunger for Identity

CHAPTER TWENTY-SIX - The Boy and the Body

CHAPTER TWENTY-SEVEN - The Girl and the City of Blinding Lights

CHAPTER TWENTY-EIGHT - The Boy, a Burial at Sea and a possible Mutiny

CHAPTER TWENTY-NINE - The Girl and a Thing of Two Halves

CHAPTER THIRTY - The Boy and the Bad News

CHAPTER THIRTY-ONE - The Girl and the New Plan

EPILOGUE

ABOUT THE AUTHOR

AUTHOR'S NOTE

Q AND A WITH HERBERT KARLINER

ACKNOWLEDGEMENTS

FOR ALL THOSE WHO STILL SEEK SAFETY

Fascism: I sometimes fear...

I sometimes fear that
people think that fascism arrives in fancy dress
worn by grotesques and monsters
as played out in endless re-runs of the Nazis.

Fascism arrives as your friend.
It will restore your honour,
make you feel proud,
protect your house,
give you a job,
clean up the neighbourhood,
remind you of how great you once were,
clear out the venal and the corrupt,
remove anything you feel is unlike you...

It doesn't walk in saying,

"Our programme means militias, mass imprisonments,
transportations, war and persecution."

Michael Rosen

CHAPTER ONE

The Girl and the Trip to the Camp

8th November 1938

The clear winter sun reflected off Alice's handlebars as she cycled along the wide roads, with grand old houses giving way to smaller apartments where the city began to close around a shrinking blue sky. She was trying not to go too fast or too slow. Anything out of the ordinary could prompt suspicion. She let the pedals spin freely from time to time, shuddering whenever her bike clattered noisily against the cobbled streets.

Each time she left the house – and her sister, hiding in the attic – Alice was forced to ride in circles from Charlottenburg. She travelled across a zig-zagging range of different areas, occasionally doubling back on herself. It was through this painstaking process, in her part-time role as an ordinary German girl, that she became familiar with much of Berlin. She maintained a steely, purposeful exterior, but inside her heart was pounding. Her blonde braids beat gently against her back.

She braved the commotion of trams and motorcars to reach the Kurfürstendamm and its stretch of luxury shop fronts. Men in suits and women with coiffed hair walked with their heads held high, their shoes tapping at the busy pavement in carefree rhythms. Wealth and privilege hung in the air, punctuated by the rich scents of husky furs and branded leather. Huge department stores – the same ones that the Party had denounced as vices of decadent and destructive Jews – remained exactly as they had been before, only now they were seized and placed under new owners with unfamiliar names. Many of those who lost their businesses in the commercial districts of the city became part of the worried and hurried throngs of Hackescher Markt, the Jewish Quarter. This was where smells of cheap meat and expensive cloth mingled to create an acrid, overpowering atmosphere that permeated through the sprawl of cluttered spaces. She didn't want to linger here too long. Not while the identity papers in her pocket remained the only barrier between herself and a permanent stay.

What unnerved her most was the quiet where there should have been bustling noise; the murmurs where there used to be shouts. Yet she knew it was an area where she was unlikely to be followed. It was a safe route. Before she started on the final stretch of streets, she spotted a large piece of graffiti scrawled brazenly across a shop wall, right next to its white J. It was a hangman cartoon of a man with a crooked nose. Another had been crudely shaped to resemble a woman. There were smaller figures, too, presumably their children. The blood-red lines of their sagging bodies glistened, ominously fresh. She told herself that it was just a tasteless prank perpetrated by bored Hitler Youth, likely no more than children themselves, looking for something to do on a cold Saturday morning; but that didn't stop the sweat from trickling freely down her back.

She paused to let a group of Hitler Jungvolk pass. Over a dozen children, some as young as ten, out on patrol, like little wind-up soldiers. Their leader set them off on a parade routine, which she, along with everyone else on the pavement, acknowledged with stiff salutes as the boys passed them by. Her arm soon began to ache in the chilling wind.

The tension in her arm matched that of the city. The threat was everywhere; from the Jungvolk, with their loud marches and louder uniforms, to the SS and their beetle-black regalia and lightning bolt insignias, stomping their mark through the streets. Worse still was the Gestapo, in their suits and swishing raincoats, biding their time, listening for whispers. With food in such short supply, there was no shortage of citizens willing to put a little extra on the table by turning someone in.

She continued on to the station, to catch the S-Bahn to Oranienburg; her aim being to spend the journey looking at no one, while resisting the train's attempts at rocking her into a state of vulnerable lethargy.

The final stages, the long walk to the camp from the station, were devoid of colour. Trees and flowers had disappeared. However sparse the season had already made them, they were now gone completely. In their place were barbed wire fences. Nature's lush, inviting gardens replaced by a brutal man-made ecosystem of concrete and steel. The building loomed ahead, its bright lights matching the lamps set around the confining barricades.

The temperature seemed to have dropped, making the air difficult to breathe, and suddenly the world looked a little darker. She wore one of her best dresses. It had been her mother's, and she couldn't bring herself to sell it. Its blue flowers contrasted starkly against her surroundings as she moved steadily across the dry landscape.

When the cabin that held the officers became visible, she took out a mirror and checked her face. Too pale. She had to look important, well-fed and definitely nothing like an undernourished fugitive. With shaky fingers, she took her brooch and pierced the skin of her thumb with the pin. The pain caused her to clench her teeth. She dabbed red on her cheeks and lips. Now all she could do was think about putting one foot in front of the other until she reached the entrance to Sachsenhausen. Her legs trembled. Her heart hammered against her chest.

A dog barked.

'Halt!' A guard stormed towards her, a shadow against the setting sun, holding up a rifle threateningly.

'I want to see the commandant,' she replied, lifting her chin and meeting his gaze.

His mouth curled into a smile. The oval of his jawline tightened as he took in each part of her body. Beads of perspiration ran like fingertips down her back as the dog snarled and pulled at its lead. The guard lowered the rifle, holding out his free hand in a gesture that would have looked friendly under different circumstances.

'Papers!' he snapped.

Handing them over, she heard a smattering of gunfire in the distance.

He frowned, examining them. She prayed that today's identity would hold up to scrutiny. The people she had paid, and paid well, said that it would. It had to. She was running out of both money and things to sell. To have one identity for too long was incredibly dangerous, but the group that was helping her could only do so much with limited funds.

Max would be furious if he could see her at this moment. She could picture him, turning from kindly, comical uncle figure to the cerebral strategist that he almost seemed born to become. He would berate her for putting them all at risk.

'There's someone I need to see,' she said, forcing herself to smile sweetly as she fiddled with the neckline of her dress, just enough to flash the gold that was tucked away inside. Her mother's brooch.

The soldier's eyes were grey and merciless, but the sight of the jewellery caused something to sparkle in them. He blinked, and then looked around to see if anyone was watching. The other guards were too far away to detect what was happening.

'Name?' he asked.

'Albert Sommer,' she said.

The guard paled visibly under the harsh spotlights. 'The commander won't respond well to such a request,' he finally said.

The dog strained to get at her. The guard spoke cautiously, but his eyes were still on the glint of gold around her neck.

She looked beyond him, to the red and pink of the setting sun bleeding through the thick iron gates of the camp.

Her father was mild-mannered and gentle in everything he did. From balancing a younger Alice and her sister on his feet as they waltzed across the room, to his delicate lab work which required precise calculations and a steady hand. The stress of recent years had put him in poor health, though. The Nazis had aged him before his time. They had transformed his laughter lines into scarred depictions of strain, contorted by the tight, permanently downward curve of his mouth. During the height of the depression, when food and money were scarce, her father had told her with such conviction that the future had to be better for Germany. Now he was here.

The barrack huts were visible from where she stood. A few figures, stooped and shaven-headed, moped around them. Barely moving. Barely human. She tried not to think about the stories of this place – about the people who disappeared, or the ashes that were posted out to families.

Alice turned back to the guard, who was still fidgeting, pondering what to do, when the sound of tyres against the rough gravel ground pierced their awkward silence. They both stood frozen as a Mercedes pulled up close by. A rear door was thrown open and a man was bundled out. Three Gestapo agents emerged from the other side. Alice's heart stopped as she watched one of them turn in her direction. His frown was discernible and familiar, even from the distance between them.

It was too late to run.

The taste in her mouth was bitter and sharp as the man, in his dark suit and long coat, headed towards them. He offered a salute to the soldier and glared at Alice.

'Would you mind helping my men get that Red processed?' he asked the guard politely, handing him a cigarette.

'Another Commie,' the guard replied gruffly, taking the cigarette and glancing in the direction of the camp as the prisoner was being dragged off by the other two agents. 'What about her?' he nodded in the direction of Alice. 'She's asking to see Albert Sommer.'

'I'll handle that,' he said.

The guard looked at her again. He seemed unsure about taking orders from a Gestapo agent on his own turf, but after a moment's deliberation he shuffled off towards the others.

Alice was left with Franz. The previously skinny, freckled Franz; her old neighbour, her old friend, who had morphed into the dreaded figure that everyone called 'the Blond Reaper'. She spat at his feet.

He ignored the insult, addressing her in a low voice. 'Are you trying to get us all killed?'

She turned away.

He brought his face close to hers, and a strong whiff of leather and soap caused her to recoil. Such items had disappeared from the lives of ordinary people that could no longer afford even the smallest luxuries. Scents that were commonplace to the point of mundane had come to represent trappings of power and privilege.

'What name are you under today?' He held out his hand.

She passed him the documents. His lips curled into a thin smile as he appraised them.

'These are good. You must have paid a lot.' His eyes flickered between her and the papers. 'Alice, my job is to look for people like you,' he said, handing them back. 'You know this. I can only do so much for you and Max. You need to leave, immediately.'

'I heard that they were letting people out of the camps if they agreed to leave the country,' she said.

'That doesn't apply to your father,' Franz said, shaking his head.

'You know he isn't well enough to work.'

'He isn't working. He has special privileges and is being taken care of.'

She caught a brief glimpse of the old Franz as he attempted a reassuring smile.

'Franz, you know my father, you know me-'

'Yes, and you use this to compromise me every day of my career.'

The friendly grin she knew so well was replaced by a hard line. The shadows beneath his eyes made him look older than his nineteen years.

He took her gently by the shoulders, the closeness of his face bringing back memories of a first kiss. How much she had trusted him in that moment, when they were alone in the Tiergarten, fresh pine sticking to their skin; but in the end, Franz knew better than to risk his progression through the Party for a mischling. A half-breed. An Un-German.

'I'm so sorry for your career,' she taunted.

His icy glare made the muscles in her stomach clench. She imagined the terror that others must feel when being interrogated by him.

'I am running out of patience, Alice,' he said matter-of-factly. 'Not to mention the means to protect you.'

'Just as well that Papa never said such things to you, Franz,' she said. 'No, instead he fed you, clothed you, read with you-'

He put his hand to her mouth, and for a second she saw a flash of humanity – the bedraggled, malnourished little boy who used to sit at her family's table, gratefully wolfing down platefuls of food – but then just as quickly the child was gone, replaced by an agent spinning her around and frogmarching her back towards the woods.

'Alice, take your sister and get out of the city before tomorrow night,' he implored. 'I promise you, with what is about to come, your father is safer here.'

CHAPTER TWO

The Boy Learns a Lesson in Courage

9th November 1938

The group took long, confident strides along the Unter den Linden, their boots beating down on the pavement in unison. The dark shadows they cast were a menacing presence in the decreasing light of a short winter's day. The boys marched in order of seniority, with those of higher ranking positioned at the front. Kurt was forced to bring up the rear – not even so much as a flag bearer – alongside his old friend and neighbour, Alfons Lehmann, who as usual was not making any effort to stay in time with the others.

They each wore the HJ winter uniform, consisting of a dark pullover, black pants and a ski cap. Even their accessories were identical, from the cross-strap to the armband, all the way down to the footwear. The neck scarf itched at Kurt's neck and the belt buckle dug into his waist, but still he was grateful for them. As long as he was in uniform, no one could tell that he lived in the worst of the run-down Litchtenburg areas – a place where smoke and sewage stood in for air and greenery. His mind drifted to the pockets of communists that were still offering futile resistance there; and then to his father, who had given refuge and support to communists and Jews alike, and what a fat lot of good that had done him.

He pushed thoughts of his family to one side. The brisk pace was becoming exhausting, even for Kurt; and this was after he had passed a fitness test which included a very long march of over ten miles, while carrying a knapsack loaded with breadbags, zeltbahns and tornisters – exactly the same as what was expected of the Wehrmacht. He was also required to pack a gas mask, although the only smells that they needed protecting from here were the distinctive scents of the city: fumes from the buses and trams, and burning steel and setting concrete from new buildings growing around them.

The paint on his palms stuck uncomfortably to his skin. He tried to rub it off in flakes. Alfons turned his head and tutted. Kurt had still not gotten used to his friend's cropped hair. After years of looking at wild blonde curls, it was jarring to see it shaved short at the sides and parted in the middle. In that moment of observation, it once again occurred to Kurt just how easily he could satisfy the demands being made on him by their corps leader. He lifted his fist and clenched his knuckles. One swift move was all it would take to prove himself. He knew that he would never be able do it, though.

They were to be treated as a threat – even the children. That's what Peter Fischer had said. He was older than them, and resembled Hitler in volume and Himmler in appearance. His regular rants about 'Un-German' activities were almost perfect mimicries of the

Fuhrer's public addresses, and his small, dark eyes glinted through tiny spectacles with such a fury that it was impossible not to see the likeness of the revered head of the SS. Every speech he made – usually about how they were duty-bound to represent the master race a certain way – was accompanied by a launch of indiscriminately aimed saliva missiles. Even the most fanatical members made sure to stand a few paces back. Alfons had nicknamed him 'Spitler'.

Despite being smaller and thinner than the other boys his age, Alfons was still capable of matching them in all physical activities. This gained him the reluctant admiration of the group, as well as the scorn of Peter – and he was already unpopular with him thanks to a reluctance to engage in fist fights. Alfons was more interested in books than batons, and he didn't care who knew it, either; just as he didn't bother to hide the fact that he only joined because his father's position at the factory had been threatened. He had, however, gone too far on this particular morning.

While Kurt hadn't exactly been happy about wasting time painting messages to the Jews on a shop wall at the Hackescher Markt, when Peter encouraged him to keep going with the hangman cartoon until it depicted a whole family – causing something to twist in his stomach – he hadn't said anything. He merely continued working without comment.

'Children?' Alfons' voice had leapt from the group. 'You're drawing hang-man children?'

'It's a warning,' Peter had stepped forward, his voice booming and spittle flying. 'The Jew is no less devious in infancy than in adulthood. They need to know that we know this – that we will not accept them and their poisonous ways. They must leave.'

'Why do you all believe this shit? Don't you question anything?' Alfons threw his arms out to the group.

His words were met with a silence that sent a chill down Kurt's spine. Within seconds, a circle had formed around Alfons. A wall of black uniforms penning him in. Peter walked over to him, and Kurt instinctively moved to lunge forward and protect his friend; but then instead of the violence that would typically follow such an outburst, Peter simply leaned forward and said something quietly to Alfons. Something which made the colour drain from his face. The leader then made his way over to Kurt.

'If you really want to prove yourself,' he whispered. 'And your family's loyalty – particularly your father's – you should teach Lehmann a lesson.'

To the surprise of Kurt and everyone else, he had then turned and instructed them to get in formation. They would be marching to the grave of Horst Wessel to pay their respects. Even more of a surprise was that Alfons fell in line with them.

As they headed to the final resting place of the dead Nazi hero, Kurt fought the urge to ask Alfons what Peter had said to him. His friend dragged his feet until they reached the wreathes in front the iron statue. Some of the other boys jostled and nudged the two of them, adding to the sense of tension.

'Halt!' Peter called.

He summoned Kurt and Alfons forward, and the black wall formed around them once again. Heavy drops of rain began dotting the dusty pavement as everyone stood and waited for what would happen next. Kurt felt a chill in his bones.

'Let's see what Lehmann and Hertz have learned about courage,' Peter said. His shrill voice had now lowered in volume.

Kurt, who was taller than most of the boys, looked over their heads to see if anyone was around. Not that any sane citizen would dare intervene. There wasn't really much of what you'd call a police force anymore, either.

The two friends had long been anticipating their Mutprobe – the opportunity to prove their bravery, usually through the completion of a daunting task, such jumping from a great height or diving into deep water. Kurt had actually been looking forward to his, to gain its reward of a Hitler Youth dagger; and while Alfons was nonplussed at the prospect of receiving the weapon, he still very much wanted to get the ordeal over with and out of the way. It was, however, not uncommon for Peter to use the tests to pit the boys against one another. He pushed his rounded spectacles up his nose and gestured towards Alfons.

'Punch him in the face,' he casually instructed Kurt.

Kurt didn't move. His feet stuck to the cobbles as though weighed down by lead as he faced his best friend. They were so alike in bone structure and sun-caught complexions that people often mistook them for brothers. Alfons wouldn't meet his gaze. His stone-grey eyes stared past him, fixated on some distant point.

'Hertz, if you don't do this, I will have no choice but to question your loyalty to the Hitler Youth and to the Fatherland,' Peter hissed into his ear. 'I may also have to report Lehmann's misguided defence of the Juden rats to someone more senior.'

Still Kurt couldn't move, and then he noticed something. The subtle tapping of Alfons fingers against his leg, one finger and then two. It was a childhood code they had between them. Alfons was tapping out letters.

'D-O, I-T.'

Peter began talking again, his voice sounding far away. 'Do it, and I'll wipe the slate clean for the both of you.'

Kurt's fists clenched and unclenched. His heart was pounding. The rain was picking up on the cobbles and blurring his vision.

Peter was in his ear again, talking about how the Gestapo were still watching his family, his father; about how this could be the final act of disobedience before they paid another visit to the shit-streaked slum he came from and took away his communist father, again. This time for good.

The other boys were watching, some with undisguised delight. This was another game unfolding before them. It was like the fist-fight fuelled platoon they often set up when camping, where the weaker, slower ones would often get pummelled for not being the first to throw a punch.

Peter was still in his ear. He was using his other card to wind Kurt up. Did Kurt and Alfons have a special relationship? One that often saw men, if they could call themselves such, dragged off to Dachau?

It was the mention of the camp that did it. The one that his father had returned from only weeks ago, ashen faced and skin and bone. Kurt cast one more look at Alfons, who remained impassive, immobile. Why didn't he just fight? Why didn't his own father fight, instead of sitting shrivelled and shaking in the kitchen? Why were the pair of them so weak? This new Germany offered them everything, and yet all they did was complain and disobey.

He raised his fist.

CHAPTER THREE

The Girl and the Art of Lying

9th November 1938

Alice nearly rode into the man wearing a wide-brimmed hat and dark suit, as he stepped out from the trees that lined the driveway. She skidded across the path. Stones flew up and dust caught in her eyes, causing her to fall from her bike.

'Uncle Max,' she said breathlessly, and with more than a hint of anger in her voice. 'I thought you were Gestapo.'

'Where have you been?' he asked. His eyes searched around her, looking for anything out of place.

At first, he had been completely opposed to Alice's idea of 'hiding in plain sight', but they hadn't found an alternative yet, and they had survived raids before. The Gestapo didn't really want them, yet.

Max was a well-built man, tall and imposing, but with a thinness to his face, accentuated by high Slavic cheekbones that would have suited a slighter frame. There were smatterings of grey in his dark hair and deep lines across his brow – more of which had appeared in the weeks since he had started helping Alice and her sister. He wasn't actually related to them, but he had always been such a presence in their lives that it felt as though he was. He was a close work colleague of her father's, another scientific genius; but Max complied with the Reich in all outer appearances. He even wore a shiny Party lapel. This helped them all.

The smoky scent coming from his suit betrayed another of his frequent visits to the Bavarian bars. This was where he picked up useful information from the police and bartenders he knew, usually after the settling of a large drinks tab or dropping of a generous tip. He was a vital link to the Berlin underground, providing access to a regular supply of forged identity papers. This fraudulent ink kept Alice mobile as she tried to look for ways out of Germany for her and Edie; and even more importantly, a way out of the camp for her father.

'Don't tell me where you've been,' he threw his arms up in the air. 'We need to talk, inside.'

She opened the door to the house where they lived in like mice, scurrying about, sleeping in the attic, ready to run at a moment's notice. It had been six weeks since the Gestapo had taken her father. She lit one of the melted-down candles. Leaving Max on guard in the hall, she treaded the stairs carefully, avoiding the sharp splinters where the carpet had been ripped out and sold.

'Edie?' she called, listening for the patter of footsteps above. 'You can come down.'

'Papa?' Edie shouted, as she always did by way of greeting whenever Alice returned. Alice shouted up no, her voice heavy. 'Franz?' Edie asked in reply.

Edie climbed down from the cobwebbed attic where they slept. The narrow door and pull up stairs allowed for some extra time to react if they were raided again. The plan was to climb down from a roof window via a system of knotted ropes. This would allow them to run to a temporary hiding place in one of the neighbour's stables. They hadn't had a chance to test it out yet.

Edie dropped onto the bare floor of the landing with a thud. Alice looked at her sister, thinking again that with her jet-black hair, sallow skin and deep brown eyes, they were polar opposites. Edie resembled their mother, and this was dangerous.

Max paced the hallway as they came down the stairs together. The candlelight bounced off his shoes, making sinister shadows of his features. Edie paused and pulled at Alice's dress.

'It's Uncle Max,' Alice assured her. The small hand released its grip.

'Hello little Edie,' Max exclaimed, overly loud and jovial, in an attempt to alleviate the little girl's reticence. 'I have a gift for you.'

Beaming up at them, he pulled out a cinnamon-speckled Apfeltorte. The sickly-sweet smell made Alice's stomach rumble and heave all at once. She had become completely unaccustomed to anything like this, experiencing them only through the display windows of the cafés that she passed on her visits to the passport office.

'Thank you, Uncle Max,' Edie said politely. She could barely conceal the excitement in her voice.

It pleased Alice to hear this, having become used to listening to Edie speak with near-paralysing trepidation. Her sister had spent most of her life in a Jews-only school, ironically having to pretend to be fully Jewish and not a Mischling in order to be accepted there; but then someone had found out, and she'd been cast out of there, too.

They walked into the kitchen. It was a place that had once been bright and busy, with a full staff led by a talented cook, serving lavish meals through the double doors to an adjoining dining room; a room where all of them had once sat at a large table and ate and drank and laughed. Now all that remained was a splintered rocking chair covered in old blankets, illuminated by the other candles that Alice was now lighting.

The fire began to flicker and crackle as Alice added some fresh kindle, cut from the woods behind their house. A small pan sat above it on a makeshift stand that Alice had built out of an old chair, ready to bubble the latest batch of rotting vegetables. A strong smell of potatoes and cabbage from the previous night's meal still floated in the room.

'Why don't you go slice up that cake for us, Edie?' Max suggested. 'I need a minute alone with your sister.'

Alice wanted to argue that Edie had already seen a lot that she shouldn't have, so what difference would a bit of listening make, but something about Max's expression stopped her. Edie raised an eyebrow at Alice but obeyed.

They stepped out into the damp hallway. Its ornately patterned marble floor gave off such a cold that Alice could feel it through her boots.

'You both need to leave this house tonight,' Max spoke in hushed tones. 'Your father has arranged separate hiding places.'

'Why can't we stay together?' There were lots of questions to ask, but this was the one that mattered most. Her voice became so child-like and desperate that she knew it must have made her sound pathetic.

'It's only temporary-' he trailed off. He waved his hand in the air, as though that could be enough to brush away her concerns.

She tried to regain some ground. 'I was already planning to leave Berlin for a few nights,' she said. 'I had a direct warning from Franz.'

'So, you did go to the camp?' he took a cigarette from his pocket and lit it, regarding her with narrowed eyes. 'I know he had business there today.'

'I had to try,' she said.

Cigarette smoke billowed around them.

'Don't put us at risk like that again, Alice,' he said, with an unfamiliar chill to his tone.

Alice lifted her head up and looked him in the eye. 'Franz said that there is danger coming.'

Max nodded slowly.

'When do we leave?' she bit down on her lip and focussed on the pain, hoping to distract from the panic in her head. 'When can I pick up Edie again?'

He hesitated. 'When the trouble is over-'

'Can we get Edie onto a Kinderstranport instead? I have been trying-'

'There's no time for that now.'

The kitchen door creaked open. Edie stood in the doorway.

'Everything's okay, Edie,' Alice said, forcing a smile. 'Let's enjoy this treat and then we have to pack. Uncle Max is taking us to a safer place.'

'Together?' Edie asked.

'Yes,' Alice lied, as she shepherded her over to sit on some piled remnants of furniture.

The ecstasy of the cake crumbs dancing on her tongue was almost enough to let Alice forget about Max. It had been so long since she'd tasted sugar.

'My car is in the next street,' he announced, once they had finished.

Alice nodded, and they proceeded to pack.

When the battered old suitcases were closed, Alice turned to him. 'Could we have a moment alone please, Max? In case this is the last time we see our family home.' Her words sounded sincere, although she had every intention of returning here, with Edie, as soon as this latest trouble had blown over. She would then continue her efforts to free their father and get all three of them out of the country together.

When Max had stepped outside, she took a small knife from the kitchen and picked at a piece of marble in the corner of the hall. This revealed a small hole that fitted in with the pattern and was barely detectable. There was too much of a risk to carry the brooch with her across such a great distance, and she knew that she would need to sell it at some point. She couldn't resist pulling out the scroll hiding the photographs and taking one last look at her and Franz. One day she might have to use them, but in the wrong hands they would be so dangerous. Edie hovered nearby, her shoes creating a gentle patter on the floor.

Max's car was a black Mercedes, liberally branded with Party emblems. Inside, the scent of leather and polish was chokingly thick, suggesting a recent valeting. Alice was tempted to ask if the car would be fumigated after two mischlings had travelled in it.

They drove across the city, lights twinkling, buildings flashing past, with the smell of smoke and petrol filling the air. Max apologised when he stopped on a dark, narrow road, telling them to avoid public transport, and giving Alice a parcel containing some sandwiches and fruit. 'Your father said that you would know the place if I told you to think of the holiday with your mother, and the funny hats.'

A family holiday. Funny hats. Schorfheide. They had camped on rural fields and went rowing on the river. She could hear the ripple of the current as she pulled the oars with her father, the smell of fresh lavender. Mamma and baby Edie, dipping their fingers into the passing water. Her mother's jet-black hair was cropped to her chin, and her skin had darkened under just a small amount of summer sun. They had passed a church attached to a large, stone building, where a bustle of young children streamed out dressed in identical black and white uniforms. They were followed by women in long cloaks and hats that hid their heads.

'I used to go to a school like that,' her father had told her.

'With those ladies in funny hats?'

'They're nuns,' her mother said. She could still see the red lipstick move on her mouth as she spoke that day.

'Where's all their hair? Are they witches?'

Their father laughed. 'I happen to know that those particular nuns are not to be feared at all.'

'Why, do you know them?'

'I was taught by nuns like those, Alice.'

'Were you taught by them too, Mama?'

'No, my dear, Papa and I had different teachers. It's why we have the Menorah with the seven candles as well as a Christmas tree. That way, you can enjoy the traditions that both of us grew up with.'

The conversation had been disrupted by a ferry heading towards them at full speed, from around the bend in the river. It was the first time Alice had seen real panic on her father's face. Alice picked up her oar and rowed with all her might, matching her father's speed.

'Thank goodness I have you, Alice,' he'd said when the ferry had passed. That easy smile was back on his face again – the one that wrinkled his skin without making him look old. 'You saved us back there, my girl.'

She came back to the present, the awful, uncertain present, but those words remained with her. He was still relying on her to be strong.

'You do know what he means by that?' Max asked, staring at her intently. 'I only have a map until a certain point, and then he said that you would know the rest of the way. He didn't want anyone to know about this place, in case any of us are... compromised.'

She nodded her understanding. She knew all about the rumours that there was an informer in the group.

Max handed her some coins, for her transport back, alone. 'When you're back in Berlin, go to the Jewish Hospital and ask for Irena,' he whispered.

It was like a different world outside the city. Folds of snow covered the woods and fields, surrounding them like scoops of ice-cream smoothed down over the landscape. Emaciated branches stretched and shook themselves bare, in their futile attempts at reaching out to touch the cloudless night sky. Germany had never looked so beautiful.

'Do we have to walk far?' Edie's rose-pink cheeks puffed out sullenly.

'Not really.'

In truth, it would be an evening's worth of walking, but lately Alice had found that the lies tumbled effortlessly from her mouth. The car started up again behind them, and then disappeared down a dark lane, back towards the city, leaving the taste of petrol on their tongues. Berlin was no more than a distant assortment of lights.

'What are you doing?' Edie asked, a frown on her face as she watched Alice use fallen branches to dust away their footprints. 'No one is following us. We're out of Berlin now.'

Alice couldn't help it. This was how she lived, like a fugitive.

They walked for what seemed like hours. The stars were much clearer than they were used to seeing from within the city, sparkling gaily across a thick, inky sky.

'Can we stop somewhere?' Edie had started to shuffle at a slower pace, her breath making shadows of ice in the air.

They had eaten Max's sandwiches, and there was nothing to pick at in the winter fields. Drinking icy water was not filling their bellies. Alice saw a farm up ahead. Its lights shined out onto the rolling fields.

The farmer's wife answered the door. She was a tall, buxom woman, with braids fixed around her head and an apron dusty with flour. The house, and the wife, smelled of baked bread and a sharp hint of apples. She stared down at them both with a slight frown, looking furtively behind them.

'You're alone?' she eventually asked.

Alice nodded.

'I can give you something to tide you over. You can warm yourselves by the fire for a short while too. Her tone was stern, but there was a softness in her eyes when she looked at Edie shivering on the step.

'Lore, prepare some food for these girls,' she commanded, before sitting down to knit in a battered old rocking chair, clicking and sighing as she did. The chair creaked loudly under her weight.

Lore, who Alice estimated was around nineteen served them with narrowed eyes, set like slits in her doughy face. Edie didn't seem bothered by the frowning glances, though, having received them for as long as she could remember. She tucked into the steaming bowl of eintopf, scooping the broth, chicken and pulses up with freshly baked bread.

When Alice got up to warm her hands on the fire, the farmer's daughter followed her and stood close.

'Juden?' She pointed at Edie.

'Don't be ridiculous,' Alice laughed.

The farmer's daughter raised an eyebrow and then went over to her mother and whispered in her ear.

'Come on.' Alice walked back from the warmth, pulled Edie up and bundled her out of the door. When she turned back the farmer's daughter was watching them, arms folded, casting an imposing shadow against the glow of the warm house.

They continued the journey. Edie explored the trees for squirrels and kept a look out for rabbits. Her eyes shone with excitement when she thought that one had appeared.

'What are you looking at me like that for?' she asked, dark, rebellious curls spilling out of her woollen hat.

Alice couldn't tell Edie that she was trying to memorise her, to record every last detail and lock it up in a memory box in her mind, to keep safe until the danger had passed. Alice had done the same with their parent's wedding photo. Mama's veil cascading down towards the floor, her face lit up with happiness; and Papa, who looked so handsome wearing a fine suit and a Cheshire Cat smile. Their feet were turned in towards each other. It had always taken pride of place, hanging prominently in the hall of their family home. It was now hidden under the marble floor, along with all of the other photographs.

Edie whizzed ahead and threw a snowball which caught Alice on the mouth. Alice laughed, and for a couple of minutes they were normal sisters again. That was until Alice looked down the barren stretch of road and her stomach flipped. She ran ahead as though it was part of the game, her winter boots trudging through the thick carpet of snow. In the distance were the silhouettes of buildings and a church spire.

'This doesn't feel much like a safe place,' Edie commented as they reached the large, grey stone building attached to the church.

The river which Alice had once rowed on was now a bed of ice. They walked up to a thick, black gate. Alice thumped at it. All around them were sad shadows of frozen plants, creeping up the walls.

'I don't like it,' Edie shivered.

The door opened with a creek, and a woman in swishing robes with a stiff white collar and hat ushered them in.

'A nun?' Edie whispered.

'You must be Edith,' the nun replied. Her voice was kind, even if they could not see her face properly. 'And you are Alice. I am the Mutter Oberin of this convent school, and you can call me Sister Catharina. Come in, please.'

Edie grabbed hold of Alice's hand as they followed Sister Catharina into the shadows of the building, where a long hall was filled with candle light. Edie's eyes were wide.

'You might like some cocoa after your long journey?' She held a chunk of keys which made a heavy, jangling noise as she moved. She used them to gain access to a kitchen with a long wooden table, and a fire heating the room. 'Please sit,' she said, and disappeared into the darkness at the end of the room.

'Why would Papa send us here?' Edith said under her breath. She was trembling.

'We're safe here.' Alice couldn't look at her sister.

The nun returned with the cocoa, as well as several rounds of buttery toast. Her face, illuminated by the fire, was pale, with the beginnings of lines that made Alice guess she was around the same age as their father.

'Do you know Papa?' Edie blurted out.

'I did, many years ago,' she replied. Her voice was warm and calming.

'How?' Edie questioned.

Sister Catharina glanced at Alice.

'Edie, remember what I said about us having to be new people for a while.' Alice took her sister's hand. 'You can't mention Papa or me, but you must listen to Sister Catharina.'

'Here you will have lessons and be treated like all the other girls in class,' the sister said. 'I will show you the dorm. We have to make sure you know a few prayers.'

'Like the prayers Papa used to say?' Edith's hands were shaking and some of the cocoa poured onto the table. 'I don't want to learn them.'

'It's important, Edie,' Alice said, looking up at the large clock on the wall. Time was going too fast.

'Must you leave tonight?' Sister Catharina looked at Alice.

'You're not staying, Alice?' Edie cried.

'I can't, Edie,' she said, placing her hand on her sister who shook it away. 'There is another place they have arranged for me.'

Edie started to sob. 'I thought we were staying together.'

'It isn't safe for us both to be here. I promise, I'll be back for you soon.'

'Why did you lie to me?' Edie was howling as Alice tried to hug her.

'Edie, please, this is what Papa wanted,' she begged. 'You'll be safe.'

Edie fell to her knees and tried to grab at Alice's ankles.

'I'll have to lock her in the kitchen while I let you out,' Sister Catharina said, fumbling with the keys. Alice could see tears in the Sister's eyes as she held Edie back and shut the door.

'No! No! Alice, please!' Edie banged on the closed door.

Sister Catharina gave Alice a hug which she collapsed into. 'You must be strong. One day, this will all be over.'

But Alice had heard that line too many times before. Reaching the river, she fell into the snow and cried. Everything inside her was breaking apart, like shards of ice.

CHAPTER FOUR

The Boy and the Fire

9th November 1938

'Our flag leads us to eternity
Our flag means more to us than life…'

The song echoed off the walls of the towering eight-storey building. Kurt's unit sang as they
threw makeshift missiles: stones, rocks, bits of gravel and bricks.

Alfons' blond hair was matted with blood, his face a stark white against dried streaks of red. Kurt was holding his friend's head up carefully, while at the same time trying to compress the wound with his necktie. It was already soaked through. Alfons' nose was bent out of shape, but it was the wound at the back of his head, streaming at an unmanageable rate, that was the main cause for concern.

All around them, glass was smashing and wood was cracking.

Only Georg, a quiet and often unsure member of the group, had come over. The colour had drained from his face when he saw Alfons. He wanted to help carry him to a hospital. It was then that the doors of the imposing building above them burst open, and more Hitler Youth spilled out from the group's headquarters, brandishing weapons and screaming bloody murder. Kurt's chest tightened at as a sea of brown shirts came surging towards him. Georg had stumbled back before turning and running for cover in the adjacent narrow streets. Kurt tried to curl his body into a shape that would protect both himself and Alfons from the onslaught of blows he was expecting at any moment. The attack didn't come, though. The mob passed them by without so much as a glance, and eventually his breath slowed to something approaching normal. Whatever was happening, it must have been big.

A gust of wind carried the stench of burning. It blinded him as he stood up and dragged a semi-conscious Alfons to his feet. The soot-filled air clogged in his lungs as he gulped it in and tried to steady himself. When the fog cleared, he saw Peter standing and surveying the crowd, a smile on his thin lips. He rocked on his heels with satisfaction, occasionally shouting a few words of encouragement. Still cradling Alfons as best he could, Kurt moved over to his leader, grabbing at his leg and pulling him down to the ground.

'What are you doing?' Peter punched him on the jaw.

'Alfons,' he managed to say, tasting metal in his mouth.

Peter stood back up and dusted off his uniform.

'Listen, you stupid son of a Jew-lover,' he leaned back down, beads of sweat dripping from his forehead. 'A little bit of blood for your friend here, and for you, will give you both some much needed honour. Now, make yourself useful and help us get rid of the Jewish swine, before I take the pair of you, along with your traitor families, to the Gestapo myself.' He strode off into the crowd.

Kurt part-dragged, part-carried Alfons around a corner. Georg and the others stood outside a haberdashery shop, its windows jagged with broken glass. The pavement was covered in sparkling trinkets, like little stars twinkling on the ground.

'What's happening?' Alfons asked, his voice faint and eyes rolling back into his head.

Kurt laid him down gently onto the floor.

'It's the Jews again,' Georg replied. 'One of them killed a General in Paris.' In a move very unlike the reserved boy Kurt had come to know, Georg spat on the ground. When he looked back up from where his saliva landed, his eyes had brightened. He seemed almost intoxicated by the violence.

Kurt turned around, his hand still clasping Alfons'. A man came staggering out of the shop and was quickly forced to the ground under a barrage of fists.

'Please, take whatever you want, but leave my husband alone!' a woman, screaming, crying and holding up glittering pieces of jewellery pleaded as she followed behind.

The street lights were knocked out, alerting passers-by to the situation. Suddenly there were looters swarming all over, grabbing what they could.

'Alfons needs help!' Kurt shouted, but his voice was lost to the frenzied sound of thuds, punches and cries of pain. He ripped off one of his uniform sleeves and tried to wrap it around his friend's head, but the loose material wouldn't stay in place. A low groan shuddered from Alfons' body as Kurt picked him up as carefully as possible. He would head back in the direction of the hospital. He knew that there was one close by.

As they reached the next section of cobbled streets, Kurt stopped to take a breath and fell down roughly onto his knees. The life was draining from Alfons. His blood seeped out onto the concrete. Kurt thought of all the times they'd had to stand in front of Peter and the group and say that they would die for the Fuhrer – everyone except for Alfons declaring it with gusto, without really knowing what it meant. *Our flag means more to us than life…*

He tried carrying Alfons again, but his legs were wobbling worse than they had done during any of their military training, or the hours and hours of marching.

'Don't worry,' he told Alfons. 'I'll get you to a doctor.'

He found the strength to pull himself up and start heading for the nearest doorway. Someone had to be inside. He didn't care who they were as long as they had supplies, or even just a phone to call for help. Tears stung his eyes. 'Bitte!' he shouted at the entrances of houses that had been closed and bolted.

'I'm scared,' Alfons' quivering voice was barely audible.

'You'll be fine,' Kurt replied, avoiding his faraway gaze. He strained to lift Alfons' upper half, and together they dragged their feet in the direction of the hospital, to an area that was now deserted.

Thick, black smoke was billowing from a nearby synagogue, making them cough and splutter. Kurt then saw that its doors had been forced open, and using every remaining ounce of strength began hauling them both towards it. Inside, the building was cold and dark, apart from a nearby fire spitting light into the room at random intervals. Beds were overturned, and bottles had been smashed against the floor. There was no one around. Glass crunched under their feet.

'Don't… don't be like them,' Alfons muttered, his breathing laboured. 'Peter told me… that he would make you like them, but I knew that if you hit me… it would change you back.' He closed his eyes.

Kurt searched the rooms for a phone, a nurse, a piece of equipment that could somehow help. He was at the other end of the building, trying the last door, when he saw Peter outside the window. He tried to get his attention, but Peter was focussed, his eyes lit up by a flaming baton he was carrying. There was a pail in his other hand. It looked like water, but when he threw it, the smell of petrol was unmistakable.

'No, Peter!' Kurt shouted, his voice hoarse. 'Alfons is in here!'

Peter looked up and saw him, and Kurt almost collapsed with relief. But then he threw the baton anyway.

A violent gust of wind blew Kurt against the wall. He got up, choked and dizzy, and made his way back to the room where he'd left Alfons. A sharp, chemical fog blanketed the building, stinging his eyes and scratching at his throat as he grappled through the wreckage.

The wall outside the room was blown to pieces. Alfons was lying motionless inside, twisted debris all around, with small groups of flames licking at his outstretched limbs. That was the last thing Kurt saw before another mini-explosion set off a chain of blasts, engulfing the room in fire and smoke.

He woke to a hissing sound, and opened his eyes to see water gushing past him in a futile effort to put out the fire which clung to everything: the bricks of the building, the air around it.

Alfons.

'I have to go back in!' He got up on unsteady legs and made to move, but a pair of strong arms pushed him back down. His vision cleared enough to see that it was a lone fireman standing in front of him.

'You can't go back in there,' the fireman said, picking up the hose again. He was a burly figure, with a distinctive scar on his left cheek that was filled-in and accentuated by the falling soot. Tear-stains streaked through the black blotches that stained his cheeks. 'I think there are still some children inside.'

'My friend is in there!'

Blurring sirens and screeching tyres interrupted them. The sound of car doors being slammed preceded the arrival of a group of shadowy figures. The fireman gave him one last look before disappearing back into the building.

'You! Don't move!'

Kurt heard the yell from behind, just as a Gestapo agent made a grab for him. The shoulder of his uniform was torn off when he flung himself away from the man's clutches. He started running. He ran until his whole body hurt. The ground felt as though it was shifting under his feet whenever he stopped. He kept going, following the sounds of the song in the distance. He found himself humming along, as he headed back in the direction he had come from, to find Peter, to make him pay. He grabbed a flag and joined in with a passing cell.

'Our flag leads us to eternity

Our flag means more to us than life…'

CHAPTER FIVE

The Girl and the Glass

9 November 1938

'They won't come here,' Irena Bauer kept insisting; but she sounded less and less certain as the smashes and screams drew ever nearer.

Alice had followed Max's instructions to meet Irena, a member of his 'team', at the Jewish hospital where she worked as a nurse. She was tall, broad and imposing. Her expression alternated between scowls for her staff and smiles for her patients. Alice had been subjected to a lot more of the former than the latter so far.

Irena threw a starched nightgown at her. She couldn't bring herself to look at the other patients in their varying degrees of ill-health. Equipment was limited and supplies were scarce. She felt like an inconvenience.

'Bloody Max and his business,' Irena muttered.

'Business?' Alice asked.

'You think he doesn't make money from looking after the likes of you?' she said gruffly.

The idea of Max extorting money for her safety, her life, produced a fresh wave of nausea, before her attention was swiftly moved to the sound of pounding boots and violent voices in the corridor. The patient opposite was shaking under her sheets.

'Take that dress off and put on the gown, so you look like a real patient – now!' Irena snapped.

She pulled the nightgown on over her dress, the rough material scratching at the skin on her arms, and scrambled under the covers just as the door burst open. The room was quickly filled with men, angry and armed. They wore civilian clothes but moved like an army, pulling the patients who were closest to the door out of bed if they couldn't move fast enough.

'What is the meaning of this?' Irena stood in the centre of the room, her voice sharp. Alice was close enough to see the trembling fingers behind her back.

One of the men stormed forward, getting almost nose to nose with the nurse. His dark hair was closely cropped, and his face so contorted by rage that it pressed his features together.

'Jewish whore!' he spat on the ground. He turned to the nearest bed, which happened to be Alice's, and glared at her. 'Get up.'

As Alice struggled to escape the bed covers, he went over and grabbed her by the nightgown, ripping it as he yanked her up. Her heart stopped as he looked her up and down.

'He's not hiding here,' a man shouted from across the room. 'They're all patients.'

Alice stifled a sigh of relief.

'What should we do with them?' the same man said, his voice broad and deep.

The dark-haired man scratched at his neck for a moment, and then awkwardly swung a baton in the air and shouted, 'Get them out!'

The ward erupted into movement.

Clutching the nightgown at its torn seam, she followed the others, stumbling through the dark corridors of the hospital. She was grateful for her boots as they crunched against the broken glass littered across the floor. Several patients could only hobble along on crutches, while others had to be carried by doctors and nurses. Some of the younger children started to cry. She tried her best to soothe them, whispering comforts and telling them that it would soon be over. Her thoughts drifted to Edie.

Once outside, it was not the freezing winter cold that made her shiver, but the sight of a baying mob. They were stood not far from the hospital, throwing bricks, stones and pieces of rubble at nearby shops and houses, their shouts of anger ringing through the air. The patients were met with threats and insults, and more than a few were caught by kicks and punches as they trudged past. Alice concentrated on the road ahead, even when she herself was struck on the shin. Her teeth clenched with pain. Head down, carry on, and look for a way out.

A woman from the side-lines grabbed her shoulders and tried to yank her forward. Alice twisted her head and found herself looking straight into the assailant's cool blue eyes. Her insides turned to liquid, but she held the stare.

The woman's rage-filled expression changed. 'You are hardly more than a child,' she muttered, before turning away and re-joining the crowd.

They were marched to a nearby synagogue. A single stone flew across the air in front of Alice, hitting the corner of a fractioned star which had clung on to one of the frames, sprinkling yet more glass across the night sky. She was pushed to the ground, alongside others who were kneeling with their hands above their head. Stones dug into her skin. An old man next to her was shoved down roughly. The cold whipped around them, gathering their collective breath into transient clouds.

'Please,' a woman pleaded repeatedly as a fire began to rise in front of them, drawing a roar of approval from the rabid crowd. A boy slightly older than Alice was kicked in the head and fell face-first to the ground. Boots continued to rain down on him until a woman in white threw herself over his limp body, crying and screaming.

The blaze spread quickly. Those in front of Alice were coughing from the smoke, flames getting closer to their faces. She dared to look around, and saw a fireman holding a hosepipe with no water coming out of it. He caught her gaze and turned away. Next to him, a woman in a feathered hat held a young boy, his face a harrowing mask of euphoric reverie, up above the crowd.

Objects were thrown through empty spaces where there had once been windows, feeding the flames. Alice had never before set foot in the place, but she still felt an ache in her heart as she watched it burn. A sudden, sharp crack to her skull caused a wetness to spread across her head. Dazed, she looked to see where it had come from, and noticed a small gap in the crowd. The fireman nodded, and without hesitation she made a run for it while he turned his body to allow her and a few others through.

The crowd became shapes and shadows against the pulsating inferno. Alice ran from Elsässer Strasse until her head was bursting and her chest was splintering with sharp pains. Shouts came from all round her. A choking, burning stench overwhelmed her senses. She paused by some rocks that had been heaped into piles.

Then she heard them. Men and women, young and old, a storm of shrieks, howls, whistles and screams, hurtling towards her. She climbed over a gate, tearing open the skin on her knee, and dropped herself into a small park. Through the gaps in the gate, she could see men hurling rocks at the windows and doors of more shops; and although most were dressed no differently than your everyday Berliner, she could spot the well-built physiques and expert aims of trained soldiers, much like she had witnessed at the hospital.

With the excited shouts growing closer, Alice sprinted for an exit at the other end of the park, her feet slipping in the wet soil. Behind her, the gates clattered, and unknown voices called out at her to come back.

'You had better run. And don't stop until you are out of Germany!' one of them bellowed over the burning air that was seeping into her lungs, filling her with the furious exhales of the city.

She didn't look back. The next gate she came to was harder to scale, and she fell into a puddle on the other side. Her nightdress was spotted black with dirty water and drenched at the bottom. It was becoming harder to breathe.

Finding a side street that was darker than most, she kept her body pressed against a wall, creeping along slowly while rain dripped onto her throbbing head. Hair stuck to her face like rats' tails, and blood trickled freely from cuts on her hands, arms and legs. A rattling sound and a shout made her start running again.

She slammed into a body. It was a man. He grabbed her, his fingers digging into her skin. She fought back, scratching at his hand. He didn't let go. He spoke in English, which she usually understood, but his words came in snatches, spoken too quickly for her to grasp. He took a deep breath and removed his brown coat, putting it around her shoulders. He looked smaller without it on.

'How old are you?' he asked slowly, with a flat, solemn tone. The language now sounded similar to how her father had taught her to understand it. She had been practising for moments like this.

'Seventeen,' she replied.

There was a sudden sound of steps coming towards them. She readied herself to flee, but the man pushed her up against a wall and held her there, his eyes fixed on her, saying more things that she couldn't understand in his strange, quick accent. Blood thumped its way through her head.

Another man appeared behind him, short and stumpy, wearing a hat and shivering in a shirt and tie. Beside him was an old woman, also in a suit jacket but with night clothes underneath. White hair tumbled down her face and past her shoulders.

'Please, come with us,' the second man spoke in Alice's native language. 'We'll help you.'

'Journalists, from America,' the old woman said. She stumbled, and Alice had to grab her hand to stop her from falling. 'I need them to-' her words were lost as the men lifted her between them and signalled for Alice to follow.

They ran through the streets. Alice's limbs were heavy, and her heart was beating too fast. Occasionally they paused to hide from passers-by, but other than that they didn't stop until they reached an apartment. A rough hand on her back pushed her in with a muffled 'hurry'.

The room was small and dark. Alice could make out a chair and tables in the centre, plus a bed and a sink over in the corner.

'You will both stay here,' the short man said. 'We'll be back soon with a doctor for her.'

They left, locking the door behind them.

'My child, will you help me?'

Alice turned to the old woman and watched her slide down the wall to the floor.

'I kept trying to tell them, those journalists, but my English-'

'They're going to find a doctor, don't worry,' Alice noticed the wound on the back of the woman's head, dyeing the white hair a mauve red. The woman's eyes were milky, and the skin around them heavily lined. There was a thin film of sweat across her forehead.

'N-no,' she patted at her chest, and Alice could see that underneath the nightgown, sheltered by the suit jacket, an envelope was hidden. 'The papers... new identities... for my neighbours – a good family... to get them away from here.'

She tried lifting a frail hand, but didn't have the strength to hold it up.

'But I don't know-' Alice began. 'Where do they live?'

The old woman gurgled and shuddered, and then became very still.

'Where do they live?' Alice shook her gently. 'What are their real names?'

The old woman's eyes had closed. Her breath was slowing.

Alice tried to stand up, but found that her head was heavy and her legs were shaking. She slumped back down next to the old woman and pressed a hand into hers, uncertain of whether she was trying to give comfort or take it. She held the papers. Three new identities. The old woman, her body growing colder, provided no information regarding who she was herself, never mind the family that the documents were intended for.

The piercing screams of those still at the mercy of the night were now permeating through the thin walls, into the room. Outside the window, the city was lit by intermittent flickers of fire. The dark sky was filled with heavy clouds of billowing smoke.

They look like signals, she thought, recalling a school lesson on Native American customs. It was a distant memory, belonging to a different girl in a different life.

Like warning signals.

CHAPTER SIX

The Boy on the Balcony

9th November 1938

A red mist seemed to be leading Kurt through the streets, his eyes always trained on Peter. He was boiling with rage, as though channelling heat from the buildings burning all around him. He kicked and smashed, shouted and roared, knowing that it would bring no attention to him. Everyone else was doing the same.

As his leader changed direction, heading away from the other boys, Kurt picked up a metal pipe, cool and solid against his fingers. He ducked back into the shadows when Peter was joined by two others. They wore darker uniforms, with SS lapels. He hadn't spotted many high-ranking men during the worst of the violence that night, so the sight of these two confused him. Cigarettes were offered around, and Kurt watched as the three were surrounded by plumes of smoke, their laughter and low voices straining his every nerve.

Eventually they walked towards the entrance of a nearby building and gestured for Peter to go inside while they walked on. Kurt waited for them to move and then tried the door, finding it locked. He went up the fire escape instead. The rails were slippery with rain, but still he clasped the pipe within his shaking fist.

Peering through the window, he could see that Peter and the SS were examining paintings and other loot. He climbed onto the balcony to get a closer look. The SS men shook Peter's hand and headed out of the room, each carrying an ornate frame. He heard them taking the stairs and lowered himself out of view. Once he was sure that they were gone, he began working his way back to standing, slowly and steadily, but the steel surface had become so wet and slick that he couldn't help but lose his footing and drop with an almighty thud that seemed to reverberate for miles. Panicking, he scrambled to his feet just as the balcony door was flung open.

Peter's twisted face was equal parts confusion and anger. 'Why are you here?' he spat.

Kurt raised the metal pole, intending to bring it crashing down onto Peter's head, but then Alfons' voice came into his head.

Don't be like them.

The moment's hesitation was all Peter needed. His fingers dug into Kurt's arms, pushing him towards the edge. Kurt felt himself going over the side, weak and winded from his earlier fall, but he managed to grab hold of Peter, hanging onto him as he fell. He became weightless, air rushing past him, until he landed unexpectedly on something soft, feathery and light. Everything went black.

'Oh boy, you are lucky. So lucky.'

Kurt opened his eyes to see a boy his own age standing over him, with dark, slicked back hair gleaming like a halo beneath the streetlight.

His whole body hurt. The skin on his arms was cracked and blistered. The boy reached forward and pulled him up. He felt the bounce of whatever was underneath him and was stunned to discover that he had somehow landed on a mattress, strewn with clothes and surrounded by other pieces of furniture.

'I'm Walter,' he said. 'That man there with his brains in the gutter, he threw my brother Heinz off a bridge. Yes, he did, can you believe that? All because he would not join the Hitler Youth. They followed him, picked him up and threw him off. He is crippled because of this. It is horrible, no? And he isn't even a Jew.'

Kurt was barely listening, although his senses were coming back to him as he looked on at the scene in horror.

'Such a brave man, a good man.' Walter clapped his hand on the Kurt's back. 'Do you want to finish the job, or do you think he is done?'

A door opened further along the street, followed by the sound of hurried footsteps.

'No matter, we need to move,' Walter said, nodding his head towards a narrow alleyway. Kurt followed as they jumped walls and landed in gardens – brambles pulling at their clothes, water-laden flower beds sucking at their shoes. Eventually they stopped, both out of breath. Walter laid his hands on his knees and spat on the ground.

They had arrived at an area of Berlin which Kurt didn't normally venture into. It held what was left of Socialism and other Nazi opponents, and was home to a number of the few Jews who still had some influence. It was a wealthy district, with a mixture of gothic and modern architecture comprised of twisted steel frames and red brick.

'You know how long I have been wanting to kill that man?' Walter asked. 'I was planning it for months, and you just go for it, and in a Hitler Youth uniform with SS in the area.' He broke off in a laugh and opened his coat, taking out rolling papers and tobacco from the inside pocket. He drummed his fingers on a door, using what must have been a secret code. He gave Kurt a long look. 'I will give you one piece of advice if you want to stay with us.' He glanced down at the Hitler Youth uniform, charred in places and blasted with soot and grime. His lip curled in distaste and his voice changed, losing its previous light-hearted tone. 'Say that you killed Peter Fischer, even if it was an accident. Make the people you meet in here believe it.'

Kurt went to speak, but Walter held his hand up to stop him.

'You will need to hide now,' he said. 'You will need us to hide you, because no matter what happened on that balcony, you will be blamed. You know how your people work.'

The door opened slowly, and a girl emerged from the shadows of a grand hallway.

'Sophie!' Walter exclaimed, kissing her on both cheeks.

The girl's large brown eyes widened at the sight of Kurt. 'Who is this? What is he doing here?'

'Don't be put off by his poor choice of outfit tonight. This man is a legend and a true ally. Let us inside so I can tell you what he did,' he smiled. 'Anyway, look at the state of you.'

Sophie was wearing the pressed white shirt, dark blue skirt and black neckerchief of the League of German Girls, the female equivalent of the Hitler Youth. The clothes were too big for her. She twisted the Fahrtentuch, which hung loosely from her neck in a sheen of lightweight brushed cotton. She placed a hand on one of the coronets of mousy brown plaits either side of her head and frowned.

'You know why I wear this hideous thing,' she said. 'I can hardly open the door in my trousers if the swine come knocking.'

Kurt noticed several other figures in the darkness behind Sophie, poised with various weapons. He could make out a knife and a club.

'Let us in then, doll,' Walter grabbed Kurt by the shoulder and pulled past the protesting Sophie.

Inside, smoky coffee drifted from a room towards the end of the hall, where a low hum of voices and the distant din of a record player could be heard. He was led down a corridor. Two boys – presumably guards – followed behind, their feet padding noiselessly on thick, rich carpet.

'Heinz, you have to hear this!' Walter burst into the room, making several of the occupants jump.

The space was packed with people. Some were wounded, cut and bruised and holding bandages to various parts of their bodies. They boys were dressed in high-waist and wide-legged trousers, as were many of the girls. Many smoked pipes and had umbrellas and long hair. A room full of degenerates.

'Such a brave man. A good man,' Walter thumped Kurt's back with unexpected force, propelling him further into the room.

There was a thick scent of cigarette smoke barely masking the unwashed smell that everyone across the city was starting to share, due to a chronic lack of soap and detergent. Walter led him through the crowd, the two boys and their weapons still close behind. One girl with short dark hair and long limbs, covered in bruises, visibly recoiled as Kurt's uniform brushed against her skin. Walter clasped a boy into an embrace and asked him where Heinz was. The boy pointed at another door and glared at Kurt.

They passed this living area of sorts, where plush and soft fur-nishing contrasted with battered, dishevelled young people, and went through a doorway into a kitchen, where a group was huddled around a table in the middle of the tiled floor. They each stood up quickly, chairs scraping loudly.

'Guys, it's OK,' Walter said breezily. 'Ignore the uniform. Believe me when I tell you, I have found a defector!'

Nobody sat down.

'Let me through,' a voice spoke, authoritative, deep and certain. At once, the group created a pathway and a boy came to the centre, with firm hands gripping the wheels at the side of his chair.

Heinz.

He had broad shoulders and a long frame, with a mop of blond hair and quick hazel eyes that evaluated Kurt without giving anything away. Walter and Heinz didn't resemble each other in the slightest.

There was silence in the room.

'Who is this?' he asked sharply, gesturing to Walter but not taking his eyes off Kurt.

'This,' Walter replied, stepping forward and patting Kurt's chest, 'is a hero. He will be a much-needed asset to our little group. He-'

'Is a Nazi,' finished one of the others.

'Let him speak,' Heinz said, clasping his hands together and nodding at Kurt.

In the dim light of the kitchen, with shadows closing in and all eyes focussed on him – not to mention the two-armed guards behind – there was nothing to lose. Besides, where would he go if these people, whoever or whatever they were, rejected him?

'I killed Peter Fischer.'

'I can verify it!' Walter shouted. 'I saw him do it, right in front of my own eyes. He pursued him to a balcony and then fought him, risking his own life as they both fell. Bravery at its finest.'

There was a pause, and then everyone erupted into cheers, applause and laugher. Everyone except for Heinz, who continued to frown at Kurt.

'Get him some coffee,' he finally ordered, before turning back to the table. 'But first,' he called back over his shoulder. 'You'd better wash up.'

Kurt suddenly felt conscious of the speckles of red on his clothes, the cuts and bruises all over his arms and legs and the gash near his ear. Walter led him to a sink in the far corner of the room.

It was Sophie who brought over the coffee, and a brittle wooden chair for him to sit on. It was not service with a smile. The coffee tasted thick and rich – nothing like the gritty roasted oats he was used to at home. He was also given some rye bread and eggs, which he took gratefully. His mother would queue for hours without getting anything close to this level of quality, and very often came home empty-handed. The shopkeepers in his neighbourhood knew about his father being in a camp, which made it difficult to find someone willing to sell her even the most basic groceries.

'I told you I'd find one,' he heard Walter say to the group gathered around the table.

His insides churned. What did they want with him? As the coffee and food brought him back to his senses, sending energy coursing through his body again, he jolted with the realisation that he had to get back to the hospital. The Gestapo would surely be gone by now. He couldn't leave Alfons alone any longer.

'I have to go,' he said.

The murmur of conversation from the table stopped.

'No, no.' Walter was shaking his head.

There was a shout from another room, and a boy burst through the door, shouldering another with a bloodied nose. 'We've got another one,' he said breathlessly. 'A girl this time – she's hurt. Where are the medical supplies?'

Heinz signalled to those around the table to go and help, and they left the kitchen obediently. Kurt looked around and realised it was just him, Walter and Heinz left, and noted that the room had quickly become both smaller and colder. A hush seemed to have fallen over the previously vibrant house, save for the low drone of voices coming from next door.

'You stay with us now,' Heinz said firmly.

'Why would I do that?' Kurt stood up.

Heinz turned to face him, a steely expression in his eyes. 'We can help you, if you help us.'

He moved towards the door and Kurt knew to follow. They pushed through the packed assembly in the living room and out the other side.

Back in the echoic hallway, where every footstep fell emphatically, the guards were still at the door and Sophie remained sat on the stairs, sullenly twisting the skirt of her uniform around her fingers. Walter kicked away the edge of a thick-woven carpet under the staircase, and then pulled away the lining underneath to reveal a trap door.

'We're hiding those who are in the most danger in the basement, in case the house is raided,' Heinz said quietly, as Walter opened the entrance with a creak. Stairs ran down into the darkness, inky black except for a beacon of faint light from around one of the corners.

'Heinz and I use our good Christian backgrounds to deflect any attention away from the Jews and other people who have pissed Hitler off,' Walter explained.

'Am I a prisoner?' Kurt asked.

'We need to know that we can trust you,' Heinz replied. As Kurt went to descend the ladder, Heinz took his arm with a surprisingly strong grip, displaying a bulging bicep. 'What was inside the house?'

'Paintings. Art.'

Heinz gave Walter a knowing look.

'We'll go back and get some,' Walter said. 'We can use them to buy visas. Your first use for us.'

Heinz gestured for Kurt to descend further into the darkness before closing the wooden hatch behind him with a thud.

The floor of the basement was cold, bare concrete. The walls felt damp to touch. Adjusting to the dim light, the shadowy outlines of people became apparent, three or four, including a girl sitting next to a solitary lamp. A variety of warm and moth-scented blankets were piled up in the corner, alongside a supply of food and drinks. He sat down next to the girl, who turned to look at him with sharp eyes. Her oval face was bruised, purple and red, with unruly dark curls shaking against her cheeks. She was holding a selection of sketches and a family portrait. They were caricaturist, portraying three strong boys, ready for battle, and a young girl riding on their shoulders.

'Did you draw those?' he asked.

'They took my brothers.' Her eyes brimmed with tears. 'We can't find my neighbour. She had the new identity papers for them – the ones they needed to escape.'

She registered his uniform and moved away from him, pressing herself tight into the wall.

He thought to ask if she was Jewish, but then decided that he didn't want to know.

The next morning, he was woken by the sound of the latch opening, as Walter climbed down into the cellar. He was carrying a pair of scissors and a bottle of dye.

'Time for a new identity,' he said. 'Starting with your hair.'

'What?' Kurt attempted to rub the fatigue from his face.

'You work for us now,' Walter said sternly, before his face broke into its usual grin. 'I never thought we'd actually get a trained Hitler Youth member under our banner. You guys are just like real soldiers, and you know how to navigate the hell out of Berlin, thanks to all your little camping trips out to the woods and forests.'

'What are you talking about?' Kurt asked.

'Well, that artwork you led us to is already on its way to buying life for some of the people trapped here. Heinz is pleased, thankfully. Then I told him how you could be like a Nazi infiltrator, and that you may even be able to tell us when your former friends are meeting next.'

'I already told you, I have to go. Why would you think that I want to work for you?'

'Because Peter Fischer survived, and now you're wanted for his attempted murder, as well as the successful murder of someone called Alfons Lehmann.'

CHAPTER SEVEN

The Girl goes Submarine

10th November 1938

'I'll take the gamble,' she told him.

'That's a bold statement from someone in a nightgown,' Max replied. He wasn't smiling.

Alice pulled self-consciously at the white material. She'd been on auto-pilot, making her way back to her home, still dressed in the hospital 'costume' that Nurse Irena had thrown at her. The house had seemed clear and undisturbed, and she'd had just enough time to retrieve her mother's brooch and tie it back around her neck before the noises from the street sent her scurrying up the stairs and into the attic.

'Alice?'

A familiar voice had called when she was halfway up the ladder. It was Max, and now they were sat together, damp and cold, the wind sneaking in with the faintest of whistles through the roof.

The guilt of having left the old woman still tore at her, despite her knowing that the final breath had left her body. Worse still was the sight of the three identity papers that she now felt like burning. Three boys, not much older than her. Three chances to escape.

'The gamble is not worth it,' Max shook his head. 'If you try and find these people, you put yourself and them in danger.'

'But-' she began.

'Who tracks down people who want to be hidden?' Max interrupted. 'The Gestapo, Alice.' As if on cue, there was a whistle from downstairs. Alice felt her body tense. It was Franz's signal. They waited in silence until he reached the attic. She could see the dark circles under his eyes, melting the ice out of their blueness. He collapsed onto a cushion, setting down a large bag by his side. She bit back a comment about how tired he must be after a night of violence and Jew-baiting.

'Last night was organised, wasn't it?' Max asked him.

'If you mean by the powers that be, then yes,' Franz admitted. 'It's only going to get harder for the Jews now.'

'You'll probably get more opportunities for honours, though,' Alice couldn't help but taunt. Some days she found it impossible to so much as look at Franz, even though her life depended on him.

'Alice, you're part-German,' Franz reminded her. 'If it wasn't for your father refusing to work for us, you would have more rights.'

She wondered if he would ever understand how the phrase 'part-German' cut through her? A second-class citizen was nothing, and the way he said 'us' instead of 'them' served to further widen the gulf between them. From her father's perspective, using his research into radio communications for the benefit of these monsters would be a fate worse than death; and even if it would set them free, he knew that it would only be a temporary respite. She had asked her father why his work was so important to the senior members of the Reich. He'd replied that it would allow the Nazis to rule the skies, taking in any countries it passed over, killing as they went.

The thought that so many people who could still call themselves German by law were at that moment travelling to start their days as normal, despite crunching over streets of glass and avoiding pools of innocent blood as they went, had created an ache in her chest that wouldn't subside.

'Where is the best place for Alice now?' Max steered the conversation back to the issue at hand. 'Do we arrange for her to leave the country?'

'We'll have to hide her until it all calms down,' Franz said. 'She can't leave by any ports or borders right now. Perhaps in a few months it could be possible.'

'I'm not leaving the country,' Alice said, sitting up straight. 'Not without Edie.'

'Edie is safe, Alice,' Max said. 'Moving her would be too great a risk.'

Alice had been relieved when he'd told her about a coded letter which had been received at a safe mailbox, stating that Edie hadn't been discovered. She was also comforted by the fact that neither Max nor Franz seemed to know that the sender would have been Sister Carolina, or even that the location was a convent. Her father had kept those who knew to an absolute minimum.

Franz opened up the bag and took out a small gas stove, a knife and some eggs and onions.

'I'm going to make omelettes', he said. He lit the stove and began chopping the food up roughly on a small wooden board, and then threw the pieces into the pan. Spliced onion was soon fermenting the attic space. He motioned for Alice to get the rest of the items out of the bag. She found antiseptic, a flask of water and a selection of fresh clothes.

Her skin stung as she washed the cuts on her arms. She dressed quickly in the corner of the room, putting on a casual button-front checked black and white dress, with a black buckle belt, calf-skin gloves and heeled pumps. She carefully folded her mother's blue and white dress and threw the nightgown to one side. Franz and Max spoke in hurried whispers.

'You are to go submarine until we can get you out of the country,' Franz said, with Max nodding along. 'Last night's actions show that no one is safe now. They will now start arresting anyone who they have previously thought could cause a public outcry, like you.'

She sighed at the prospect of being permanently underground in the city where she had lived her whole life. A stranger in her own hometown.

'You'll hide out in safe houses until the heat is off you,' he went on. 'And then you'll do jobs for us, carrying messages, things like that. We'll get you some new papers that can be used long-term.'

'I'm still not leaving until I know Edie is on a Kindertransport,' Alice insisted.

'Edie would need someone in England to act as a guarantor for her, because she is too young to earn a living there,' he answered. 'For that, you need more money than any of us can spare.'

The pan spitting in his hand and the smell of fried egg reminded Alice that she hadn't eaten since the night before. He tipped the omelette onto a plate, the steam rising as he brought it over. He rested a hand gently on her shoulder, and as though reading her thoughts, added, 'Your father will not be released any time soon.' He said it with such sympathy that she was almost able to believe once again that the old Franz was still in there somewhere.

'Did you have to queue for those eggs and onions, Franz?' Max grinned down at his portion, knowing full well that the Gestapo helped themselves to what were now rare food items.

'Good food is still available to Germans,' Alice muttered. She took a large mouthful, and then became annoyed with herself for accepting the pleasure it gave her. Glancing over at Franz, she noticed how, sitting with a plate of food on his lap and wearing simple civilian clothing, there was a vulnerable normality to him that she was happy to see. 'Is there absolutely nothing we can do to get my father out?' she asked.

'Don't try anything like your visit to the camp again,' Franz warned. 'You're worth a lot of money right now, and that will continue to be the case for as long it takes your father to give up his knowledge and expertise to the Luftwaffe.'

'Who would have thought physics would be so in demand?' Max laughed. 'The coming war will be all about radio beams and bombs. Shame it's not my area of expertise.'

'May father won't allow that,' Alice declared.

'He might decide that he wants to save some of his friends,' Max suggested. 'Quite a few Jewish scientists and intellectuals were arrested last night. He could offer them some of his radar techniques in exchange for a few lives. A kind of payment for knowledge.'

Alice put the food down. She took a deep breath before asking the next question. 'Is my father paying you both to look after me?' she said. 'If so, what happens when the money runs out?

Max's fork clattered to the floor. 'I have to pay people for information, so we can stay one step ahead. Your safety comes at a price, yes,' he sounded hurt. 'But I don't make a profit from you.'

'I'll always protect you,' Franz whispered, taking her hand. He had avoided the question, but the warmth and contact reassured her. 'Where are your real papers?'

'I destroyed them,' she lied. She hadn't been able to let go of her original identity, her real name in paper, nor the photo of her and Franz, or her parents' wedding photo. They hadn't been discovered in the numerous raids on the house that followed her father's arrest. She would keep them under the floorboards in the hall until this whole thing was over. If it ever would be.

Max gave her a look, and she thought for a moment that he was going to say he'd seen her stashing those things away. 'Let's see the identity papers you found on the old woman,' he said.

Reluctantly, she handed the documents over. Holding them in his hands, a grin grew across Max's lips and he smacked them and laughed.

'But these are brilliant!' he waved the Aryan certificates, which confirmed that the holders were each a member of the German race, with birth and baptismal records of parents and grandparents, and a genealogy table going back to 1850. 'They are the best Ariernachweis card forgeries I've seen. We can sell them and change the photos. It's easily done.'

'We can't sell them,' Alice stood up and grabbed them back. She had cried leaving the old woman, and had wanted to take her to the morgue to try and identity the body and secure a proper burial for her. Instead, she'd climbed out of the apartment window and down the fire escape when she heard men smashing their way into the building. She would have to go and see if the death had been recorded when she got out of here. Maybe that could be her way of finding the family that the papers were intended for, or perhaps she could find those American journalists again and ask for their help. She had seen queues of desperate families waiting outside foreign embassies for visas, clutching small suitcases, with hard lines tattooed across their faces. 'I can't take away this family's chance,' she said. 'They must have spent everything they had to get these.'

The two men shared an exasperated glance.

'She'll change her mind,' Max said.

CHAPTER EIGHT

The Boy and the Final Dance

6th May 1939

The pulsating beat was near-palpable as the teenagers, dressed in their long coats and tilted trilbies, jived and gyrated to the sound of Benny Goodman. Chairs and tables, pushed to the edges, framed a dance floor filled with revellers and illuminated by dim lights. A heady mix of cigarette smoke, liquor and perspiration flavoured the air. Boys with slicked back hair and girls with faces painted in colourful make-up wiggled their lower halves with wild, free, unpredictable abandon. The saxophone upped its tempo and the crowd picked up the pace, clapping their hands, jumping up and down and rolling their heads in time with the music. Kurt sat on a table off to the side, tapping his foot and sipping at a tumbler of whiskey which burned his throat. Across the room, Heinz raised a glass and gave him a smile.

For many of them, this was the goodbye party. He felt again for the tickets in his pocket. His lifeline. His way out. He had certainly worked for it over the past six months, starting with sewing papers, rings, necklaces and trinkets into the linings of hats and coats for people who they were helping to escape Germany. He thought of Walter standing over him and repeatedly saying, in the mock American drawl he found so amusing, 'we all need to learn new skills, pal'. Then, once they trusted him enough, he'd helped devise a plan to break into the house where the valuable art pieces were stored. They sold the paintings through connections of Heinz's uncle, a police officer, who wore a party badge and a wary look whenever they turned up at his house. There was never any mention of Heinz's parents, or any other members of his family for that matter.

Kurt's orienteering and survival skills, courtesy of what Walter called his 'misspent Hitler Youth', did come in handy when leading other fugitives out of the city. There was a thrill that came from seeking out secret locations for people to hide, despite it being difficult to mix with most of them socially – these Jews, Commies, degenerates and anti-Nazis. They really were a motley crew, comprised of just about everything he'd ever been taught to oppose.

He did, however, surprise even himself by forming a handful of genuine friendships, most notably with Greta. She had risen from a state of abject despair to become a useful member of the group. Particularly helpful were her sketches of important people that they needed to look out for or trail. She was a highly skilled artist, taking after her father, who had himself been a renowned painter. He, along with her mother, had died when she was still a young girl, leaving her three older brothers to take care of her. He admired her work and enjoyed stories about her brothers' struggles to make her dress like a girl, until they finally gave up and let her wear long shorts and a shirt, resulting in her being mistaken for a boy most of the time. Kurt often caught himself forgetting that she was Jewish.

They hadn't yet found her brothers, and Greta was adamant that she wasn't leaving without them. Heinz was staying, too. Kurt had tried to persuade them both that it was too dangerous to remain in Berlin, but neither was willing or able to look beyond their loyalties to those they were helping.

He ran a hand through his hair, which, now free from dye, was blond once again, after Heinz had received word that those who were looking for him had been tipped off about his previous change of colour.

'What's the matter, my friend?' Walter slumped down in a chair next to him, sweeping back his long hair and revealing a chain of beading sweat across his brow. 'You are used to watching people dancing like there's a stick up their arse, like your old Hitler Youth pals?'

'What's up?' Greta had spun off the dance floor, twirling and laughing as she landed next to them. She raised a pencilled eyebrow and put her hand on Kurt's arm.

'I thought you weren't coming?' she said quietly. 'You were supposed to go and see your mother one final time? Wasn't that your plan?'

The changes Greta had gone through since the time when they'd first met had been remarkable. With dyed blonde hair and pale make-up that lightened her dark eyes and sallow skin, she'd developed a kind of ethereal beauty, and many in the group admired her. Armed with false papers, she used her feminine charms to cosy up to HJ leaders and, more dangerously, SS men; and with such endeavours came serious consequences – the nights she'd come back bloodied and bruised, her clothes ripped. The times when Kurt had helped her back into their various hiding places, with lipstick smudged and stockings torn. He'd try to talk to her about what happened, but she would always brush it off as nothing.

'I'm going soon,' Kurt replied.

'Kurt's not enjoying his final party,' Walter shouted over the din, while casting an approving eye over Greta's short dress. He reached into his double-breasted suit jacket and pulled out a packet of cigarettes, flashing a Union Jack pin badge that glittered in the light of the cafe.

'One last dance before you leave?' Greta took Kurt's hand before he could answer, adding, 'I wouldn't like to think that all of those lessons were a waste.'

He blushed, reminded of the times they'd swayed along together as she taught him to waltz and jitterbug; but no matter how close they got, there was always something nagging, holding him back; and no, it wasn't anything to do with her nightly ventures.

And this face is the face of the Devil. In the middle of this devilish face sits an enormous crooked nose. Behind the glasses glare two criminal eyes. And a grin runs across the protruding lips…

Greta and the other Jews didn't match up to the descriptions that had been loaded onto him by teachers, Hitler Youth leaders and his own mother. Kurt still wondered about the other lessons, though, on subjects such as the German defeat in 1918 being the work of Jewish and Marxist spies that had weakened the system from within, or how Jewish saboteurs had undermined the nation's economy before the Fuhrer stepped in and stopped them. The Jews had a proven history of usury, malevolence and conspiracy, with the aim of destroying Germany and keeping the rest of the world under heel through corrupt, immoral banking systems. They couldn't help themselves, even if they wanted to. These practises were in their blood.

He'd gone back to see his family a few times, watching from a distance as his mother and brother, Amon, went about their day-to-day lives; only now she took in mounds of additional laundry for extra money, giving off a musty smell that seemed to be constantly emanating from the open window, while Amon worked on perfecting an aggressive marching style, his face tight with obedience. There was no sign of his father. He asked Heinz to look into it, and it was soon confirmed that Paul Hertz had indeed been rearrested and sent to Dachau for anti-Nazi activities. He knew who would have been responsible for this.

'Are you okay?' Greta pressed a warm hand to Kurt's chest.

He smiled, but it didn't feel like the right time to bring up this or the other faces that haunted him. His father. Alfons. Peter. Christopher.

Christopher.

Christopher had been a member of the group, a friend in fact, until they discovered that he'd been meeting secretly with a Hitler Youth member. It was Greta who'd caught him, and she was adamant that he had also been behind previous infiltrations that had led to a series of seemingly random attacks by the SS and Gestapo, breaking up parties like the one they were having now. He had protested his innocence, pleading with Heinz and grabbing at his shirt, begging to be believed. Heinz had remained silent, unsure, but Kurt had seen it with his own eyes. They'd followed him to the outer part of the city one night, where he met with Dieter, a boy who Kurt remembered from his own HJ. Dieter, who was all fire in the eyes, singing about flags, banners and battlefields at the top of his voice, was barely recognisable out of uniform, but there was no doubt that it was him they had spotted whispering into Christopher's ear.

'He is my-he is a close friend,' Christopher had tried to explain at his 'trial'. 'He's not like them. I have to see him... I... but he knows nothing of us, I swear.'

Kurt couldn't speak of Dieter's character either way. All he knew for certain was that the boy was generally all bark and no bite.

'You're too close to him to promise that!' Heinz erupted. 'He knows your schedule, and therefore so do the enemy. You've put us all in danger.'

When Christopher finally left, Walter stormed the room, smoking furiously, kicking at furniture. 'Bloody homosexuals,' he muttered.

Kurt had flinched at the term. Until then, he hadn't realised what Christopher was.

Since they had expelled Christopher from their protection there had been no more attacks, and no one had heard anything from him. The whole ordeal still weighed on Kurt's mind, though, alongside the threat of Peter calling for his execution, and the false accusation of killing Alfons. Something wasn't right, he knew. It made him feel uneasy, like they were all living on borrowed time. When he'd asked Greta about it, she'd looked away and said absently, 'We need to have a system of justice. Christopher got what he deserved for betraying us.'

'Greta, why don't you come with me?' he asked. Holding her in his arms, he realised how much he didn't want to leave her.

She drew back. 'Kurt, you don't know what you want from me,' she murmured.

She was right, of course. Handing Kurt his new identity papers at the start of the party, Walter had said with a wry smile, 'You'll have to get over your thing with the Jews, you know. Apparently, it's easier to get on this ship as one of them.' The J stamped across the papers caused his stomach to flip.

Kurt still struggled with why Heinz and the other non-Jews did any of this. He'd tried to talk to them once about how the Jews had stolen victory from Germany in the 1918 defeat, thinking it was something they wouldn't be able to argue against. Walter had started laughing, but Heinz had given him a serious look and asked him to explain what he meant by that. Unused to being questioned, or hearing anyone question this, he found that he couldn't answer. Walter had then asked Greta, who was passing, how she felt about Communists, and she'd replied, 'They're responsible for our country losing the war.' This had confused Kurt to the point where he didn't try and bring anything like this up again.

Realising that Greta had danced him practically to the exit, he unlocked himself from her arms, and without a word turned and headed back to the table where Heinz was sat. It was too hard to explain how he felt about her. He didn't know how he felt. He looked back to see her still standing in the same place, arms by her sides, lonely and lost. For a second, he was tempted to go and try and convince her, plead with her to come with him. But he just couldn't do it. He didn't know what he wanted from her.

'So, your last night,' Heinz addressed Kurt as his eyes surveyed on the room.

'My last night.' Kurt nodded. A heaviness had settled in his heart over the last few hours. Even though he had spent six months un-dercover – or 'U-boat', as they called it – in his home city, with the permanent prickled senses that came with being hunted, he would miss Berlin.

'Chocolate for the journey,' Heinz said, passing a solid bar to Kurt under the table. 'A goodbye gift. Some thanks for all your help in saving many lives. I'm sorry to see you go, but if you stayed much longer, we couldn't guarantee your safety.'

There was nothing to do but agree. The net was closing, and if he didn't leave soon he would be putting others in danger, too. He felt the weight of the chocolate bar in his palm.

'I hope that one day you can come back and clear your name against Fischer,' Heinz added, taking a sip of his drink.

Kurt felt the falling sensation that came whenever Peter Fischer's name was mentioned.

'I trust you still have your Hitler Youth uniform? You'll need it for the train journey.'

'Yes,' Kurt replied. It was out in the alleyway behind the café, hidden from sight. He also had Alfons' papers. Hopefully it would just be a train conductor checking them, who wouldn't recognise the name. 'You could still get a ticket, you know?' he said, already knowing what the response would be.

'There is too much work to be done here – too many people to help,' he took off his glasses and wiped them with his shirt, leaving more marks than there had been before. 'Most of them have next to nothing now that all valuables, and even war medals, have been confiscated.' His lip curled in disgust.

But would they help you? Kurt wanted to ask. Instead, he watched quietly as Greta glided into an effortless spin with Walter.

'Your time on the St Louis will challenge what you've been led to believe.' Heinz replaced his glasses. 'It took losing the use of my legs to teach me how to see life from an untermensch perspective. I hope it doesn't take as much to convince you.'

They sat for a moment, the silence between them emphasised by the laughter, shouts and cheers flying around the dance floor. Kurt eventually put his hand out to Heinz, who took it and smiled, causing a knot to build in his throat. He wanted to soak in as much of the warmth and affection as possible, while he still could, but his ruminations were cut short when the doors at the opposite end of the room blasted open.

Men in uniform piled into the room, their dark fatigues contrasting against the bright colours of the dancers who fled in frantic waves. They crushed furniture under heavy truncheons, throwing chairs up into the air as they closed in on the boys and girls. Some fought back using tables as barricades, while others pulled black cloths down from the windows and smashed their way out. The brown shirts moved quickly, bringing the jazz music to a screeching halt, and replacing it with a soundtrack of echoing screams and crunching bones. In the wake of this brute force trailed a group of long-coated, suited men.

Gestapo.

Once the initial commotion died down, another shadow entered. He was younger than the others, but wore the same leather coat, and his icy stare seemed to be looking past the violence all around him. His skin appeared corpse-white under the lights that bounced off his yellow hair. He was the perfect German poster boy – the ultimate secret police success story. His enemies knew him as The Blond Reaper.

'Franz Muller,' Walter whispered, his face rigid, eyes unblinking.

It was to their advantage that they were positioned in a dark corner, but Kurt knew that it wouldn't hide them for long. He scanned the room for potential exit points.

'Help me,' he hissed at Walter, snapping him back into action. Together, they grabbed Heinz under the elbows and carried him over to the bar behind them. Kurt jumped across, his feet stinging as he hit the ground, and held his arms open to take Heinz. They both landed in a heap, with Heinz groaning as his head bounced off the hard floor. A rush of relief at seeing the open door to the kitchen was soon replaced by a churning in the pit of his stomach. Where is Walter?

While Heinz crawled slowly towards the kitchen, Kurt raised his head above the safety of the bar. Ahead of him, he saw that a pile of necklaces, rings, watches and papers was forming on top of a desk where Franz Muller was sitting, head bent over, absorbed. The intruders had shifted their focus to pulling apart hat and coat linings, spilling out more jewels, visas and ID cards. There looked to be no sign of Walter, until the sound of choked breathing caused Kurt to turn and see him being dragged along the floor, back into the middle of the room, by two Brownshirts. His head was bleeding and his eyes were wide. He looked over at Kurt and mouthed, 'Go!'

Before Kurt could decide what to do, someone threw themselves over him, sending them both crashing to the ground. Raising his fists, he came face to face with Greta. Her face looked drained, but she appeared to be uninjured.

'Is there a way out, Kurt?' she asked.

He took her by the hand and pulled her into the kitchen, where Heinz was waiting. A heavy door shut out the bar, and Kurt shouldered a steel cabinet up against it for good measure.

'There's no exit,' Heinz said in the darkness, his breathing fast and irregular.

Kurt pawed at the walls, scratching until he found a part that wasn't solid. When he finally arrived at a window, he ripped down the curtains, allowing the dim moonlight to trickle in. He cracked the glass with his bare fist, wincing as hot, wet blood made a crimson glove around his hand. A loud thumping started at the door, shaking the steel cabinet. A crack of light appeared at the angle of the doorframe.

Heinz looked towards it. 'You won't have time to get me through,' he said, his face contorted with pain.

'I'll get you through first,' Kurt said.

'No! Greta first!'

'I'll get you both out!' Kurt made a flat base with his hands and lowered, motioning to Greta that she should use it to climb up onto the worktop.

'Offnen sich!' the shouts from the bar grew louder, and the glimmer of light wider. An arm curled around the door.

'Even if you get me outside, I can't go any further,' Heinz spoke quietly and calmly, without a tremble in his voice. 'I don't want all three of us to end up caught.'

Kurt felt bile rising in his throat when he saw what Heinz was doing. 'I can't,' he sobbed. 'I ca-'

'You can,' Heinz snapped. 'And you must.'

Before Kurt could do or say anything else, Heinz had popped a small capsule into side of his mouth, ready to snap and break the poison in at a moment's notice. He felt the air suck out of his lungs.

'Remember, Kurt, you're not theirs. Don't believe what they've told you, and-' the door burst open, cutting Heinz off. 'Go now, and don't look back,' he implored. 'It's easier that way'.

Kurt scrambled up onto the window ledge before the screaming SS men could reach him. He landed in the alleyway, the impact of the hard ground vibrating up through his shins and rattling his knees. His mouth tasted like copper. Greta was nowhere to be seen.

CHAPTER NINE

The Girl and the Boy on the Train

12 May 1939

'Papers please!'

The shout rang through the carriages, and Alice, alone in a compartment designed for six people, scrambled to locate her documents, dropping them with fumbling fingers. Thankfully, no one had witnessed this moment of panic. She'd walked through the connecting corridors of the train, slowly and carefully so as not to tear her stitches, until she arrived at an empty cabin – one which came with the added bonus of a jammed window, trapping enough damp heat to turn away the rest of the passengers. One sniff was all it took for each potential new occupant to decide to look for a seat elsewhere, muttering complaints under their breath. Alice just smiled back at them and exaggeratedly fanned herself. She would have sat in a cabin full of livestock if it meant that she could avoid having company.

She looked out at the station clock, leisurely ticking its way towards midday. Edie should have boarded her train at the same time she had got on this one, if all had gone to plan. It had to have gone to plan. Her stomach tightened. She moved to touch her mother's brooch for comfort, only to be reminded that it was gone, leaving nothing but an empty space behind. It had been sold, along with the identity papers belonging to the family she had failed, to fund Franz's last-ditch effort to get her out. She closed her eyes at the thought of it all, at memories of dark corridors. The instruments on the table. The pain which had caused her to pass out. She comforted herself by remembering that Max and Franz had said Edie could have to go on another train, depending on timings.

The inspector came in and held out his hand. These checks were becoming more frequent, but at least she could be glad that he wasn't SS, even if he did wear a Party badge. He was a stout man, with a twisted moustache that hid his lips well enough but did a poor job of disguising the stench of tobacco and whiskey that tinged his breath. The door opened behind him and a teenage boy slipped in.

The sight of a Hitler Youth uniform sent a shiver down her spine.

Although pale and thin, the boy possessed a number of features that were synonymous with the idealised German – not least a full head of dishevelled dark blond hair. It was her own blonde hair, now teased into loose curls, that had enabled her to put Alice aside and become Anna.

He started rummaging through his pockets, displaying an air of panic. He took out a piece of paper which the inspector barely glanced at before leaving the cabin, and then shoved the battered brown leather carrying case into the luggage rack.

She tried to concentrate on her book – an Agnes Miegel, which she was able to stomach due to its focus on places rather than people – but still couldn't help but steal glances in his direction; whereas he just kept looking straight out of the window, only occasionally turning to check the cabin door. Whenever he ran a hand through his hair, her eyes would be drawn to patterns of tiny cuts that covered his fingers and knuckles, criss-crossing like tiny diamonds. He caught her looking and stuffed his hands into his pockets. As the train started to move he let out a deep breath, which Alice thought was awfully careless.

The train rocked them gently across the countryside towards Hamburg. When it rolled into the next station, a succession of soldiers ran past the window as the wheels screeched to a complete standstill. Alice put her head back in the book and tried to stop her hands trembling at the trampling of heavy boots and shouts and screams from the other cabins. She met the boy's eyes. They were wide with fear, and for a split-second, a shared panic passed between them. Suddenly, he leaned over and grabbed her, pulling her across to his side of the cabin. She tried to kick and squirm but knew that anything approaching screaming was completely out of the question.

'Shush, or this will be worse for us,' the boy said, his lips almost close enough to touch her cheek. 'What's your name?'

'Anna Gerber.' She had practised responding with this name many times.

'Alfons Lehmann' he spoke briskly and formally. 'That is what you'll call me if they ask. Now, sit on my knee.' He seemed used to being obeyed.

She didn't answer. She couldn't win.

'Please,' his voice softened. 'They are almost here.'

Two of them entered the carriage, state labour service types who were barely out of the Hitler Youth themselves. They wore sneering looks on their faces, knowing that they could treat people however they wish and get away with it.

'Gentlemen, please,' Alfons addressed them in a jovial tone. 'A little privacy for me and my girl.' He leaned back casually against the seat, but Alice could feel that his hands were sticky with sweat.

The boys hesitated, seemingly not knowing what to make of the scene. They appeared to have come across two blue-eyed, blond haired poster children, and one of them was dressed just like they were.

'Come on,' Alfons implored them. 'We never get a carriage to ourselves.'

'Papers,' the taller one demanded, stepping closer.

Alice could see that the man was uncertain of what the correct course of action was. He smoothed down his dark hair and fixed his attention on her. The shorter one lingered behind, shifting his weight from one foot to another.

Her papers would hold up under even the most intense scrutiny, she knew; but it would still be dangerous if she were to be taken to Gestapo headquarters for being associated with this mad boy, whose forgeries were unlikely to be of as high a quality as hers. She rearranged the material of her dress as she took out her papers, revealing a little more of her legs and cleavage. The young men's eyes lowered in response, and both of their faces became visibly reddened.

Alfons dug his hand into his pockets and pulled out a document, which as it turned out wasn't even an official proof of identity. It was a Hitler Youth membership.

The dark haired one continued to stare, causing Alice's smile to narrow. He looked like he was about to say something, but then a round of shouting broke in from the next carriage and diverted his attention. He threw the papers back at them without a word, as he and his sidekick stomped off to investigate.

Out of the window, a man and woman were being dragged and kicked along the tracks. The men were pulling off the man's shoes, tearing off the soles to reveal a wad of money that went rolling into the waiting hands of a smiling soldier. Jews weren't allowed to have bank accounts, the man was desperately trying to explain. The train started up again, leaving Büchen station and its unfortunate victims behind in a cloud of steam.

Alice let herself breathe again and moved over to her own seat. The train clattered as it picked up speed.

'We live another day,' Alfons said. He had a low voice, almost smoky, which moved through the carriage slowly and hit all her nerves.

'Why did you have to get me involved?' she stared at him in disbelief. 'Do you have a death wish, acting like that?'

'You know, some days I think I do,' he said. 'But really, when it comes down to it, I don't.' He looked at her carefully. 'You could have denounced me.'

Her stomach flipped. This conversation wasn't safe. No wonder her father had always said she was her own worst enemy.

'You needn't worry,' he smirked. 'You look like a perfect little Bund Deutscher Mädel girl. Where are you off to, a hike? A climb? Perhaps a lesson on becoming a wife, a mother, a homemaker?'

There was a playful warmth to his words, but she wasn't sure whether to trust it; otherwise, she would have told him about her experiences with the League of German Girls, and how they praised her sporting prowess and energy. That was until they found out who – or what, as they saw it – she really was. There was time when she had been so eager to be accepted by such groups, but that was before. She was a different person now. She knew better.

'I heard that camping is banned now, though,' he continued. 'After, what was it, nearly a thousand girls came back from Nürnberg with the beginnings of a new army for our Fuhrer inside their bellies?'

'I've never camped,' she replied, trying to keep the conversation neutral; and then blushed, realising that it sounded as though she was referring to something else, which she also hadn't done before, as a matter of fact.

'Is that right?' he raised an eyebrow and lowered his voice.

Alice couldn't meet his eye, knowing that she would flush even more. In a way, it pleased her. Even after all that had happened, she was still capable of frivolous emotion. In some ways, she was still just a normal seventeen-year-old.

He stood and removed his leather satchel from the shelf, taking out a small object and sitting back down again. It was a bar of milk chocolate. He broke some off.

'Here,' he said, leaning across and handing it to her.

Their fingertips brushed. She popped a small piece into her mouth and swallowed without really tasting it. He looked up at her, his clear blue eyes staring right into hers. She felt the heat rising in her cheeks.

'Nice, isn't it?' he asked softly as he sat back.

'W-what?' she stammered.

'The chance for normal conversation,' he replied. 'So, Anna-

'So, Alfons,' she cut in, matching his sarcasm.

'What should we discuss? The meaning of life maybe?'

'The people who know the answers to that have been taken away,' she blurted out.

He raised his eyebrows and for a moment she panicked, thinking that this had been a trap all along.

'I don't think that would be a normal conversation at all,' he said shaking his head. 'Could we not just be two young people going on a trip? I won't ask about your destination, and you don't ask about mine,' he shot her a serious look. 'Are you going to eat the rest of that?'

She followed his gaze to the remaining chocolate, which was starting to melt in her palm, and felt suddenly compelled to stuff it into her mouth in one go, almost choking in the process. She made sure to savour the taste of it this time – a brief reminder of a forgotten pleasure.

'Maybe you are not such a good BDM girl after all,' he laughed.

It was a nice sound, laughter, she thought; and she would have laughed herself if she hadn't been fighting to regain some semblance of ladylike poise.

'Sorry,' she said, mildly embarrassed.

'Don't be sorry,' he said. 'You actually looked happy for a moment there, even if you did nearly kill yourself.' He started fidgeting in his seat. 'We should pretend to be a couple.'

'Why?'

'Oh, I just think it could be fun. It'd be like living again – properly, I mean. The way people used to.'

There was such sadness in his voice that she had to look away from him. Fun belonged to the past, before life became purely about surviving. She had spent so long thinking of death that the purpose of life had become something she couldn't quite grasp anymore. Life seemed like so much effort and caused so much worry and anguish that it hardly seemed worth the trouble. No, life was not about living – not about enjoying yourself, making friends, being yourself or going out to eat and drink and laugh, like it was for other teenagers.

It was all about death.

'What does a normal couple in Germany talk about?' she asked, wanting some reprieve from her own thoughts, however temporary.

'You like art?'

'I like sport.'

'You should wear this uniform,' he pulled at his collar.

She noticed the slight burn marks embedded into the material of his shirt, faded but still visible.

'You run?' he spoke slowly.

'Yes.'

'How long have you been into this running?'

'Six months, officially. And you?'

'Same.'

'How do you...not give up when you feel...tired? How do you-' her voice broke on the last word.

He tilted his head, looking at her in a way which told her that he understood everything; about leaving people, losing people, never really getting to know people and living in anonymity.

'It's easy, he said. 'I just never look back.'

He was trying to sound casual, but it didn't quite work.

Tears started to prick at her eyes. She pressed her fingers against them to stop the flow.

'We are making each other sad,' he said gently, and then leaned across the carriage again, whispering, 'you want to hear a joke?'

She nodded.

'You'll have to come over here,' he said, patting the empty seat next to him. 'I don't want to say it too loudly.'

She got up cautiously and moved across. They were so close that she could smell the mustiness of his well-worn uniform.

'Hitler visits a lunatic asylum,' he began. 'The patients give the

Nazi salute. As he passes down the line he comes across a man who isn't saluting. "Why aren't you saluting like the others?" Hitler barks. "I'm the nurse, mein Führer," comes the answer. "I'm not crazy!"'

She laughed, and he smiled in response. They sat in silence for a moment. He was looking somewhere far off in the distance.

'Are you okay?' she asked.

'That is a beautiful laugh,' he said, his focus snapping back to her.

'How can a laugh be beautiful, you fool?' She gave him a playful punch on the shoulder.

He seemed as surprised at the gesture as she was. A part of the old her had slipped back in. Alice had regained territory from Anna. It was a momentary return of 'the ruffian', as her father would affectionately refer to her.

'You hit hard for a girl,' he mockingly rubbed his arm, causing a patch of the sewn-over material to come away. She caught a glimpse of skin that was abnormally smooth and pink in colour, raised up over the rest of his pale arm.

'Old war wound,' he said, visibly uncomfortable.

He stood abruptly, as though he was about to leave, but instead of heading for the door he again fetched his bag down from the rack. He then pulled off his shirt, revealing a lean, muscular body, and sat back down with what she realised was a small sewing kit.

'Will you have a rest from running soon?' he asked, while at the same time expertly looping a thread through the battered garment, fixing the patch back into place. 'Or maybe you will give it up completely?' The rhythm of his voice altered in time with the needle as it moved in and out.

'Yes,' she said. 'Very soon.'

'Me too.'

'You're good at that,' she remarked, watching him work. 'My

father says that I had no patience for sewing.'

He stopped for a moment. 'And what does your mother say?'

Alice tried to form the words to explain about her mother, about what had happened to her. But aside from the grief sticking in her throat, it would be too dangerous.

'Is she-' he looked up from his work.

'Yes,' her eyes were filling up again.

'I am sorry for your loss.'

'What about the rest of your family? Are they still...here?'

It was a risky question that she wouldn't blame him for avoiding. She averted her gaze as he rose to slip his shirt back on.

'I think so,' he said, sitting back down and fastening the front buttons. 'Although some days I do not know. People can disappear and still be there, you know?'

She knew.

'Almost there,' he said.

Out of the window, metal lines fell over themselves to form the archways of Hamburg station. He brought down her luggage along with his bag, handing it over with a smile. Inside her small suitcase were a few neatly packed dresses, skirts and blouses, as well as a toothbrush and some cosmetics.

The cover story she had been given was that she was visiting a friend in Hamburg. She was wearing the same black and white dress and heeled pumps that Franz had brought her that night in November. Franz. There had been no time to warn him that her real identity papers were still under the floorboards of the entrance hall to her family home, right next to a photograph of the two of them together. She had spent months deliberating over what she should do with them, and then, in the haste of fleeing, she had left them behind. No one will ever discover them, she reasoned with herself for the thousandth time. Franz is not in danger.

They left the carriage, and Alfons helped her down onto the platform from the train's high step. Her heart pounded and her stomach lurched at the sight of all the people; the uniforms, the informers, the hidden trouble-makers who wanted to make money from finding the vanished. Perhaps there were also some like her, whose insides were so used to jittering that they never really stopped. As he let go of her hand, she looked at his face and saw the same alertness – a fear so palpable that she wondered if she could reach out and touch it. It was unlikely that they would meet again, she knew. She hoped his path would be safe.

She turned to him. 'It has been-'

He cut her off with a hug that warmed her from head to toe. She buried her face in his mended sleeve and bit her lip so that she wouldn't cry. She hadn't been hugged in so long.

'My name is Kurt,' he whispered into her ear as he released her.

She didn't answer. To reveal her true name would be too dangerous, no matter the circumstances.

He stepped back and gave her one last smile, and she made a mental note to store this image of him with the few good memories she still had. The ones that she was constantly battling to prevent from being pushed out.

'Goodbye Anna,' he spoke quietly. 'I wish you the best of luck'.

With that, he turned and walked off into the darkness. He didn't look back.

CHAPTER TEN

The Boy and the Girl on the Deck of the Ship

13 May 1939

The ship was a black and white cliff rising out of the dock.

Kurt stood in line, listening to the smashing of valuables and cries of despair as people's luggage was ransacked in the wooden shed that they were all queuing to enter. The mournful tune of a brass band, present to give the ship a traditional musical farewell, provided a depressing backing track. A woman wearing a bright yellow dress – faded and patched in places, but still incongruous to the dark threads of the other passengers – hummed along to a popular German song.

The brown-coated back of an elderly man with thinning grey hair shook in futile attempts at suppressing a bone-rattling cough. Kurt had been stood directly behind him for more than half an hour and had still not seen his face. No one dared turn around.

'Umzug!'

The shout to move was bellowed into Kurt's ear, as an SS Officer pushed him roughly into the shed. Inside, the pungent stench of several hundred tired and scared people that had passed through, and were still passing through, took his breath away. Hanging around the edge of the room, conspicuous in their expensively tailored suits and hats, stood members of the Gestapo. A uniformed official cast narrowed eyes over his papers and opened up his suitcase. The man's hair was parted in an ode to Hitler, but a matching moustache had failed to thrive above his thin, cruel mouth.

'Enough!' cried a small man in crew member's uniform, who had stepped inside the shed. 'I would remind all of you to follow the captain's orders,' he said, dusting his hands off at arm's length, and looking pointedly towards the SS. He turned to the passengers. 'I am the ship's purser. My men and I will be on hand to look after you during the voyage. There will be an evening meal waiting for each of you when you board.' He projected an air of authority, but there was a kindness to his pale, freshly-shaven face that set him apart from the other officials. 'My men will remain here until you are finished, to ensure that the captain's directions are followed.'

Kurt looked to the suited Gestapo men, who were staring at the ship's purser with interest. One of them had written something down in a notebook. The agent inspecting Kurt's suitcase zipped it up and threw it back at him. There were now only a few more steps to the gangplank, to freedom, and yet his anxiety did not subside. He could smell his own sweat, which continued to pour out of him profusely, mixed with the thick odour of rotten food, as well as the animal hides that lingered on him, after he'd spent the previous night sleeping in an unguarded shack that was filled with them. His back stiffened at the sight of more men in suits waiting by the gangway, beneath a swastika flag flying proudly at the stern.

'You see how the Jew smells?' a crewman muttered as Kurt walked past.

He looked down at his papers again, at the distinct 'J' stamped next to the new name and surname, both still so alien to him. He had to fight against his innate revulsion at the symbol, and also at those around him, with all of their pleading and wailing. Why didn't they all get together and fight against what was happening to them? At least he was fleeing because he did something brave – a real act of resistance. He was not simply running away.

'Halt mal!'

A shout came from behind, and a hand gripped his shoulder. He turned around and found himself face to face with a Gestapo agent wearing thick-rimmed glasses on a long nose. The man shoved him out of the way and stormed past the other passengers, knocking them aside like bowling pins as he homed in on a girl of around Kurt's age. She wore a blue floral dress, with her blonde hair pinned up in unsteady curls that were rapidly unravelling as she stumbled down the plank, ahead of an official who was shoving her roughly back onto the dock. Her tear-streaked face was marble-white. She looked defeated. Everyone had something to hide, and the Gestapo weren't going to let them all get away with it. She was most likely being made an example of. Kurt hoped they would let her back onto the ship, but he wouldn't have bet on it. People lowered their eyes as she passed.

Kurt carried on walking, but tripped over something and found himself sprawled on the floor, as his chin smashed against the hard wooden floor. Through blurred eyes, he saw the long, sneering face of a skinny crew member hovering above him.

'What do you think you're doing?' he barked, as he scrambled up to his feet and shoved the man, sending him stumbling into the small crowd behind them.

The sailor's feet thudded along the deck like rumbling thunder, but he quickly regained his balance and began to laugh. Blood filled Kurt's mouth, metallic and thick.

The purser was on the scene in a flash, reprimanding the crewman who had attacked Kurt, and summoning another to attend to him. 'Please show this gentleman to his room,' he instructed.

He then proceeded to welcome the rest of the passengers on board, or at least he attempted to. He smiled at two twins, who in turn retreated into their father's arms; he tried to greet an elderly man, who responded by putting his suitcase in front of his chest for protection, before he finally gave up on the exercise after a man with a shaved head flinched when he offered him his hand.

Kurt followed the man who had been assigned to guide him through the throng of grimy and grubby and sharp-boned people, all pushing their way hurriedly through the corridors.

'Here you are, sir,' the steward nodded as he held the door open.

The room was simple and small, but spotlessly clean. The pillows and bed linen were crisply laundered and crackled slightly as he touched them. The harsh mix of engine oil, gasoline and salt air that filled the deck was softened here by the scent of soap and fresh linen. He took off his suit, tossing the stinking jacket to the floor, and lay down on the bed. Closing his eyes did nothing to stop the guilt, or any of the other assaults on his senses. Smoke and felt fire: Alfons. Weightless falling: Peter. The chalky taste in his mouth: Heinz.

The ship shrieked as it readied to move off. It was a welcome distraction. He had never been abroad before. In fact, he had never really expected to travel more than a few miles from his dank bank-alley apartment in Berlin; and now here he was, leaving the country on a grand ship and being called 'sir' – by a man who thought he was Jewish, no less. He had no intention of watching as Germany grew smaller and more distant, but the rumblings of the ship, the footfalls of passengers and the general commotion outside combined to make it impossible to rest. He ran the taps, rubbed a damp hand towel over his face and headed for the main deck.

A thicker crowd had formed, hunched around the view of the port. A piercing blast of the horn, shouts from the crew, ropes slipping away.

'Goodbye Germany!' A little boy waved happily, while a man with tears streaming down his face squeezed his narrow shoulders. It was a strange feeling, to be sad about leaving a country that didn't want you, Kurt knew.

'Have we really made it?' An old man whispered to another. 'Will they not come and take us back again?'

'We have a wonderful new life ahead of us,' proclaimed a woman dressed in furs and finery, despite the breezy heat. She was speaking to a little girl in a pink coat, whose attention was fixed on the endless procession of mini-waves that pawed feebly at the hull. 'And Papa will follow us,' she added. The woman's voice was calm, but her eyes were red. A constant sniffing betrayed a lack of conviction in her own words.

He thought about his own mother – her soft caramel hair, the worry lines, which had increased at a worrying rate over the last year, and the warmth of her embrace. He was leaving her at the mercy of the Fatherland, and his brother completely under Hitler's spell. There felt a strong pull inside, urging him to go back to shore and take his chances. He knew that he had no choice but to resist it, though.

Smoke rolled out from the twin stacks of black, red and white. The crowd surged forward, some of them coughing with the fumes. A girl pushed past him, her face inches from his.

'Anna?'

Her eyebrows knotted in confusion.

'Anna, it's me, Kurt.'

She didn't respond – hardly even looked at him, and instead roughly shoved her way towards the gangplank, which was still being removed by the crew.

'No!' she screamed, sending a ripple of panic through the deck. Kurt managed to grab her before she could pull herself over the railings.

'Get off me!' she yelped, swinging wild punches that caught him about the head.

'She is crazy, let her jump,' a man next to them said, before moving away like everyone else had.

'Stop it!' Kurt hissed into her ear. 'Do you want the Gestapo to come and take you?'

'I have to go back,' she said, sobbing, but her punches were weak and her legs weaker still. Forlornly, she pulled herself up using the rail as the ship moved away from the port. 'My sister,' she whispered to the disappearing shoreline of a place that she had once called home.

CHAPTER ELEVEN

The Girl tries to get off the Ship

13 May 1939

Alice sat on the deck, head in hands. Different sensations washed over her. The unsteadiness of the ship. The sun sparkling against the sea below. The never-ending blue sky above. The feeling of watching everything slip away. Edie not making it out.

The boy from the train – Alfons or Kurt or whatever his name was – stood awkwardly over her. He held out his hand to help her up. She ignored it.

'I need to get off,' she said, trying to use the cold steel railing to pull herself up, only to find her legs too leaden to shift. The hardwood deck had bruised her when she fell. She got back up, knocking

against people, who in turn avoided her, not wanting to draw attention to themselves through the mad girl who wanted to go back to
that land. Layers of anticipation and anguish made up the crowd.

A blast from the ship's great horn pierced the still morning air.
The crowd at the railings went quiet as they began to tremble away
from Germany.

'It's too late,' the boy shook his head. 'We're moving.'

She considered her options, such as they were.

As though reading her thoughts, he said softly, 'The Gestapo are
watching. They've already taken one girl, and I don't think they let
her back on.'

He didn't need to expand on that — to say what everyone who
could hear them must have been thinking. A girl who would have
done anything to stay on here was taken away, and here you are
trying to get off and jump straight into danger. She accepted his
hand and got back to her feet.

'The best thing you can do for your sister is stay on this ship,' he
said. 'I know how hard that is to hear, but it's true.'

'Don't presume to tell me what's best for my sister,' she shook her
blonde curls. 'You don't know her. You don't even know me.'

'I saved you on that train.'

'No, I saved you. All you did was take liberties and put me in
danger. My papers were fine, otherwise you'd have got me hauled in
front of the Gestapo.'

'Then why are you on this ship?' He held out his hands.

'I could go back and get her,' her voice was growing quieter as her
throat constricted. 'We could wait for another ship.'

'What other ship?'

She pushed back the tears, hiding them behind a fresh mask. It
was harder than ever now that she was leaving the country where

Edie and her father both remained, trapped. She had thought that she would be better equipped to deal with the emotion of it all, given that she hadn't seen either of them in months, but some wounds were beyond the healing powers of time. 'I'll get off at the next port,' she said decidedly, remembering that they were due to stop at Cherbourg, France. From there, she would be able to get back to Germany by train, and then collect her sister and look for other means of escape. It didn't have to be by ship. All wasn't lost. A sigh of relief escaped her body.

She took a proper look at the boy who appeared to be following her around, and for a moment, anxiety gripped her. Could the Gestapo have planted him? No. If that was the case, the ship wouldn't have been allowed to set sail with her still on it. She relaxed again.

He was dressed in a smart brown suit which softened his features, sharp and angular as they were. She guessed that they weren't his clothes, but then who really owned anything these days? Many of their fellow passengers would have sold everything but the clothes on their backs just to get on board. A woman brushed past them wearing a well-worn fur coat with a strong musky scent, but that soon gave way to another, even more pervasive odour when she was nudged closer to her unwanted companion. It reminded her of Berlin, after Hitler made everyone choose war over washing.

'You smell like a farm,' she told him, wrinkling up her nose.

The lines of worry and hunger faded from his face as he laughed.

'And your real name is Kurt?' she asked

He nodded.

'At least you're not wearing that Hitler Youth uniform.'

'Thought it best to throw it into the sea,' he said.

'How did you manage to get hold of one of those anyway?'

He opened his mouth to reply, but then the crowd suddenly surged forward, and she found herself pressed right up against him. Even though he smelled like cow hides, there was a warmth emanating from him that she couldn't help but find comforting; and realising that he was just as bony as she was made her feel a little less self-conscious about her own body. Nevertheless, she still felt the betrayal of a blush on her cheek as he looked at her closely.

'It's getting too busy out here,' he said.

She agreed, and they pushed their way out and walked around to the other side of the deck.

'They'll be watching at the next port, and you know they'll arrest anyone from this ship who tries to go back,' he spoke softly and calmly, his face creased with concern. 'Get to Cuba and then America, like everyone else is doing. Make some money there and use it to get your sister out.'

It was the same plan that Franz and Max had convinced her to agree to, after the night when she realised that she couldn't stay in Berlin any longer. She shuddered at the dark memories that were forever reaching out to touch her.

A boy edged past them, muttering inaudibly and taking zigzagging steps that made harsh little taps against the wooden floors. He took off his hat, revealing a shaved head with early bristles of hair that was trying to grow back. Alice could see that most of his fingernails were missing as he ran a hand over his scalp while moving closer to the railings. He leaned over the side.

'He's going to jump!' she shouted, rushing over and grabbing his arm.

He turned, and she had to fight to stop herself from gasping as the sun lit up his face. There were flesh wounds bursting across his skull, and bruising of all colours painted his skin, from dull yellows and deep blues, to angry purples and harsh reds. His eyes were sunken, and his mouth was taut and twisted. A thin red line ran around his neck.

'Don't jump,' Alice said as calmly as she could. The boy flinched as though her words had cut into him, and started shouting in garbled sentences, like two languages merging. His features became distorted as he grabbed at the wounds on his face. He started to climb over the railings again.

'No!' Alice screamed as she threw herself forward and grabbed his leg.

He was too strong for her, and she found herself being dragged over with him; but then she felt Kurt getting in between them, and together they forced the boy down onto the deck, where he landed with a thud. He tried frantically to get back to his feet as they held onto him, until another boy appeared from around the corner, panting.

'Please,' the newcomer said to Alice and Kurt, gesturing for them to move out of the way.

They obliged, and he leaned over the boy, grasping his hand and speaking in a reassuring tone.

'Gus, it's Eli. It's okay.'

'Have you seen it? Have you seen it?' Gus was shouting in clear German now, pointing towards the stern of the ship. 'It's all a trick. They'll take us to a camp.'

Eli turned to Alice and Kurt. 'It's the flag on the stern,' he said. 'It's got a few of the passengers worried – especially those who had been interned until now.'

Alice nodded. She couldn't help thinking of her father. Was he in a similar state? No, Franz had assured her that he had special privileges, whereas this poor Gus had probably been subjected to the worst of it. Kurt was completely still beside her. She glanced at him and saw the horror and fear in his eyes. His gaze was riveted to Gus's wounds.

'I won't let them take you back there,' Eli soothed. 'You're safe now. The ship has left.'

Gus continued to simply shake his head.

'Did I tell you that I saw the captain?' Eli continued. 'It's true that he doesn't wear any kind of party insignia on his clothes. Some of the crew are grumbling behind his back that he isn't loyal to Hitler, especially with all the trouble he's gone to in order to make this a comfortable voyage. He's even converting the social hall for the Sabbath. It's a lot of effort to go to for a trick, no?'

Gus sat up, blinking, confused, but free of the consuming panic of moments earlier.

Eli got up too, putting out a hand to Alice and Kurt in turn. 'Eli-yahu Lewim,' he said, smiling. 'Call me Eli.'

Alice was immediately taken aback by how striking he was. His sallow skin looked chronically deprived of daylight, and his hooked nose was much like those that the Nazis drew on their ridiculous posters, as were his dark, brooding eyes and carefully parted black hair. Such bold features, along with a powerful, confident aura, combined to make her find him incredibly attractive. She realised then that she was staring at him.

'Anna Hermes,' she replied, the name sliding more easily off her tongue each time she said it.

Kurt didn't offer his name or his hand.

'I'd better get Gus to his cabin to rest,' Eli said.

'Do you want us to help?' Alice asked.

'No, that's okay,' he replied. 'But, please, come and join me and my friends later on B deck. Everyone is welcome.'

Alice stiffened at the word everyone. He'd nodded at them both pointedly when he said that. What did he suspect? Before she could think of anything else to say, Eli and Gus left, walking slowly towards the cabins, their tattered shoes making shuffling sounds on the deck.

Kurt remained silent beside her.

'Are you all right?' she asked.

'I'm just tired, I think,' he said, somehow looking even paler. 'I'll walk you to your cabin.'

'We should both get some rest,' she suggested.

On the way, they passed an older woman wearing a shabby black pinafore dress that would have once been grand, asking if there would be kosher food. Her voice shook over the words.

'Regrettably not,' a crew member informed her. 'But we do have plenty of fish and eggs.'

'This is a strange ship,' Alice said, but when she looked around for a response, Kurt was lagging behind her, holding onto the wall.

'That may be the case,' he tried to force a smile, but his strained voice gave away the discomfort he was in. 'But promise me you will stay on it.'

'Do you need to sit down for a minute?' she asked, but he shook his head and they carried on walking.

When they reached her room, he collapsed onto the floor outside; and although he pulled himself straight back up, Alice could feel the heat coming from his body in waves.

'I'll get you a doctor,' she said.

'No, please,' he gasped. 'Don't. If you could just help me-'

She opened the door to her cabin and he stumbled onto the second bed. The one that had been meant for Edie. She ran the taps in the small sink and soaked a small towel, dabbing it over his feverish skin. He sighed with relief, but his eyes remained closed.

He spent the next day drifting in and out of consciousness. She had been worried about how they would get food, but every so often she would find a tray outside. It could contain anything from steaming soup to freshly baked bread, and sometimes even cakes, crumbling and glorious to taste. She never saw anyone coming or going.

Kurt seemed to dream in memories. He talked about fire and falling and complained of chalk in his mouth. He shouted out names. Alfons. Heinz. Peter. Mostly Alfons, though. He called for his father and mother. He told people to leave his father alone. He shouted at someone called Amon to stop, always stop. Eventually, she called on the ship's doctor. He said it was common for the body to collapse in on itself after a period of stress was lifted. He'd been treating a lot of passengers who'd been either in hiding or held at a camp.

Just as Kurt seemed to be coming around, Alice felt the tinge of a fever starting up in her own body. Later, lying on her own bed, her skin caked in sweat and with the world a dizzy, toppling place, Kurt served her a broth, and sleep brought forth her own memories. She found herself shouting out, too; and was hazily half-aware that she was telling him something that she shouldn't have been. She was telling him her real name.

CHAPTER TWELVE

The Boy and the Pact

16th May 1939

He found her sitting outside in the cool sea air. She'd pulled out two deckchairs, and he knew she'd been waiting for him. Something had shifted between them, and an unspoken bond had developed; one which had started to form on the train, but had become more solid during their sickness. He had been so used to living in fear, barely trusting anyone. This was strange. Welcome, but still strange. She would be feeling the same way, he knew, and now he wanted to reassure her.

'Alice, I-' he began.

'So, I did do it, then,' she said, twisting a napkin in her hand. 'I missed the port, and I told you my real name.'

He sat down, steadying himself before replying. The rolling waves hitting the ship still affected his barely settled stomach. 'Yes, you did,' he said. 'But you don't need to worry.' He wanted to reach out to her, put his hand over hers.

She turned to face him, her intense blue eyes looking fully into his. 'You also told me things,' she said.

It wasn't a threat, but she was holding his gaze. He could tell that she was used to bargaining for silence, using secrets to survive.

'You only gave away your name,' he said, thinking it was better to admit everything, and hoping that she'd do the same in return. 'I promise.'

She sighed. 'You only talked in names, too.'

'I won't tell anyone,' he said. Not that he had any idea who would ask. He had no intention of getting to know anyone else on the ship.

'Thank you,' she replied.

They sat quietly for a few moments. Children were playing on the deck, dancing over chalk squares. Their laugher was more muted than would be expected, given their age. It was as though they were only just waking up to freedom, and slowly shaking off the need to keep quiet in order avoid the wrong sort of attention. Several of the boys were wearing skullcaps.

'Are you Jewish?' Kurt asked, tentatively. He had to know. He'd almost said, 'are you one of them', but had managed to stop himself in time.

She shook her head and looked out to sea. 'Does it matter?' She titled her head to one side, studying him. 'You are, I presume?'

'Yes, I'm Jewish,' he said, the words sticking in his throat. He didn't think that his feverish shouts had suggested otherwise.

She turned away again.

'That boy Gus,' she said. 'The camps. I can't stop thinking about it.'

He didn't want her to say that – to bring up what had been haunting his own thoughts.

'My father is in one,' she added.

'Mine too.'

He didn't want to talk about it, and he could tell that she didn't, either. If she wasn't smiling her eyes were heavy, and her skin still had a pallid post-fever sheen. When she'd fallen ill, right when he was getting better, her sudden vulnerability had scared him; but just as she had fed him the broth that kept appearing at the door, he in turn had sat and patiently coaxed her into taking small mouthfuls. He felt that it was his responsibility to take care of her, even though she was already showing the strength and resilience he'd first witnessed on the train. The steeliness in her voice and alertness in her eyes were creeping back in.

'Who do you think kept leaving the food?' she asked.

'There was probably a crew member instructed to look after us,' he concluded.

'Strange, though,' she reflected.

'Only because we're not used to being looked after, but we have paid for this voyage after all.'

Even as he said it, the very idea sounded odd. It had only been in the last six months that he'd found himself as a 'non-citizen' of his own country. Before that, everyone had treated him okay, or as a human at least. Even if she was not Jewish, as an enemy of Germany she would have been treated poorly, he knew.

'I wanted to make a pact,' she said, turning to him suddenly. There was a fire in her eyes, but also the smallest hint of fear that he could see she was desperate to hide. 'A pact that we both look after each other on this voyage.'

He nodded, and she relaxed slightly, her shoulders loosening.

The corners of her mouth turned up into a grin. 'You made a

pretty good nurse, you know.'

'I was certainly better than you,' he smiled. 'It took three washes to get that soup out of my shirt.'

'Well you kept moving around,' she was still grinning. It transformed her face, releasing the shadows. 'But you survived, so I must have got some of it in.'

'I never said thank you for going along with my story on the train.'

'Who was Alfons?' she asked, but then saw his face. She bit her lip and gave a nod, acknowledging silently that it wasn't a question for now.

The fire, he thought. It was never far. It felt like his breath was stuck inside his chest. Maybe the way to extinguish it would be to forget everything.

'OK,' he said. 'So, the pact also has to be that we live on this voyage, and not just survive.'

She furrowed her brow inquisitively.

'We wipe the slate clean,' he went on. 'We're Kurt and Alice.'

Her eyes widened, and she quickly scanned the area, searching for anything other than children and chalk nearby.

'Sorry, Anna if we're in public,' he corrected. 'And we're on holiday, and for these two weeks nothing else matters.'

The loud lunch gong started and shook the ship.

'I don't feel like any food,' she said, shaking her head.

'But that would be to reject living,' he said, taking her hand in his and helping her up. 'We're not eating purely to survive now, remember? We're here to enjoy it. Let's take a walk around the ship and then sit down for a real lunch. We've been cooped up for days between us – although I must admit, your cabin is superior to mine. You must have better contacts than me.'

A shadow crossed over her face, and he worried that he'd said the wrong thing again. He didn't even know why he'd added the last part. No one wanted to talk about the things they'd done to get on this ship.

'Although at least mine will smell better,' he joked, and was relieved to see her laugh.

'You're the one who obviously hadn't washed in months before getting on here,' she retorted. 'At least you've had a bath now, so I can walk next to you without holding my nose.'

He smiled, remembering the glorious feeling of warm water against his skin in the bathing facilities of the ship. It was cheap soap, but still better than anything he'd had at home, and it was enough to loosen some of the knots in his joints. By the time he'd finished, the water had turned a murky grey, like the ocean all around them. He almost felt as though he'd cleansed himself of some of the past.

The wheelhouse windows of the cabins receded as they entered the ship, heading for the social hall. They walked over plush carpets, under crystal chandeliers, past gilt-framed windows and polished woodwork. Some of the passengers turned their heads away from the luxury, walking quickly over the carpets as though they didn't want to leave an imprint. Many were allowing themselves to relax, though, acting like they had once been used to lavishness such as this. Kurt felt awkward and out of place, as though his poor roots would be sniffed out by the others. It was a scent that he feared no amount of washing could scrub off.

He turned to see how Alice was coping, and was surprised to see that her head was held high. She glided along the first-class area as though she had every right to be there. She was used to this, so much so that when a crew member asked to see their tickets, she waved him away confidently with a rapid recital of her room number, naming Kurt as her guest.

They sat down, and she ordered assertively, barely glancing at the menu, and he noticed her accent properly for the first time. His guttural Berlin had taken a kicking with Heinz and Walter. He'd even picked up a slight Anglo accent, thanks to the slang habits of the swing kids. Hers was inherited, ingrained. Bought and taught.

A waiter brought over coffee and arranged the cups, saucers and spoons. Minutes later, the table was teeming with fresh bread – an aroma he found intoxicating – and a variety of cheeses and fruits. This was where Alice's upbringing seemed to disappear, as she joined in him in cramming down everything at once, each of them letting the butter and the juices from the mango and melon run over their fingers.

Kurt couldn't remember ever eating like this. His family's butcher shop had never thrived because of one of three reasons: the depression, according to his father; the Jews, according to Hitler; or the Nazis, according to no one.

But he wanted to shake all that from his head for a while. Alice's eyes were bright, and her shoulders lowered with less of the tension they usually held. She was focussed on the food, and not calculating if, and when, she would need to run again. He could tell she felt safe. He felt safe.

'I'm going to ask you a question,' he said. 'And I want you to forget about what Germany is like now when you answer.'

Her shoulders rose again slightly, but she nodded.

'What do you love most about Berlin?

She put down her fork. 'Going for early morning runs about the park,' she began. 'The best time was spring. It was like being in a different world, seeing the green light of the sun through the glades, the smell of pines, hearing deer running through the undergrowth… Nothing but nature around me.' Her eyes closed for a moment.

When she opened them, she was smiling. 'What was yours?'

'Those times in camping when it felt like just a trip with some friends. Peter would be snoring away, nothing would wake him up, and we could all just be us. Alfons used to do a bit of a comedy routine, like Charlie Chaplin, who we all thought looked like Hitler, but no one would say it outright. Alfons used to make himself look like a tramp and march up and down, barking out ridiculous orders. He didn't care that some of the boys threatened to report him.'

Kurt swallowed. He could almost taste the fire again, and he needed to change the subject. Alfons would want him to be brave.

'The last time I was able to relax in such a place was with my father and my sister, Edie,' Alice told him, sensing that the mood had changed. Her eyes slipped down onto the plate and she chewed on her lip, still holding a small piece of warm bread slathered with butter and brie.

'Tell me about them. What does your father do?'

She hesitated. 'He's a scientist.' She picked up her coffee and hid her face with the cup. 'I thought we weren't going to talk about the past?'

'I'm sorry,' he said sheepishly, remembering that she hadn't made him talk about Alfons; and with that thought, his appetite departed.

They sat in silence for a few moments, pieces of bread and snatches of fruit and cheese spread across their plates. Neither of them touched anything.

'This pact is working out well, then?' she eventually spoke.

'We just need distractions,' he insisted. 'Remember that somewhere in the world, someone is running and they're not doing it to save their own lives. Someone else is camping in the woods and they're not doing it to train for a war. We will have that world again one day. Look at us now, how quickly we have been able to loosen up and just eat. This ship shows that the world isn't all the same.'

Looking around the room, something caught his eye. A clumsy notice, hastily written in scrawled writing. It was the details of an evening ball. 'Do you dance?' he asked.

She laughed and dropped her bread. 'I'm a terrible dancer,' she said.

'We live in the moment – forget the past. Here you can be a good dancer,' he stood and extended his hand. 'Come on.'

The clattering of knives and forks and the droning hum of conversation faded as they stepped outside the dining room into a light sea breeze.

'Could we go somewhere quiet?' Alice muttered, tilting her head in the direction of a small group.

He looked over to see Eli, the boy they'd met on the deck, watching them. He always seemed to have an entourage surrounding him. The others, both boys and girls, fawned over him like he was their leader. Tall and dark, in his worn but obviously expensive suit, he always seemed to be giving speeches that got the others either fired up or misty-eyed. The set-up reminded Kurt of a Hitler Youth meeting, with the key difference being that Eli was one of the most Jewish-looking people he had ever seen. He did his best not to listen, and they spoke in Hebrew a lot of the time anyway. He mainly just avoided them. They never saw the boy who had tried to jump.

He was more than happy to oblige Alice in going to the other side of the ship, and when they got there, he realised that he was nervous. His mouth went dry as they stood opposite each other on the deserted deck, which creaked underneath him as he moved towards her. Then, mercifully, the sound of music floated out from the social hall. It was a lively number, a quick step, and he took Alice into his arms, still maintaining a distance, and led her around the small space. She was breathless, laughing hard. Her eyes emerged from their shadows as her limbs grew loose. Then the music changed, moving into a slower Glen Miller tune – the type that you could only sway to.

When he felt her cheek on his shoulder, he thought of Greta; of the times they'd dance together at parties, and how she'd show him what to do. For what felt like the thousandth time, he went through that night, wondering if she got away, until he remembered the pact, and pushed those thoughts away. He had to live in the moment. Thinking about the past would kill him. He concentrated on the light touch of Alice's fingers on his back, and the way her hair caught the breeze and tickled his neck. It felt warm and safe. The music stopped, and they parted self-consciously.

'Danser jusqu'au bout de la nuit vi,' he heard himself say.

'You speak French?' she asked, startled. 'What does that mean?'

He enjoyed the surprise on her face. 'Sometimes, when you feel really good, you just want to dance the night away.'

'How do you speak French? I understand English because of my governess, but not when people speak it too quickly.'

After hearing that, he was hardly going to admit that his mother had taken in washing for a French family for a number of years. They were professional dancers, and he'd listened to their conversations while he waited to pick up the money. Languages had always come easy to Kurt. Even in his short time with the swing kids, he'd managed to pick up a little English, as many of them liked to talk American-style.

There was a sudden bang, like something had been knocked over in the shadows close by. A scurrying of feet. Alice looked at him. She didn't need to say what they were both thinking. They were being watched.

The days passed. They regularly saw Eli with his flock, which was growing in number by the day, and would nod in recognition but not converse with them further. It worried Kurt that whenever he passed with Alice, a few of them would whisper to one another and call over to Eli. He got a lot of stares from a boy with brown hair swept back from his face, emphasising a long forehead; and while he was used to intimidation, it was a new experience to have it caused by Jews. He tried to just ignore them and focus on his blossoming friendship with Alice. Somehow, it was easier to breathe when talking to her. The air around them felt calmer, and he could even relax enough to appreciate the taste of the sea salt mist carried by the cool breeze as it landed on his tongue. It was still hard to shake off the feeling of being constantly under surveillance, though; and as it turned out, he was right to be cautious.

They were almost a week into the voyage when Alice sat him down and asked if they could talk about something serious. She smiled as she said it, but her tone made him uneasy and his nerves seemed to tighten again. He studied her face, tanned by the sunshine they had been enjoying. A lightness had replaced the shadows that she had boarded the ship with. Her clear blue eyes shone at times now, with a touch of mischief and a hint of happiness. He loved to see these sparks in her. It helped to drive out what he still saw and felt in his dreams: the smoke, the ash and the weightless panic.

The words flowed out of her, hard and passionate, like hammers to his brain.

'So, if we join Eli and his friends for the poker game tonight, I can build up to asking Gus about the camp he was in,' she concluded.

'Why?' he asked.

'It's the same one that my father is in.'

'It's a risk.'

She acknowledged the point with a small nod while she fidgeted with the material of her trousers

'You may have to tell them who you really are.' The absurdity of the situation wasn't lost on Kurt. Even he didn't know who she really was. All he knew was that she was Alice, not Anna, and that she was undoubtedly Aryan. This would hardly make her welcome amongst that lot.

'I don't have to say it is my father who I'm asking about,' she said.

'Do you think he'll let us join them?'

She looked away again, out to sea. 'I got talking to him. I asked how Gus was doing, and apparently, he's much better – coming out of his cabin again. Eli invited us to meet him properly, along with the rest of the group.'

Kurt felt like he'd been punched in the stomach. 'When did you talk to him?'

'Does it matter?' she snapped.

He didn't react. He had become completely absorbed in trying to be someone else and living in the present, and he wanted so badly for it to last for the duration of the voyage. He had planned to tell Alice the truth about who he was when they arrived, but now he feared that it would be taken out of his hands. He felt as though they had worked him out – Eli, the staring boy with the hair swept off his forehead and the small groups of whisperers.

There was no need to mix with these people, he thought. It was an over-ambitious plan for her, and a dangerous one for him. If he spent time with them, would they be able to tell he wasn't a Jew? Would he give himself away somehow? He had never been around them in such circumstances – outnumbered and not in control. Most of Heinz's group were non-Jews. The loudspeaker in his head mimicked Minister Goebbels, whose voice he had heard repeating

'Juden', the term itself a warning, day and night across the city for years now.

However, the look on her face, the fleeting optimism that he saw there, had changed something in him; and so, when her burning eyes started to dull again, and she began to withdraw into the same shell that he had worked hard to keep her out of, he knew that if he could give her hope, he would. He would just have to be very careful.

CHAPTER THIRTEEN

The Girl takes a Gamble

19th May 1939

Alice's nerves were in knots as they approached the group and its hubbub of multiple conversations. A string of fairy lights had been rigged up, and a collection of tables and chairs were scattered about on the deck. The seats were already occupied by girls with curled hair and rouged lips, wearing the best dresses they had, even if they were faded and patched in places; while the boys were mostly dressed in suits – some of them tattered and worn, or simply too large or small. The alcohol and smoke-filled air, alongside the careful conversations of people used to watching their words, indicated an atmosphere of subdued celebration. She looked at Kurt, whose blues eyes drank in the scene without his pale, stoic face betraying any hint of emotion. She couldn't really understand his reluctance to mix with Eli and the others. He'd have something to hide, of course, but then so did everyone else on the ship.

Initially, she had wanted to avoid the group too, in case they discovered that she was a half-Jew, as it was said that after years of forced segregation, they were always able to sniff out one of their own. It had been hard to keep her distance, though. She liked listening in on their prayers, led by the one who'd introduced himself as Eli. His voice was powerful, yet calming; levelling, but inspiring. He talked about a homeland, giving sermons in Hebrew – her mother's tongue. It was when she overheard them mention a camp, the camp, that she knew she had to do it. She had to know. It didn't have to mean compromising her own identity. She could slowly get to know Gus, and then ask offhandedly about her father. She could say that he was an old employee or a neighbour.

'Welcome,' a voice broke into her worries. It was Eli, speaking softly, lyrically and in German, not Hebrew. 'I hoped you might have joined us sooner, after you both recovered from your sickness some days ago?'

There was something accusatory in Eli's tone. Alice felt her cheeks grow hot. He held out his hand and Alice went to shake it, but he shook his head and lowered his eyes.

'I'm sorry about this,' he said. 'But I must check your papers.'

Alice suppressed her panic as she handed them over, relying on her well-honed skills of staying stony faced, appearing untroubled. Kurt passed his over without a word, but Alice could feel his unease next to her. Eli lingered on both their papers, but Kurt's in particular.

'Kurt Josef,' he said, tapping at the name on the page with his index finger. 'I knew of a Josef family in Wedding. The father is a rabbi, wife called Rebekah and a daughter called Sarah. Any relation?'

'No,' Kurt said shrugging. 'It's a common name.'

'I suppose it is,' Eli replied. 'A common Jewish name.'

To her relief, he didn't ask what Alice, as an Aryan, was doing with a Jew. She knew there were a few passengers on the ship running for reasons other than race or religion, so perhaps it didn't look so suspicious after all.

Kurt snatched his papers back, which made Alice grimace. Don't act too rash. Hadn't he been trained?

'Would you both like a drink?' Eli spoke in a more casual tone, as he led them into the middle of the group. Everyone greeted him with a form of reverence and respect. The boys nodded towards him or shook his hand, the girls cast him approving glances. All of them regarded Alice and Kurt with distrust.

The table they finally stopped at held a tumbler of liquid that filled the air with a liquorice smell, with two boys sat on opposite sides arguing. One of them was Gus. His hair had grown back slightly, so that small curls has started to frame his head. The thin red line around his neck had faded, and some weight now hung off his bones. He looked better. He looked human again. But he was talking in a hurried, agitated manner

'Anna and Kurt,' Eli interrupted by way of introduction. 'We will make them welcome.'

Everyone fell silent. Gus's companion stood up. He had a thick mop of light brown hair swept to one side, revealing a long forehead, eyes set close together, and a scar that ran down the side of his cheek, into a thin mouth sucking on a cigarette. He was tall and broad, with muscled arms and thick thighs.

He raised his eyebrows at Alice. 'You need an Eva Braun now, Eli?'

'Don't mention that woman,' one of the girls said with a shudder. She was long-limbed with flaming auburn hair, and had wrapped herself around a chair at the table.

'Why not, Leah?' Josiah turned to the girl.

'Because when you mention her, we think of her boyfriend, don't we?'

'Well, we can hardly forget the Fuhrer when his portrait hangs in the social hall, can we?' Josiah retorted. There was a scraping of a chair and Gus got up and left.

'Watch yourself, Josiah,' Eli said evenly.

A few of the others stopped what they were doing and stared. Eventually Josiah looked away and took a swig out of a glass. 'Gus doesn't like strangers,' he said. 'Especially two perfect candidates for a propaganda poster. Real Germans.'

Alice found herself taking a step back.

'Josiah,' Eli's tone was so sharp, it cut through the group like a knife.

Josiah sat back down and shuffled the cards that lay in front of him. He was trying to appear unfazed, but Alice could see lines of frustration and anger on his face.

'You can sit here,' offered a boy with a slightly stilted voice, like he wasn't used to talking, or that he watched every word. He was wearing round-rimmed glasses which he took off and polished using his shirt, hands slightly shaking. 'Until Gus comes back.'

'He won't come back for a while, Malik,' Josiah said. 'He already thinks that everyone is out to get him, and with these rumours of Gestapo spies on the ship-'

Eli thumped his fist hard on the table. A glass toppled over, and the liquid poured out onto Alice's arm. She didn't dare move to wipe it clean. Josiah dipped his head down again. All the chatter around them had stopped.

'Gestapo?' Kurt asked. He didn't betray any fear, but Alice was sat close enough to see his cheek muscle tighten.

'They are rumours, no more, borne out by the paranoia many of us felt having to run for our lives to get on this ship,' Eli said with a wave of his hand. 'So, stop fanning the flames, Josiah.' His voice was completely calm again, totally composed, and it restored the relaxed atmosphere back amongst the group. It was as if the flash of violence and the unsettled drink had never happened.

'What have I done? I am only here to play poker.' Josiah opened his arms up in mock outrage, before taking the cigarette holder from a nearby girl and breathing in a long drag. The girl had watched the conversation carefully, stealing appreciative looks at Kurt. Her chestnut hair was cut into a neat bob, which bounced back red in the dimming lights of the ship.

'You are a poker player?' Josiah addressed Kurt.

'Not really.'

'We are all taking a gamble being on this ship, so why not be a proper Jew and make some money out of it?' Josiah laughed before turning away from them and back towards the table, swinging the brunette girl back around with him so that she had to take her eyes off Kurt.

Alice picked up a glass of strong herbal liqueur that Eli had put down beside her. It hit her throat hard and she muffled a cough. 'I'll play,' she said, trying to make her voice sound strong. She cast a look around to see if Gus was coming back to claim his seat.

'You?' Josiah jabbed a thumb towards Kurt.

Kurt nodded reluctantly, and Josiah shuffled the deck.

'Did Gus board the ship on his own?' Alice asked casually, although no question could really be seen as casual under such circumstances. 'Or did he already know the girl who went after him just now?'

Eli shook his head. 'Most of the men on here are travelling alone.'

He sat down next to Alice. She noted how strangely intimate his presence felt, despite them not touching. He had a way of making anyone near him feel both important and at ease, demonstrated by the fact that everyone around the table, apart from Josiah, hung on his every word.

'They were released from the camps on the condition that they left Germany immediately,' he continued. 'So, their families had to stay behind until they could raise money for more visas. Leaving also means that they can try and make money themselves from Cuba or America, which is a more likely source. It was too dangerous for them to stay and wait.'

Alice nodded. She knew this. She was living it.

'Can we not talk about the camps for one night?' Josiah growled.

'What shall we talk about?' Eli asked, his arms outspread. 'What makes you happy, Josiah?' Eli managed to say this in a way that came across as genuine and not pandering.

Josiah gave a sly smile and had a quick look in Kurt's direction. 'I like your talk of a new homeland,' he said to Eli. 'What Jew would not, when we are being driven out of our own country?'

'This is not to leave you out, Alice,' Eli said, briefly touching her arm. 'We know that the Nazis have made many enemies, and not just Jews.'

There was a hush around the deck area. An air of expectancy.

'I am running,' Alice said, aware that the eyes of the group were on her. 'I would hardly sell everything I own for a ticket to Cuba if I wasn't.'

'What did you do?' Malik asked.

'Well,' she paused, considering how she could say this. 'My father was a journalist-'

'Aryan?' Josiah interrupted.

Eli waved his hand across the table in a dismissive gesture and turned back to Alice.

'Yes,' she said. At least this answer was true, and the strength of a lie was its basis in truth after all. She held her chin up. 'But, along with my father, I resisted the Nazis, and now he's in a camp. I would have been in one too, soon enough, if I hadn't made it onto this ship.'

'What's his name?' Malik spoke more confidently now, throwing questions. 'Which paper did he work for?'

Alice felt a lurch in her stomach. Why hadn't she picked a different profession to align her father to? Simply telling the truth, that he was a university professor, would probably have been safer; but then her father was so well known for his resistance, and the death of his Jewish wife had been common knowledge, so it wasn't a truth that she could hint towards.

'Malik wants to be a journalist,' Eli explained.

'Would you let Alice into this homeland you speak of, Josiah?' Kurt said suddenly.

She knew it was to deflect the attention from her, and was grateful for that, but Josiah frowned, and his mouth opened in what Alice could see would be a burst of anger.

Eli got in first. 'Everyone who is in danger and needs somewhere to call home is welcome.'

'Then the same problems will just happen again,' the girl called Heidi said. 'We'll be driven out if we let them in.'

'Us Jews need our own place,' Josiah agreed. 'Or we'll always be running.'

'We must be better than that,' Eli said. 'For this time in history, we must be more.'

'Why should we?' Josiah bristled. 'Because a madman has

convinced a whole country that we are evil and to be feared?'

'That is exactly why,' Eli replied.

'How did you get on the ship?' Josiah turned to Kurt. 'Is it anything to do with that scar on your hand?'

Alice had tried not to pay much attention to the criss-crossed diamonds on Kurt's right hand, due to their pact. She'd stopped herself asking several times, but it was something she knew must link to his fever-induced shouts of fights, fire and falling.

'Yes,' Kurt answered. 'I had a fight with a Hitler Youth leader. The scars are deceptive. I won the fight.'

There was a hush over the group. Alice found herself stunned, too.

'And because I won the fight, it became important that I left Germany sooner rather than later.'

'Of course,' Malik nodded. 'Did you kill him?'

Something tightened in Alice's chest.

'No,' Kurt answered.

'A Jew who attacked a HJ leader,' Josiah exclaimed. 'You have almost equalled the calibre of my scar!'

'The story of the scar again,' Malik muttered, eyes downcast.

'One of the highest-ranking Nazi officials gave me this.' Josiah traced the thin red line with his finger.

'He won't tell us who,' Leah said, her attentions away from Kurt again.

'We don't care,' Malik said quietly.

'Some of us have internal scars just as high-ranking, Josiah,' Eli quipped. 'Should we get on with the game?'

'Don't be jealous, Eli,' Josiah playfully rebuked him. 'No one can beat you as hide-and-seek champion of Berlin, my friend.'

'It's not as though he wanted the title,' Malik said.

'I suppose going submarine isn't an option when you have a nose shaped like one, eh?' Josiah burst into laughter and slapped his thigh.

Leah tutted. Josiah patted her arm and added, 'He knows I am joking, such a handsome man as Eli. He has good Jewish looks. It's just a shame that they aren't fashionable in Germany at the moment.'

The group waited for a reaction from Eli, but he just smiled and shrugged.

'What you did was brave, Eli,' Leah said.

'What did you do?' Alice asked.

'He organised a protest,' Malik beamed.

'It was a peaceful one,' Eli said, taking a sip of his drink. 'I wanted to get people from all communities involved, to show the Nazis that they had opposition – that many of us weren't willing to go along with their plans, and not just Jews, either. We were betrayed, however, and when they attacked us, I was sought out as the leader. I had to go into hiding.'

'How long did you hide for? Kurt asked.

'Almost a year.'

'How did you do it for so long?' Alice said.

'Contacts, friends, Jews and Gentiles alike, who still wanted to fight in some way, but realised that it would have to be through hidden, secret means, rather than public demonstrations. Berlin is a place being built up and knocked down all at the same time, so as long as you keep moving, it is possible to hide for a while.'

Alice wanted to tell him that she knew this well.

'And you don't think the Gestapo could be on this ship, looking for you?' Kurt said.

'If they wanted to arrest me, they would have done it at the port,' Eli said. 'Or when the ship docked at Cherbourg.'

'Ah, but there is no telling how they work,' Josiah said. 'Or what links they have with the Cuban authorities.'

'We do not know that yet,' Eli replied, his brow knotted.

'Whatever the outcome, I still believe that a homeland is needed.' Josiah lit a cigarette, sending smoke across the table. 'I mean, look at how it is on this ship. The crew are nice to us up top, but one of the first-class passengers who has an interest in engines and things went down for a tour, and heard them all singing Horst-Wessel-Lied.'

'Never!' the girl with the chestnut bob gasped.

'They did, Heidi. They sang when Jewish blood flows from the knife, things will be better in full voice, accompanied by a piano.'

'I do not believe that,' Leah cut in, shaking her head.

'Why? Is it because the crew have been sneaking you smiles and chocolate, or that you know they are saying that, despite the threats to their German blood and honour, you girls are the hottest to ever come on the ship? Even Hitler cannot control what goes on in their pants.'

Josiah laughed, and Heidi blushed and left the table. Leah gave them all a furious look and followed her.

'This evening is becoming very boring,' Josiah went on. 'I want to find out what the Gentile thinks about the homeland idea.'

'I think we should take Germany back instead,' Kurt remarked.

'I asked the Gentile,' he pointed at Alice. 'Just because you look like a good little Christian, doesn't mean you can answer for them.'

'It is a question for everyone,' Eli calmly interjected. 'I do not think that we should drive others out or be forced away for good ourselves. I too believe that we should take back Germany.' He nodded at Kurt.

'Did you two know each other before the voyage?' Josiah asked Alice.

'We met on the train to Hamburg,' she said, thinking it best to be honest where possible. She saw a look pass between Josiah and Eli.

'You sat in the same cabin?' Josiah asked.

'Why, is that important?' Alice said, aware of how the sea bucking and rolling the ship was adding to the unease in her stomach.

'Well, anyone with Jewish papers would be travelling in one of those specially marked cabins, wouldn't they?' Josiah proclaimed. The contents of his drink sloshed over the glass, and Alice realised how drunk he was.

'I used false papers to board the train,' Kurt said.

'I am sorry for all the questions,' Eli said. 'It is just that everyone is so jumpy, wondering whether we actually will be allowed off at Cuba.'

'Why wouldn't we be?' Kurt asked.

'More rumours and hearsay, like the Gestapo spy.' Eli waved his hands.

Kurt stood up, knocking the table slightly, and went over to get another drink. Alice needed a break from the questioning herself, but she let him go ahead. Eli left too, and was soon thick in conversation with a small group who were stood close to the ship's railings, including Heidi, who was visibly upset. Eli was talking, making gestures with his hands, pointing out to sea and eventually raising a smile.

'You admire him, no?' Leah was beside her, whispering into her ear.

She did, thought Alice, but on a deeper level than what Leah meant. She had watched Eli throughout the voyage, checking on the children, making them laugh, soothing struggling faces; and with those his own age, he would pat shoulders, listen to worries, talk of resolution and revolutions.

'Did you know him before the ship?' Alice asked.

'No, but I knew of him,' Leah said. 'He helped forge papers to get people out, and found ways for those who couldn't afford it to raise money for tickets. Did it all from his hiding places.'

Alice found herself standing up, moving towards him. The others had dispersed, and he was alone, arms resting on the railings, watching the swirl of waves below. The sky was as dark and dense as her own secrets.

'Did you leave soup at the door?' she asked.

He turned around, his dark eyes focused intensely on her. He nodded slowly.

'Why?'

'You are Alice Sommer,' he said, softly, so no one else could hear. 'And you have a price on your head.'

CHAPTER FOURTEEN

The Boy is reunited with an Old Friend

19th May 1939

The tension was rising, along with Josiah's alcohol intake. Kurt knew that it would only be a matter of time before one of the boy's sharp jibes towards him led to something physical.

The conversation had turned to war. Nearly everyone wanted it, but for different reasons than Kurt was used to. In the Hitler Youth, it was welcomed as a way of Germany getting back at the world. Here, it was a way for the world to get back at Germany.

Alice was off talking to Eli at the side of the deck, their heads bent low together. They were whispering closely, and he felt the stabbing pain of jealousy. He was almost tempted to go over and tell her that Gus had unexpectedly returned, so that they could get this whole uneasy charade over. If she asked him about the camp, like she had planned to, they could leave. He turned back to the conversation at the table.

'Germany will be at war with the world soon anyway,' Malik said. 'We'll have everyone on our side then-'

'Oh, you idiot,' Gus snapped. He was one of the few who didn't seem keen on a second global conflict. 'Things will only get worse with war!'

'Why?' Leah's brow furrowed.

Alice slipped into the seat next to Kurt. As she picked up her drink, he noticed that her hand was shaking. Eli looked completely at ease.

'Because then they can do what they want to us – ban the international press completely, starve us, arrest more of us.' Gus's cheeks were turning red, his hands drumming unsteadily on the table. Josiah placed a steadying hand over his in an unexpected gesture of kindness.

'That is why Eli's big plan involves studying English and French,' Josiah said, as though this was a waste of time in his opinion.

'I know some English,' Alice said quietly. 'Kurt speaks French.'

Kurt turned to look at her. What was she doing, giving out information like that? The less this group knew about them the better. He spotted another glance between Eli and Josiah. It was barely perceptible, but it had happened a few times now, whenever there was something new revealed about him and Alice.

'I want to help as many persecuted people escape as possible before war breaks out,' Eli explained. 'We will need America, Britain and France for this. We need to speak their languages.'

'I think you should just concentrate on helping your fellow Jews,' Gus said quietly. His fist was clenched, and his teeth gritted together.

The red line around his neck looked more pronounced.

'Eli has controversial views, you see,' Josiah stumbled as he stood to refill his glass. 'It makes him both clever and awful.'

'What's awful is that we now have conversations like this,' Eli said.

There was more than a hint of sadness in his tone as he ran a hand through his hair, in what Kurt had come to recognise as a gesture that he was unnerved. It reminded Kurt of something his father would have said, prompting an unwelcome memory to reappear. It was of his father, head bent, on his knees scrubbing the streets with the old Jewish women who the SS soldiers had forced to the ground. His mother had been furious.

'You've put us all at risk,' she'd cried, as he washed the dirt off his hands back at the apartment. 'And for people you do not even know!'

'Stop it, Esther,' his father had implored her. 'They want us to argue between ourselves, instead of standing up to them.'

Kurt became aware of a stumbling shadow standing behind him. Josiah was leaning over him, the slice of the scar on his cheek illuminated by the moonlight, like a glint of glass across his cheekbone.

'You don't look like a Jew at all,' the drunken boy exhaled heavily. 'You know, they stood me next to someone like you at school once. They measured my nose, and then they measured his. They measured my head, and then they measured his.' He moved closer, breathing that strange liquorice and vodka scent into Kurt's face. 'And the funny thing was,' he dropped his voice to little more than a whisper. 'I was the one with the more German measurements. The other boy was a skinny rake, like you.'

Kurt's back stiffened, and he gave Josiah a long, cold stare, before looking beyond him to see how easy it would be to get away without the inevitable fight. Eli and Alice were once again locked in a private conversation.

'Quickly, everyone, follow me!' Heidi was shouting breathlessly, having ran back from the other side of the deck. She was waving at people to follow her.

The group moved as one – a chaotic tumble of bodies that were used to escaping at short notice. Chairs were knocked to the side. Josiah threw his drink to the ground and ran with the crowd, the smashing of glass lost in the stampede that followed. In the panic, Kurt found his priority was finding Alice. She had opted to take cover, rather than flee. He discovered her, crouched in a corner, holding a chair out as a weapon. She stood up when she saw it was him. Her skin had taken on a paler tone that made the shadows under her eyes stand out in violet smudges.

'I don't think even this lot would be stupid enough to run towards danger,' he said.

She smiled weakly, and without thinking he reached out and offered his hand. She accepted it, and they walked in the direction of the others. What they saw took Kurt's breath away.

'Why did you get everyone so panicked, Heidi?' Josiah was reprimanding her. 'It's only the Azores.'

'Only the Azores?' Heidi exclaimed. Her bob was now dishevelled, an effect of sea salt dust and excitement. 'We are half way to Cuba, half way to freedom! And look how beautiful they are.'

The white windmills whisked in the distant, little mounds on top of the bigger mountains. The port side was crowded with excited passengers. Alice stood close to him. As she turned to see the windmills, he could feel her faint, hot breath on his neck. Her blonde hair moved gently with the wind.

'It's going to be okay, isn't it?' she spoke suddenly, rapidly and hushed, but she was smiling. 'We'll make it, and then gather enough money and support to get our families out. We're halfway there.'

He closed his eyes and experienced a warm, bubbling sensation in his chest. Happiness. He wanted to ask her what she had been talking about with Eli, what had made the blood withdraw from her face, but he didn't want to ruin the moment. A sudden rush in the crowd separated them, and he found himself alone, further back as though deliberately pushed by Josiah, who turned and smirked before heading to the front again. It was then that he saw her. He had to look twice, blink the salt air out of his eyes, and still he thought he must have been hallucinating. Yet there was the oval face, the sharp eyes, the dark ringlets now free of blonde dye. It was her, standing in a doorway.

Greta.

She placed a finger on her lip, and then beckoned him inside the ship. Within the silent shadows of the empty corridors, she put out her arms and enveloped him in a hug. She still wore the lilac scent that he associated with her. She was more fragile, her bones more pronounced than when he had last seen her only a few weeks ago. He had so many questions to ask.

'Heinz survived the attack,' she said, pre-empting his most pressing concern. 'His uncle helped me get out. I didn't know that you were heading for this ship as well. Heinz didn't tell anyone where you were going.'

'Where is he?' Kurt asked, looking around as though his friend might miraculously materialise, too.

'He's in hospital. He's safe,' she said, a tremor in her voice. 'Walter... his family bailed him out of jail, so he is okay, too.' She placed a hand on Kurt's arm. 'But we must not think of that now. I am here to think of you, to warn you.'

'Of what?' A chill reached down his spine.

'There is a Gestapo spy, Kurt... and they think it's you.'

He took a step back. 'Who does?'

'Josiah, Gus and some of the others. The ones who could make trouble – and this idea is spreading. They won't bow down to Eli for much longer. I wanted to warn you, but I have been too scared to leave my cabin.'

'Why have you been afraid to leave your cabin?'

'Because I think the spy is targeting me. You know all the- the work I did within the SS? Well, my cover was blown, and now they want to silence me… Eli will say that he'll protect you, but he doesn't have as much power as he thinks,' she added.

'Why does he want to protect me?'

She rolled her eyes in a familiar gesture that was more like the playful Greta he knew. 'You must already know his need to have a sense of "justice", Kurt.'

When she said the word 'justice', he was reminded of Christopher – of the terror on his face when they cast him out. He recalled Greta's own words: 'we need to have a sense of justice.'

The shouts from outside broke into the corridor as a door swung open in the wind. It slammed shut with a violent bang. They stood quietly for a few moments, her hand still on his arm.

'I'm not going to tell anyone who you really are,' Greta said, pressing her lips together. 'If they found that out, you would be as likely to be lynched as the actual spy.'

'Your brothers are with you?'

She shook her head. 'Only one left, and he has been… captured.'

A rabble of voices, getting closer.

'Go back out there, pretend this never happened. You don't know me, and I don't know you.' She pushed him then, back towards the deck, towards the hope and happiness of the others. He looked at her. She smiled silently and then took a deep breath. He waited.

'One final word of warning, Kurt,' she said, looking at him straight in the eyes. 'You're putting that girl in danger by always being around her.'

With that, she was gone; the wispy scent of her lilac perfume the only evidence of her ever being there. Outside, the wind did little to ease the swirl of his thoughts. His first instinct was to look for Alice, despite Greta's words. The air bit at his neck. He was tired, and it still felt like there was a long way to go. He'd had enough of the games, playing to stay alive.

He felt someone close in on him. It was Eli.

'Why did you invite us tonight?' Kurt asked quietly.

They watched the thick white clouds, the shadows of mountains against the blackening sky. Peaks of land and glimpses of shore.

'You're not who you say you are,' Eli said.

'I swear on my mother's life that I am not a spy.'

'But you are not a Jew, either.'

Kurt prepared his standard answers within his mind, calculating the danger, but before he could protest Eli turned to look at him. It was a look that held no menace.

'I will not tell anyone,' he said. 'In fact, I think we could help each other. But you'll have to convince some of the others that you're not selling anyone out to the Gestapo.'

A steady drizzle picked up, splashing specks of cold onto their faces. They watched the waves roll back and forth, fighting against the ship and the islands

'And you need to stay away from her,' he added.

For a second, he thought Eli meant Greta, and his heart hammered against his chest. Then he saw the direction of Eli's gaze, which was trained on Alice as she leaned over to look at the Azores, her face not as taunt. It was the most relaxed he had seen her since the voyage started.

'Why should I?' he asked, turning to face Eli head on. He noticed more figures in the shadows, and the glint of a knife. He was surrounded.

'Because if you don't, she will end up dead.'

CHAPTER FIFTEEN

The Girl is reunited with an Old Friend

21st May 1939

The smell of hot metal stung Alice's nose. She'd ventured down into the engine rooms in search of Kurt, certain that she'd heard his voice in the echoes of the corridors. But she couldn't get through the latest steel door, and there were footsteps behind her. As usual, it was Eli.

She sighed. He had probably been following her all along. No one knew the ship better than he did. He was the one who'd told her that five of the decks reared above the water line, and then another three, filled with machinery, storage tanks and compartments, plunged deep below the surface. Hiding places; or places to take someone and hide them. A couple of days had passed since the Azores night, when Kurt had gone missing. Eli had reassured her constantly that he wasn't being held prisoner.

'He's fine. He's safe,' Eli would always say. 'And so are you.'

'Why are you hiding him, then?' she'd respond.

He never gave anything away, though. When she demanded to know why she herself was under 'protection', he would say that this wasn't the time for questions, that he would answer everything later. She felt compelled to go along with it because he thought that he knew everything about her, which he didn't of course. He didn't know about the terrible thing she'd done to get onto the ship, and the terrible thing that had been done to her in return. Would he have been so keen to protect her if he did?

On the third night without Kurt, she took her bed linen and pillow out onto the deck. Eli had been encouraging her to sleep outside, right in the middle of all the passengers, for her own safety. The sticky heat was drawing people out of their cabins, but even with the sprinkles of sea salt washing across the deck, it was still impossible to sleep. As always, Eli had made a space for himself to rest for the night, near the other men, and, also as always, instead of lying down, he was sitting at the edge, away from everyone else, with just the one eye on a book, or perhaps not even that. He didn't flick many pages.

She glanced around to see if anyone else was guarding her. Even the girls were not exempt from duty, and one of them, usually Heidi or Leah, would accompany her on trips to the wash rooms. When she questioned them over why they were looking after her, they admitted that they didn't know. Eli had a connection to everyone, and everyone followed his orders implicitly.

'He got my school friend's family out,' Leah had told her as they stood at the washbasins. 'And he's promised to try and get mine out, too.'

'And you believe him?' Alice challenged. It wasn't that she didn't believe that Eli meant to help. It was just that very few people had the power to make such things happen.

Leah had given her a sidelong glance. 'What else can I do?'

Now, she moved carefully between the sleeping and unsleeping bodies to reach Eli, with a plan to ask for information in a composed manner. However, despite her best efforts, the words still came tumbling out a fraction too fast. 'You said I could ask questions when everything had calmed down,' she said. Trying to calm her breathing, she took a place next to him and drew her knees up to her chest.

He put down his book. 'What do you want to know?'

She wanted to say that it was the same ones she'd already asked without getting answers, but she swallowed her pride. 'Why are you protecting me, and who are you protecting me from?'

'I'll start with the why,' he said, turning to face her. 'I know your father.'

She could hardly say the words. 'My f-father? You know him?'

'That is to say, I know of him – his reputation as a scientist, and the fact that he married into the Jewish community.'

'We were never part of the-'

'I know,' he said gently. 'Your mother was cast out after she married your father, Albert Sommer.'

She could feel the anger burning up in her. Eli must have sensed it, and he placed a cool hand on her arm.

'Your mother was still a respected member of our community, even if she did marry away from the faith, and a lot of people didn't agree with what happened to her,' he added.

'Did you and your family agree with it? With her expulsion?' Alice could still remember her mother in tears after seeing her grandfather, who greeted her with barely a nod on the busy shopping street of Kurfürstendamm.

'I didn't agree with how she was treated,' he said, avoiding her gaze.

'But you would never do what she did and marry away from your faith?' she asked.

'No', he admitted, shifting uncomfortably. 'And especially not now.'

They were silent for a moment. The sea threw white foams of water high into the air and back onto them. Alice felt a heat build-up inside her.

'Then you're just as prejudiced as those you preach against,' she finally burst out.

'You know what's happening,' he said. 'Many, many more of us are going to die.' His voice was soft, apologetic in a sense, but filled with conviction.

'What about people like me? The half-breeds.'

She could see that she had unsettled him. For once, he didn't have an answer straight away. This was disconcerted. Even in the short time she'd known him, there was a certainty about Eli that was more than just strength of will. Unlike many of them, even the ones who put on a brave face in public, like she did, Eli wasn't affected by the Nazis telling him who they thought he was. Despite his own country, and now other sections the world, turning against him, Eli still knew who he was, and remained unshakeable in his commitment to his faith. He was a dreamer, and yet he didn't know where Alice's place was in the world any more than she did.

'You know how my mother died?' she asked.

Eli nodded slowly. 'Do you want to talk about it?'

She shook her head. 'Tell me more about how you know my father. I've never seen you before.'

'My own father worked at the university with him, before-' Eli

We Are of Dust

started. 'After the Nazis barred my father and the other Jewish professors from teaching, Albert Sommer became a legend for speaking out and for… refusing to divorce his Jewish wife.'

Alice felt a lump in her throat as the loss resurfaced. The memories were too vivid. She recalled her parents talking in the kitchen about the Nazi stormtroopers at the back of his lecture theatres, the other outspoken professor who was thrown into Prinz-Albrecht-Strasse, the Gestapo HQ, and returning with no fingernails and scars on their bodies; her mother being followed home by men in long trench coats, the day she went out in the car alone because their father was late and she was worried; the knock on the door from the still-sympathetic policeman, who was off-duty. She couldn't think of it, or it would kill her. Kurt's advice to live in the present was the only way to survive. Kurt. She wanted him here now.

'So, you are protecting me because of who my father is?' She felt a shaming stab of pain that it wasn't because of how Eli felt about her as a person – if he even considered her a person, knowing her half-breed status.

'I saw you with him after your mother's funeral,' he said. 'I knew I wouldn't forget your face.'

There was something in the way he said it, the way he looked at her, that made her feel a buzz of a connection between them, one that went deep. It surprised her after hearing his views. She had to look away.

'Who are you protecting me from?' she asked.

'I don't know yet,' he admitted. 'One of the crew members told me that your name is on a list of wanted refugees with a high price, so it could be anyone, passengers or crew.'

'You think it's Kurt? You think that's why he has stayed so close to me until now?' The idea of this hurt Alice more than she thought it would. Kurt becoming her friend, her confidante, and all the while ready to trade her in. It couldn't be true.

'No, I don't think it's him,' he said. 'In fact, I know that it can't be.'

'How do you know this?'

He took a deep breath. 'It's up to him to tell you that.'

'When you let him go.'

'It's for his own safety that we keep you both apart. Tensions are high. I try to make a joke of it, to stop Josiah's influence increasing.' He broke off as the sound of footsteps from the otherwise slumbering deck interrupted them, but no one came their way, and the only other noise they could hear was the lapping of the waves and the snores and murmurs of people trying to sleep. It was still oven-hot, and Alice felt light-headed from the strain that the conversation put on her nerves, as well as the lack of rest.

'Josiah believes the rumours that the spy can speak different languages,' he said. 'And that they used an Aryan ticket on the train from Berlin to Hamburg. Josiah is convinced it is one of you.'

She'd wanted to seem as useful as possible when she said that Kurt was good with languages, and that she knew English herself. It had backfired.

'I've told Josiah that I'm handling it,' he continued. 'But I think someone is feeding his ego, building him up as some kind of vigilante avenger.'

Josiah paced the ship on a daily basis, his entourage increasing, and a new girl, Greta, on his arm. She didn't have any idea where this Greta had come from, but Alice had been alarmed by the harsh looks the girl frequently gave her. She assumed it was because this Greta thought she was Aryan at first, yet there seemed to be a deeper hatred, something that Alice didn't want to investigate further, and so she stayed out of their way. No matter how long she'd been hated for, sometimes from both sides, it didn't seem to get any easier.

Eli seemed to be regarding her carefully. She met his gaze. She knew by the look in his eyes that he'd experienced the same sort of pain she had. There was a deep underlying sadness, suddenly seeming so obvious that she could almost reach out and touch it.

'Where is your father?' she asked.

'My family has Polish roots, and were sent to their national border,' he replied. 'My father suffered a heart attack when he was forced to cross it. My mother couldn't live without him. She only lasted two more weeks.' He ran a hand through his hair. His dark, brooding eyes were dull.

'I'm so sorry, Eli,' Alice said. She wrapped her arms around herself despite the heat, as though it could offer some protection from what they were facing.

Eli had read her thoughts. 'Your father will be okay. They need him too much to harm him, and he's what they now consider as German.'

'I'm sorry. I didn't mean to make this all about me,' she said. 'You were talking about your family.'

Her eyes were closing as exhaustion overpowered her, willing her limbs to give up and surrender to sleep. She could hardly speak. The fresh smell of salt and the rolling of the waves were no longer enough to keep her awake.

'Are you okay?' he asked.

'I need to go to my room for a moment.'

'Malik will take you,' he said, and whistled a signal, prompting the boy to appear out of the shadows, his glasses gleaming in the moonlight and a kind expression on his face.

'We're still alive, Alice,' he said, holding onto her arm as he helped her up. 'And each one of us has a chance to defy all those who have harmed us, by living.'

Malik walked a couple of steps behind her until they reached the cabin and she shut the door, collapsing against it for a moment. She washed her face in the cabin sink, the cold bringing her back to life. She saw herself in the mirror, thin streaks of tears on her cheeks, eyes shadowed by constant worry, areas where there wasn't enough flesh to stop her bones becoming too pronounced; but she was alive. She was here. She had a chance.

Things didn't get any easier the next day, and there was still no sign of Kurt. As they ploughed through gentle seas towards the Bahamas, she tried to integrate, to stay safe in the centre of everything, as Eli had suggested. The feeling of being constantly watched had shaken her more here than it had done in Germany, and there was still the issue of the bounty on her head. Twice Josiah had approached her, asking about Kurt, and then lingered as though wanting to ask something else, but Eli, Malik or another of their group was always nearby. Without Kurt, it was like she'd lost an old friend.

At the behest of Eli, she had thrown herself into helping the other girls with preparations for a masquerade ball, and it was through this that she found herself on the deck, watching the excitement build as the worry in the pit of her stomach increased. Incongruous to how she was feeling, there was a bustle across the ship, a sense of enthusiasm in the air. Harem and geisha girls giggled along the decks in costumes cobbled together from swimwear, bed clothes and hand towels. Many of the passengers were going dressed as pirates. There were shouts of Ahoy, me Hearties! across the ship. Josiah and another boy staged a mock fight with wooden swords. With each impact came a clunky sound, accompanied by the rumble of feet as they moved up and down, mobbed by a small cheering crowd.

'Ta-da!' Leah spun into the middle of the group, wearing the full white uniform of a crew member, with gold buttons that sparkled in the sunlight, and a hat which covered her auburn hair.

'Where did you get that?' Heidi asked, taking the cap and running her fingers over the crisp white rim. 'Surely they're not throwing these away?'

Leah reached over and snatched it back. The scent of perfume moved with her, so strong that Alice felt like she was swallowing it.

'Where did you get that new perfume from?' Heidi asked, narrowing her eyes at Leah.

'Ah, my good friend, Reinhold.' She danced around the table, making the children laugh before catching Heidi's eye. 'What? I cannot help it if the Aryans cannot resist me.'

'Why you cannot see through the crew members is beyond me,' Heidi muttered.

'What about Josiah?' Alice asked. She was conscious, of course, of the fact that he now spent his time with Greta, but she wanted to find out anything she could about him, as a form of protection.

Leah sniffed. 'Oh, I am finished with him. He is always so negative. I want to enjoy myself.'

The pre-ball celebratory mood was intensified by virtue of some of the passengers having already received their landing cards; a few had even packed. Within the jumble of people, dressed in his usual clothes, was Gus. He walked with his head down, arms dangling by his sides like he didn't know what to do with them. Alice glanced around quickly, and noting that Leah and Heidi were too busy with their costumes to notice if she slipped away, she decided that she couldn't pass up the chance to talk to him on his own.

Gus's bony shoulders rose up and down, betraying an ingrained sense of caution, like he was trying to make himself look smaller as he walked. He looked up, saw Alice, and his face turned grey. He skirted through a group dressed as Arabs and headed in the opposite direction. She chased after him, and grabbed him by the bones of his skinny arm.

'Gus, you do not need to be afraid of me,' she said. 'My father is in a camp. I understand.'

'You don't understand,' he spat. 'Who are you? Not one of us. And now you want to compare stories. Ever seen anyone castrated, or woke up five mornings in a row to a hanging at breakfast? Have you? Have you?' His voice got louder as he spoke. Several people stopped in their tracks and looked over.

'Please, my father is a prisoner-'

'And what did he do? Did he do something? Because I never did anything but be who I am!' His shouts echoed across the ship.

'Enough,' came a stern voice from behind them. It was Eli. He took Alice by the arm and led her away.

'Get off me!' she shouted. 'I've had enough of all this.'

He refused to let go, and marched her around to his cabin, opening the door and forcing her inside. In the small room stood Kurt. He was dressed in a pirate outfit made of black material that was roughly stitched into a waistcoat and hat, accompanied by a wooden sword. There were dark shadows under his eyes, indicating a similar lack of sleep to what she'd experienced.

'Ready for the ball, are you?' she asked. Her relief at seeing him again, the warmth in her stomach, was outweighed by anger.

'Eli said I should come back out into the open as normal.' He gestured towards his outfit. 'Pretend that I'd been ill again.'

'You know about the price on my head,' she said. 'Why would you leave me if you knew that?'

She turned away from him, but he moved and stood in front of her. She could smell a mix of tar, diesel and engine oil, and wondered how far in the depths of the ship Eli had taken him for questioning.

'I've been watching you, looking out for you,' he explained. 'At first Eli thought I was going to sell you to the Gestapo, that I was the spy. So, they separated us, kept me down below, away from you. But they questioned me and realised I was innocent. I was assigned to watch you instead, to see if the spy gave themselves away, but there has been nothing.'

'How did you prove it wasn't you?'

'Eli found out from a crew member that the spy is a Jew.'

She realised then that Eli hadn't told him of her real identity, that he had been true to his promise not to tell anyone. 'How does that prove anything?' she asked.

'I'm not a Jew,' he said.

The room started to spin. Alice put a hand against the wall to steady herself.

Kurt was still talking. 'When I met you, I was so relieved to find someone like me on here.'

Someone like him. Who was she like? Not like Kurt. Not like Eli and the others. She almost did it then, blurted out who she was – in Hebrew, just to see his face.

'I feel better now,' he was concluding. 'I feel that everything is finally open between us.'

She wanted to cry. She couldn't remember ever feeling worse than this, but then he put his arms around her and the comfort was so warm and unexpected that she found herself kissing him. It was forceful and desperate, like she had nothing to lose. Her body pressed against the length of his and he kissed her back even harder. It was a feeling she had forgotten, and it sent an electric pulse fizzing through her. It was a kiss of utter certainty. Her lips tingled when he pulled away, and they stood not quite looking at each other. It occurred to her that he didn't know he had kissed a Jew. Her mind started racing again. The confession started to form in her throat, but she couldn't do it. She had to get out of the room, away from him.

She opened the door and almost tumbled out of the cabin.

'Wait,' he said, following after her. 'Where are you going?'

'I just need some time on my own,' she said, heart racing.

He took her in his arms again. 'But we're going to the ball.'

There was such an intensity to the look of care in his eyes. It made her break apart inside to think how that would fade when he knew she had Jewish blood.

'We can't go together,' she insisted. 'It's too dangerous.'

'We're stronger together,' he said.

Stronger together. It sounded nice, but he didn't know who she was, what she was. The voyage was nearly over. She would tell him when they got off the ship, watch his face crumple into disbelief and anger, before she walked away, alone again, as usual.

The sun was melting like caramel across the sky as they stepped out onto the deck. Eli's cabin was close to the social hall. He was nowhere to be found. They saw other passengers dressed in a variety of homemade costumes, juxtaposed with flashes of wealthy pasts. Alongside geisha girls and pirates came men and women in their best suits and finery, the clothes adding gloss to the people who walked the decks by daytime, heads down, biting lips, barely suppressing tears and clenching fists. Tonight, they smiled, held their heads up high. The hum of excitement from around the ship came to a head here. The voices and shouts were at their highest volume.

For Alice, the breezeless air was choking.

'I realised how much I… while we were apart…'

Kurt was talking, but Alice could only concentrate on trying to breath. She caught a glimpse inside the social hall. Streamers and balloons suspended from the ceiling and hanging over gallery rails; the wicker-work chairs pushed to the side to make room for a dancefloor; a spray of flowers on each table, and still the portrait of the Fuhrer. Steps swept down into a double set of wide, curved staircases. Trumpets and saxophones maintained an upbeat tempo.

Kurt slipped his arm through hers. 'Are you all right?'

Suddenly, she became furious. She wanted to lash out at Kurt, make him understand how it felt to be an outsider, but then out of nowhere, Josiah appeared in front of them

'Ah, I am glad the two of you could make it,' he said, patting Kurt on the shoulder. 'We have been waiting for you both, to get this whole thing started.'

A trap.

She broke away from Kurt and pushed through the pressing crowd, feeling like the air was being squeezed out of her lungs. Alone on the edge of the deck, frantically thinking of a hiding place she could get to quickly, she saw a girl approach her. A girl in a mask that covered most of her face. Blue crushed crystal lips simmered in the reflection of the dimmed boat lights, while buds of gold and cream spiralled into painted flower buds. Her gown was long, and its skirts gathered on the floor like a royal blue puddle. She was blocking Alice's path.

The girl removed the mask and put it on top of her head. Her pretty, oval face broke into a grin. It was Greta. Despite the smile, there was a hardness to her features which the light should have made softer. She tossed her head angrily, and then closed her eyes as though in pain.

'He was my brother,' she said, grabbing hold of Alice's arm and digging her nails in. 'You sold his life, and now I'm going to sell yours.'

The shock of the words almost took Alice's legs from under her, but she somehow managed to run. She had to run.

CHAPTER SIXTEEN

The Boy hears talk of a Monster

25th May 1939

Kurt had felt Alice's hand slip away from his. When he turned to find her, she had melted into the crowd. Something was seriously wrong and he had to get to her, but he couldn't get past Josiah, who stood like a blockade in front of him, flanked by number of his entourage.

'Let me out of here,' he protested.

Josiah shook his head and pushed him further into the social hall, until he was on the edge of the dancefloor. Couples brushed past him, laughing and enjoying the music. The beat of the band was worse than any headache he'd known. That was when he saw her.

She moved slowly through the hall, wearing a mask of blue and gold, with her royal blue gown trailing behind her. Like an electric current, she sent a fission through the crowd. Josiah and his cronies parted to let her through.

'Dance with me,' Greta said upon reaching him.

It was a command. Everything and everyone else was a blur of shadows. He let himself be led into the middle of the room. Her penetrating gaze was more intense close up – the scent of her lilac perfume so strong that he could practically taste it. The noise of the band faded. She had a strange half-smile on her face.

'What's going on?' he forced himself to speak.

'I could ask you the same question,' she spoke through barely parted lips, her words a whisper against his neck.

'Have you told them who I really am? Where's Anna?'

'They don't care about you anymore. No one is going to hurt you now. You're under my protection – and you can call her Alice in front of me, by the way. We all know her real name. We know more about her than you do.'

He stopped. 'What have you done?' he asked. 'Is she safe?'

He tried to break free, but she gripped him tightly.

'That girl is a monster,' she hissed.

'What are you talking about?'

'For a start, she's a Mischling,' she spat the words out. Her voice was flint sharp now. 'Not a full Jew, or a German, like you, but a bit of both. Look at your face,' she laughed cruelly. 'You won't want her now, just like you didn't want me.'

Questions clogged in his throat. He couldn't get the words out.

'I don't believe you,' he finally managed. 'You're lying.'

She spun him around and aimed his head carefully in the direction of the main door, her red fingernails reflecting like drops of blood against the lights. Josiah was watching, arms folded, a satisfactory grin. A few of the other boys had gathered to the side of him. One of them whispered to Josiah, whose expression changed to anger as he headed across the room with three others following behind.

'They believe me,' she said. 'Because they know that your little half-breed girlfriend is out to betray us all.'

'What do you mean?' He was still trying to shake her off. 'If you harm her-'

'Your Anna is the spy.'

The words bit at him.

'She's the Jew catcher,' she went on. 'And I can prove it.'

CHAPTER SEVENTEEN

The Girl finds herself Hiding Again

Saturday 27th May 1939

The shadows of the ship barely touched the shore, but they were still close enough to see the bustling port markets. There was fruit being lifted over the heads in the crowd, and then laid down into bursting baskets of bananas and overflowing crates of oranges. The salty air filled Alice's lungs, with the wind adding a hint of warm spices. Havana was so close, she could almost taste the freedom, but she couldn't move. The gap where the cover reached the lifeboat provided her with a slice of a view. Just enough to see that everything had gone wrong.

Some of the passengers called out to loved ones in the market crowd, and a few even got shouts and waves back in return. Their words were barely audible, but the mix of frustration, confusion and fear was evident.

Alice had been watching and listening all morning. No one had been allowed off the ship. The police lined the edge of the land in their beige uniforms, carrying guns that sent out blinding reflections of the harsh sunlight. They weren't the only source of danger, either.

'How could you lose someone on a ship?' Greta's voice had reached her while she'd been hiding in the kitchens, pretending to the staff that it was all part of a game, one that she mustn't lose because there was money at stake.

'What can you expect from a Jew?' she'd heard one of the cooks mutter, making her feel less guilty as she slid leftover food into the underskirts of her dress when no one was looking, before slipping back to the lifeboat.

As night turned to morning, and then back to darkness again, with a beam from the Bahamas Lighthouse acting as a guide, Alice skirted along the ship's dark corners and hidden crevices, bypassing crew members with flirtatious glances and unspoken promises of how she would repay them for allowing her to 'look around' the forbidden areas that were usually off-limits to passengers.

Kurt, meanwhile, was with Greta and the others. The sight of him, eyes darting, blonde hair tucked behind his ears as he followed Josiah and the others, created a heaviness in her chest which almost led her over the edge of the ship and into the dark waters below. Exhaustion threatened to close her eyes, which ached with the lack of rest, but she knew that whenever she drifted off, she'd relive what had happened back in Germany. Being pinned down while the straps were fastened, everything falling into darkness, and then the burning in her body when she woke.

A sudden movement from below made her stumble, and her head

cracked against a wooden board. Ignoring the warm blood that spread over her fingers, she pulled herself back up with one hand and watched as the St Louis rejected the Cuban shores. The ship erupted into action as the great horn sliced through the air, eliciting a burst of screams and cries from the surge of passengers that poured out across the deck. A voice crackled over the loudspeaker: 'Please try to stay calm'. Near the lifeboat, a woman burst into tears, while a man rubbed his shaven head over and over, muttering prayers in disjointed Hebrew.

Using the chaos as cover, Alice climbed out of the lifeboat, pulled a scarf from the head of the crying woman and ran through the stream of bodies while wrapping it around her head. The stairs were packed with people watching the water rushing past as they pulled away from port. Alice pushed against the crowd with her head down, knocking into unreactive bodies standing helpless as their dreams moved further into the distance. She was filled with panic, knowing that she had to get off the ship, but aware of the guns kept ready for anyone who tried to jump and swim to shore.

'Where are you going?'

A hand grabbed her shoulder as she reached the top, pulling her back. She fought past. The cabin was heavily guarded, a sheet of white uniforms with flashing gold buttons. She forced her way through the others. The papers inside her brassiere scratched against her skin.

'Please let me in,' she begged one of the men. 'I need to speak to the captain about my papers.'

'You cannot speak to the captain,' he said. 'You think that you are the only one demanding an audience with him?' He turned his head away from her.

Even through the rabbled noise of the crowd, she heard the clear call: 'Alice!' Looking below, she saw Kurt, his arms waving as he stood on top of the lifeboat she had escaped from moments before. He was alone. He gestured for her to head towards a door leading into the ship. Cupping his hands across his mouth, he shouted out again, but his words were lost in the pandemonium going on around him.

The crowd surged again as Alice dipped down between the shuffling legs and got closer to the edge of the deck. She had one foot on the step when she saw Greta slip out from behind Kurt. Her steel gaze bore into Alice, and she raised her arm and pointed towards the stairwell. Out of the shadows of the lower deck came Josiah and the others, knocking the other passengers out of the way. Alice stumbled back, falling against a man's back; her face pressed into the cloth of his coat, choking her as the mass of people surged forward again. With each push, more of the breath was knocked out of her, until eventually she fell to the floor and felt herself sink under the weight of those above. The smell of old clothes, sweat-stained and moth-balled, surrounded her. The scarf fell from her head.

Taking a deep breath, she clawed and pulled her way towards the cabin until a pair of strong arms pulled her up.

'Are you okay?'

She was face to face with an old man, who had kind, tired eyes. He held her up as the dizziness passed. Behind him, Josiah was working his way closer, reaching his arm across so that it almost touched Alice's hair.

The old man was still looking at her. 'Are you hurt?' he asked.

She would have to do it. The scream she released as she scratched at the wound on her head, digging deep into the skin, was so piercing that it ripped apart her own nerves along with the splintering pain. 'Let go of me! Don't hurt me!'

The commotion set off panic waves strong enough to wrench Josiah away and send the man tumbling to the ground, his face ashen with shock.

'Please, help me!' She pushed up against one of the crew members guarding the main cabin, her blood-stained hand against his uniform.

He looked down in horror at the red stains on his tunic, at the crimson covering her head and palms.

'They are turning against me. Please, let me in!'

He hesitated.

'Check my papers,' she pleaded, pulling them out of the top of her dress, further spreading the blood across herself. 'They know I'm not Jewish. They will kill me.'

The crew member examined her papers, and then grabbed her roughly and shoved her inside the cabin, slamming the door shut behind them. Alice said a prayer of thanks under her breath. Inside, the captain and several senior staff were bent over maps. The steady throb of the ship's controls vibrated under their feet.

'What is she doing in here?' a voice bellowed from across the room.

'Captain, look at her,' the crew member said. 'They are turning against the non-Jews on the ship.'

The captain strode over, his brow furrowed. 'Get something for her wound, and make sure she is kept safe,' he ordered. His eyes met hers for a moment. 'I am sorry,' his voice softened as he addressed her directly. He turned away and walked briskly back to the small group, who were poring over sheets of paper.

'Captain, communication from Miami!' one of them shouted.

'Miami?' Alice whispered.

'She must leave this area now!' the captain boomed.

The crew member who had brought her in spun her around so that she faced the door opposite, and with two strong hands on her shoulders marched her over to it. 'I will take you to the crew quarters,' he said. His voice was low, commanding. His fingers trailed down her back.

She stiffened, wondering if there would be a price for his care. She saw another crew member, a slim figure with bright blue eyes and hair slicked into a side-part, whisper something to the captain.

'Halt!' the captain's voice thundered once again. 'Eichel, I need you here. Berger, you take the Fräulein below deck to safety and then get back up here.'

The one named Berger took the place of Eichel with a curt nod. 'You are ready, young lady?' He motioned for her to move.

He didn't touch her, instead leading the way while maintaining a respectful distance. She caught the smell of sweet sweat and sharp salt as they went along a narrow corridor, past cabin doors, every area below deck deserted. The shuffling of the bodies above drowned out the echoes of their footsteps as they reached a door. Berger took a set of keys from his pocket and opened it. They descended down steep stairs, and a musty, suffocating smell grew stronger the lower they got.

Eventually they reached the dim interior of the crew's quarters. She could make out rows of bunk beds through a second door at the end of the room, but they stopped in an area consisting of little more than a table and some chairs. A game of cards lay suspended in the middle, the chairs roughly pushed to the sides. The heavy scent of rum and smoke created a mingled and suffocating aroma. She looked around to see any potential hiding places or ways out, and she almost cried out in relief when she spotted a second door.

'Please sit down,' Berger gestured towards a chair. He gave her a warm smile. She noticed that he was greying around the temples.

As she sat down, her gaze fixed on a noticeboard, where a copy of the anti-Semitic newspaper Der Stürmer alerted readers of a Jewish plot for world domination, at the cost of the rest of the world's wealth. It was the most recent issue before they set sail, May 1939. The cover depicted a business man on the floor, being held down by a boot which led to a pair of trousers that had the Star of David hanging from the middle. In the distance, the Statue of Liberty observed the scene. The text underneath carried a typical warning: Where one is ruled by the Jews, freedom is only an empty dream.

Berger, who was searching through a first aid box, noticed the direction she was looking in, and ripped the paper down fiercely from the board, crumpling it into a ball before tossing it into a nearby bin.

'Don't worry,' he said. 'You're safe here. I'll go and find Eli.'

She froze. 'You know who I am?'

He nodded, and she realised that this must have been the crew member who told Eli about the price on her head.

'Please don't tell him where I am,' she begged. 'They're all out to get me. They're convinced that I'm the spy.'

'Not Eli.' He shook his head.

'You can't be sure.'

'You must trust him,' he said, pulling some cloths, bottles and bandages from the box and setting them down on the table. 'I knew him in Germany. He told me about this ship, and how I could join as a crew member.'

'Why would you want to be on this ship?' she asked.

'I had strong links to the trade unions. I'm what they call an enemy of the Reich. Of course, the rest of the crew know nothing of this.'

He passed her an alcohol-soaked cloth and instructed her to dab at a wound on her head. The sting made her grit her teeth.

'It hasn't proved to be a safe crossing, though,' he continued. 'The crew are being watched, too. They want to arrest anyone who has certain sympathies. Of course, many of the lads down here are happy to put their allegiances to one side for a pretty face.' He paused, and even in the low lighting, Alice could see him redden slightly at what he'd said. 'Do you need a bandage for that?' he said, changing the subject.

'Yes, but I can do this myself. Thank you.'

He looked down. 'I will have to lock you in here.'

She felt the panic rise in her chest again. 'Why?'

'There is no one to guard you while I go to get Eli,' he explained. 'Eichel is a Gestapo agent, monitoring everyone on this ship. I managed to persuade the captain not to leave you with him, in case he knows who you are.'

'What if he comes down here after me?'

'The captain will keep him busy.'

'What is going on? Why have we sailed away from the port? Are we going to Miami?'

He avoided her eyes. 'I'm not sure, but the captain will do everything in his power. He is a good man.'

'Do everything in his power to what?'

He hesitated, one foot on the stairs, leading back up to the chaos of the ship. 'I can't go back to Germany, either. It's the same story for some of the other crewmen. We'll all fight to get this ship landed.'

Before she could ask anything else, he disappeared, taking the staircase with light, quick steps. She put the bandage down, and despite the warm air in this bottled-up section of the ship, she began to shiver. Berger's word rang in her head: go back to Germany. It couldn't possibly happen. She had to get off the ship, even if she died trying. She must try to live, to get to America, for Edie, for her father.

She had to forget about Kurt's betrayal.

A few moments later, she heard heavy footsteps. It was too late to seek out a hiding place, or escape unnoticed through the other door, leaving her no choice but to confront whoever was coming. It was Eichel.

He gave her a slow smile that made her shudder as he stepped forward, looking down at her with distain. He was a perfect SS clone, with wide shoulders pushed back to accentuate the thick musculature of his torso.

'I can help you get off this ship, you know,' he said. 'The Cuban authorities are due on board soon. It is only really the Jews who they don't want in their country.'

She held back a sigh of relief. He didn't know who she was. Unless he was playing with her – in which case, she could handle a game like this. It would buy her some time.

He took the crumpled-up newspaper out of the bin. 'That bloody Jew-loving Berger,' he growled.

She watched as he smoothed the front page back against the board and pinned it into place, and then turned and regarded her with cool scrutiny.

'May I?' He extended a hand towards her, causing her to draw back automatically. 'Your papers,' he explained.

She took them out of the top of her dress, aware that his eyes were trained on her exposed flesh. As she handed them over, his fingers brushed against hers, turning her insides to ice. He seemed satisfied with what he read and leaned closer, his leathery hand brushing against the skin of her neck and working down lower towards her breast. The scent of his cologne, a mix of cloves and cinnamon, threatened to choke her as he reached up and released some of the pins from her hair, allowing a lock to trail through his fingers. Her breath stalled in her throat as she prepared for the worst, only for his hand to suddenly drop to his side.

'I am longing for a drink,' he said. 'Would you like to join me?'

It wasn't a question. He made that clear as he picked up a bottle of rum and poured it into two tumblers, still dirty from prior use. He didn't take his eyes off her, and in an attempt to suppress her rising terror, she accepted a glass and smiled as sweetly as she could.

'We should sit,' he said, downing his drink and guiding her by the hand around the table. 'You did hurt your head after all. Those damn Jews will pay soon enough, don't worry.'

She gave a little tug to free her fingers from his grasp. This sent a flicker of irritation across his brow, but he leaned back into his chair regardless. She was aware of every movement of his body. Her skin prickled with sweat. There was no way out of this.

'I can get you on a little boat that will take you straight to the officials, who will see you are a real German,' he said. 'You know, some of the boys have been compromising themselves and their duty to the Reich while on this ship. They will pay, too – but I do have some sympathy for them. I have seen how the Jewesses work, how they seduce you, hook you in.' He paused and regarded her, tilting his head back and narrowing his eyes. 'Yet to be on this ship at all, Fraulein Gerber, or may I call you Anna? You must have done something against the Reich yourself.' He reached across and grabbed her arm, forcefully this time.

'I am on a special mission,' she said smoothly. 'One of great importance to the Reich. I am to head back to Germany on another ship, but there is some information I need to get from a contact in Cuba. So, you see, I must get off this ship as a matter of urgency.'

'Oh, and why should I believe you?'

'I am telling you this because I can see that you are a man of integrity, adding value to the cause of making positive connections with our Cuban friends. You can call your contacts back in Germany if you so wish,' she said, hoping that this would be enough to buy her some time. 'But they won't be happy that you're drawing attention to me being here and risking unnecessary interceptions on the line, when the ship is already being monitored.'

She could practically see the cogs turning in his mind. He wasn't as stupid as she'd hoped. There would doubtless be a price.

'I'll get you off this ship, Fraulein.' He stood up suddenly, and extended his right arm from the neck into the air with a straightened hand. 'Heil Hitler!'

'Heil Hitler!' she replied, raising her glass to hide her face as she said it. 'You'll be well rewarded for this.'

With a smug expression on his face, he held out his arm. 'I'll escort you somewhere more private.'

Stifling her revulsion, she nodded. She stumbled a few times as they climbed the stairs and headed through the passageways, the dull rumble of the engine vibrating beneath her feet. It was then that he took out a set of keys he kept in a long-looped rope around his neck and opened the door. She wondered which other doors those keys opened. It was a welcome distraction.

The room was sparse and clean, as though barely slept in. There was a packed suitcase in the corner, indicating that Eichel had plans to leave the ship soon himself. He moved behind her, placing clammy hands on her bare arms and planting a clumsy kiss on her neck. His breath was hot. She tried to force her mind to focus on something else, but a tear had already escaped down her left cheek.

A bang on the door brought them both back to reality.

'Eichel,' a voice boomed outside. 'The captain wants to see you.'

Tutting loudly, he released her from his grasp. 'I'll be back soon,' he said quietly as he headed for the door.

When he left, she collapsed to the floor, trying to keep her sobs silent. She couldn't go through with this. There had to be another way. She stood up, took a deep breath and tried to remember everything Max had taught her about identifying opportunities to escape, and how to get the most from any given situation. She would have to act fast.

The room was so perfectly untouched that she had to be careful – any creases in the bedlinen, or smudges on the white walls and washing facilities, would be telltale signs of her activity – but eventually she found it, hidden behind a wooden panel in his wardrobe. A small safe. She shook it, but nothing rattled. No gun, no coins; just the light thud of paper hitting the sides.

A noise in the corridor, the sound of multiple footsteps, almost made her drop it. She pushed it back into place and closed the wardrobe. The cabin door swung open, making Alice jump. It was Josiah and two of his more brutish followers.

'The Jew-catcher is caught.' He smiled.

CHAPTER EIGHTEEN
The Boy makes a Decision

28th May 1939

Kurt was outside when they brought her to Josiah's cabin. There was dried blood in her hair and across her dress. She turned her head away from him, stumbled and fell to the hard ground, forcing those who were leading her into the room to stop. Instinctively, Kurt bent down to help.

'Alice-' he whispered close to her ear.

She pushed him away without looking.

'Keep moving,' Josiah ordered, forcing himself between them and hauling her back up. He turned to Kurt. 'Guard the door with the others.'

'No, I want him to see this,' Greta said, taking Kurt by the arm.

In her other hand she clutched a pile of papers and photographs.

He shrugged her off and tried to get to Alice, who still had her back turned to him. Josiah stepped in front and tilted his head, his expression a challenge, a dare. It reminded Kurt of Peter and the others in the HJ, when they were geared up for a fight, a bloodbath.

'Greta, let her go,' Kurt tried again. 'At least hear what she has to say.'

She ignored him, and turned to Josiah and the boys guarding Alice. 'Tie her hands together,' she said. 'And if she tries to get away, don't hesitate to use these.'

Greta grabbed at the kindling-shaped-into-batons that the boys held. The wood was rough, and Kurt saw how it spiked at her smooth skin, causing her to pull her hand back quickly, and leaving speckles of blood dotted across her palm. Josiah took off his tie and wound it around Anna's wrists before shoving her into the room, from which a rumble of voices and the shuffling of feet was becoming louder.

Kurt grabbed Greta and forced her to look at him.

'What are you going to do?' he demanded.

'Kurt, she is guilty,' she said. 'She's got plans to turn so many of us in-'

'You have no proof, Greta. You said if we caught her that she would be treated fairly, that you would stop all this hysteria and-'

'And I have proof.' She looked straight at him. The usual pain, the misery which was so apparent that you could almost feel it from her gaze, was still there, except now her mouth was set into a hard, unmoving line, too.

'I don't understand-'

'You can't understand, Kurt.' She shook her head sadly, dislodging some of the wilder dark curls from the pins on her head. 'So please, just stay out of this. I've been trying to protect you. I told you to stay away from her.'

'She was only hiding out of fear. Anyone would do the same. Let me talk to her, and leave that brute Josiah out of it.'

'I'm warning you for the last time – stay out of this.' Her tone had shifted, and it was the detached Greta he saw before him again, the version of her that he wasn't sure of; the one who had so easily dismissed Christopher from the group; the one who had perfected a steely expression for the SS parties that she attended as a spy.

She placed her fingers on his arm again, and Kurt realised that there was no choice but to go in and watch whatever she had planned unfold, and wait for his chance to rescue Alice. Greta led him through the tightly packed crowd to the front. Her long blue velvet dress crushed up against the floor like a thick wave as she walked. The whole time they had been looking for Alice, Greta had not changed clothes, leading this ridiculous 'hunt' as a queen guiding her subjects, with some of them were more than willing to obey. It was Josiah who had suggested the batons.

The cabin, which belonged to Josiah, was much grander than those found where Kurt was staying, and heaving with bodies. Alice had been thrown onto the bed and was slowly getting to her feet. Josiah's henchmen stood in front of her, forming an official guard, their faces blank as they held up their weapons in readiness. Eli was standing at the back, and gave him a look that was frustratingly unreadable. He too had taken part in the hunt, and when Kurt had tried to question him about his allegiances, he'd murmured that he would speak to him once Alice was found. Further towards the front, Kurt caught the eye of the sharp-tongued Leah, whose rouged lips were turned up in a snarl. Heidi was standing next to her, looking at the floor.

Greta moved ahead of the rest, climbing up onto a chair near the side of the bed to address the crowd. 'You've all been brought here today because we have found the spy,' she proclaimed, pointing at Alice. Her voice was clear, calm, cold. 'The Jew-catcher.'

The initial silence that followed was broken only by the sounds of the ship's engines, and feet padding on the deck above their heads. Then, the room exploded with voices.

'What proof do you have that I am this "Jew-catcher", apart from her word?' Alice said, her voice breaking across the waves of noise.

Kurt was close enough to hear the quiver behind her words.

'You turned in other Jews!' Josiah shouted from the back of the room. 'Not only to save yourself, but to make your fortune.'

'I did not,' Alice protested. 'I'm not working with Eichel.'

'We found you in his room.' Josiah smirked.

The crowd shifted, creating a feeling that the room was rocking from side to side, as though they had hit a patch of rough sea.

'If you'd just listen to me, I can help you all,' Alice tried to speak over the tumult. 'The ship, it isn't-'

'I can prove it!' Greta shouted, drowning out Alice's words. She held the papers she'd been carrying up in the air. Kurt was close enough to see how they shook in her hand as she separated one from the pile. 'Here is Anna's, or should I say Alice's, real ID card.'

The colour drained from Alice's face, setting it into marble. She moved back and used a hand to steady herself against the wall.

'That doesn't prove anything,' Malik called out. 'Many of us had to leave with false papers.'

'But why not tell us when she was safely on board?' Leah retorted.

'Would you?' Malik asked. 'We don't even know what is happening with the ship. What if we all get sent back to Germany?'

'Let her talk,' Kurt found himself shouting above the racket.

Greta glared at him. A hush descended, and the papers came

back to the front.

'I had to get out,' Alice's voice made him snap back into the moment. 'My father is in a camp, and they wanted to use me to get at him. I was working underground in Berlin, helping to get people out until the Gestapo caught up with me. Someone betrayed us-'

'Or you were betraying our people with the help of Franz Muller?' Greta interrupted. She had a different photo, held in the direction of the bed, away from the crowd.

Alice visibly recoiled at whatever Greta was forcing her to look at. Kurt tried to reach for the it, but Leah was the first to take it from Greta. She looked at it for a moment before the spit left her red lips and landed on Alice's cheek. Someone else picked it up and others crowded around. The volume of bodies crushing forward created chaotic surges across the cabin until the photograph was turned towards the room. Kurt moved to see the profile shot of a boy around his age. He was plain-clothed, but wore the unmistakable long leather coat of the Gestapo. He looked familiar. A sense of fear made the air in the room seem thicker. People started to step back.

'Step forward if you know who this is,' Greta said, her words carrying across the subdued room.

Several people shuffled to the front, heads bowed in collective terror, as though they expected the image to come to life, and the strong-featured, broad-shouldered Aryan agent to somehow climb out of the picture. Kurt realised that he had been looking at the so-called 'Blond Reaper', the source of so much strife for Walter and the others, who was sent from Berlin to 'clean-up' rebels against the state; the one who had led the raid on their dance during his final night.

'So, can anyone confirm that this is in fact Franz Muller?' Greta asked those who had moved forward. 'The Blond Reaper, who has torn apart so many of our families — who, many of us know, cannot be operating without a Jewish spy at his command.'

There were nods, and several quiet and quick confirmations.

'Is this the man who took your father away, Heidi?' Greta's voice dropped to almost a whisper as she looked to her friend, whose eyes remained cast down to the floor as she nodded forlornly in response. 'Alice worked with him to betray our group in Berlin,' Greta added. 'She would do anything for him, and for herself.'

Kurt's head snapped up at this. He remembered how Greta had said the same thing about Christopher, in almost the same words. He looked at Greta now, smiling without any guilt over banishing the wrong person out of their group, condemning him to almost certain death. Kurt's fists drew into his hands so tightly, he thought he must have drawn blood.

'How can an identity card and a photo of a Gestapo member prove that she is the traitor working with them?' Kurt's words rang out, bringing Greta's attention back to the crowd as a few people murmured their agreement.

She shot him a look of warning, and then pulled out another photo and handed it directly to him. This time it was a younger Alice, her soft curls teased into braids, smiling at the camera. Next to her, also younger, was the boy from the other picture, dressed in a Hitler Youth uniform, head bent close to hers.

'Let me see that,' said Heidi, who, to his surprise, snatched the photograph from him. The others who had stepped forward crowded around her, and the rest of them shifted forward to try and see what was happening. Heidi turned the photo around and held it up towards the bed.

'That was before h-he changed,' Alice said, her words uncertain, the terror evident in her eyes. 'I wasn't working with him. He was protecting me.'

The scream pierced through the air so sharply that it caused Kurt to momentarily close his eyes and dip his head down. When he looked back up, Greta was flying at Alice, grabbing at her and pulling back with clumps of hair in her hand. Alice didn't fight back. Nobody else moved. Kurt jumped up until the bed and separated the two girls. Greta scratched at his arms, tried to get past him, her sharp nails in his skin. He could feel her tears wet against his face as she tried to force him off the bed.

He fell, grabbing Alice and taking her with him. Kurt felt a sharp tug on his leg. He looked down to see Eli, his eyes wide, gesturing to the side of the room where a few members of the crowd, the ones most closely associated with Eli's group, including Malik, had formed a pathway leading right to the door. The last of them held a baton up and nodded purposefully at Kurt.

'Where did you get this information from?' someone asked.

'I was in the resistance in Berlin,' Greta screeched. 'This intelligence, these papers, were brought onto the ship by a contact before we left Cuba. He warned me to be careful, as this Alice we have here is working with a gestapo crew member on the ship, and then we found her in his room.'

It was then Kurt made his decision. 'I don't believe you.'

'What?'

'I don't believe you,' he repeated. Although he couldn't understand why Alice had been in a crew member's room, nothing Greta said added up to what he knew of her in Berlin; and Alice couldn't have had anything to do with what happened at the dance.

Eli pulled at him again, and gestured towards the door as the corridor at the side of the room grew narrower.

'He doesn't believe me,' Greta said slowly, looking out into the crowd. 'It would seem that there is someone else I have to expose today.' She held up another photo for all to see. 'This is Kurt Hertz, of the Hitler Youth.'

Someone pushed the photo in front of Kurt. It had been taken before a camping trip. Alfons was next to him, a fake smile, reserved for times such as those, plastered across his face.

Greta was still talking. 'The resistance sent me these so that you and Alice wouldn't be able to turn us in – to betray us and kill us, even as we reached safety, in exchange for money.'

A punch caused Kurt's vision to blur, and he fell off the bed as the crowd gathered and kicked around him. Each impact shuddered through him. His body crumpled, vomit choked him, and just as blackness was closing in, he felt strong hands pull him up and hoist him through the crowd. He reached back to find Alice's arm, grasping it tightly as he followed Eli through the crowd. The sound of his own blood drummed in his ears as he fought his way to the back with Eli and Malik, the latter handing him a baton and shouting at him to fight – to protect Alice, whose hands were still bound together.

They somehow made it to the exit. Outside, the 'guards' were tied up, with a grinning Gus standing over them. Malik pushed the door closed and Gus pulled a container across it.

'That won't hold them for long,' Eli said, pushing Kurt in the direction that Gus was already running in. 'We have to move fast.'

They entered a side door along the passageway and found themselves descending stairs, deep into the darkened bowels of the ship. It was different from the previous room Kurt had been in, where they'd questioned him about being a spy. The hissing and spitting of the engines grew louder until they came out into a room filled with pipes, but with enough space for several deckchairs, blankets and a stash of food stored in the corner. The air was melting with hot oil.

Gus, Malik and another boy called Freddie sat down on the chairs. It was then Kurt noticed that the room was set up like a court, and that standing against the door they had just entered through, Eli was holding a gun.

CHAPTER NINETEEN

The Girl is given a Choice

28th May 1939

'I thought you trusted me,' she could hear Kurt saying to the small crowd gathered in the room. Her head throbbed, and every part of her body ached.

Eli's pupils were dark, unreadable; his sallow skin waxy in the low light. She took a deep breath, trying to slow her frantic heartbeat.

'Why were you in Eichel's room?' Eli asked, and Alice realised that the gun was pointed at her. She felt Kurt move beside her, pulling himself between them.

'Step back, you Nazi bastard!' Gus shouted, standing up. His feet kicked across the dusty floor to join Eli.

Kurt stayed still, raising his hands so that they became long shadows of surrender on the walls. Eli stepped around to the front of him as Gus locked the door. The gun clicked.

She glanced at Kurt. His arm was scratched to shreds and a bruise was forming on his face. She could hear his damaged lungs wheezing as he tried to breathe.

'We know all about him and who he is,' Eli spoke impatiently, pulling her attention back to him. She realised now that it was her on trial.

'I'm not working with Eichel,' she said. 'I couldn't trust anyone, and he offered me a way off the ship.'

'I bet he offered you a way,' Gus sneered.

Kurt jumped up and grabbed Gus by the shirt. They squared up, nose to nose, before Gus backed off, laughing in a way that bounced around the room against the rumbling mechanics of the ship.

'I admire the way they are trained,' Gus said. 'They will insist on blood and honour even when the odds are stacked against them, like machines.'

'Gus,' Eli's voice was cold, with a tone of warning. He turned back to Alice. 'Did Eichel... did he touch you?'

Cheeks burning, she shook her head. Her scalp felt like it was on fire, each hair follicle pulled and strained as though singed. Her arms ached, but she fought to keep them across her chest, to keep the torn material of her dress up. Her hands shook from the effort.

'Fetch her something to wear,' Eli instructed Gus, who sat nearest to a pile of blankets.

Underneath the blankets was a selection of clothes. He threw a jumper over to Alice. She turned around and put it on, the soft wool a small comfort against her skin. She was shivering, despite the heat of the room. The smell of burning oil was so pungent, it felt like it was melting her tongue.

'I'd get rid of both of them myself,' Gus spoke up again. 'I already told you that I don't trust the Nazi. No one will hear a gun shot down here.'

Alice knew this was true. A shot would barely be felt against the throbbing of the mighty engines. 'I'm not working with Eichel,' she said once again. 'If you brought me down here to try and get information, you'll be wasting your time.' A thin bead of sweat ran down her shoulder blades. 'Eli, if you know of my father and what he stands for, then you know me,' she continued, looking him dead in the eye. 'I know Eichel is a Gestapo spy. I found evidence in his room – a safe that I think holds important documents. Let me prove it. You must have a use for me, otherwise why not let Greta and the others just deal with me themselves?'

'Because that bitch is just as bad as you!' Gus spat. The hiss of the engines seemed to get louder with this action.

'Gus has been shadowing Greta on my behalf,' Eli explained. 'He saw her with Eichel. They were arguing, saying something about a deal.'

'A deal?' Alice said.

'Probably something like the one you were cutting with Eichel in his room,' Gus accused in a leery tone. 'I mean, why else wouldn't Greta have just told him who you are?'

'She'll be holding out, trying to save her brother,' Kurt said, his breathing even more strained since the flare up with Gus. 'I knew her back in Germany. She kept my real identity hidden until now. She used to move between groups, and even risked spending time with SS members to get information on him, the only surviving one. Her brothers were forming an underground resistance in the Jewish community. The forged papers that they were going to escape Berlin with went missing. They were trapped in the city, and the Gestapo picked them off one by one, until there was only Isaac left.'

'I had those papers.' Alice realised that she was shaking. 'I tried to find the people in the photos. I even risked going into the Jewish ghettos to ask if anyone recognised them.'

'What happened?' Eli asked.

'I think Franz used me to get to them,' she admitted.

'Because he was your boyfriend?' Malik chimed in. 'No one can deny that it is you with him on the photograph.'

'I grew up with him.' She swallowed. 'He protected me, got me on this ship, but I… I know how he feels about Jews… about us. I'm not blind to that.' She stopped, took a breath. 'That photo was hidden in the floorboards of my house… I couldn't bring myself to destroy it, and I couldn't carry it with me, either. I wanted to keep it to use against Franz, if I had to. Someone must have found it.'

'Unless it was Franz who betrayed you,' Malik suggested.

The thought had occurred to Alice before, but she hadn't been able to face the possibility. Eli lowered the gun and sat down, running a hand through his hair.

'And Kurt, Greta turned you and your girlfriend in,' Malik was still talking. 'I wouldn't say that you should be defending her.'

'Ignore all of this bullshit,' Gus said. 'Greta is probably holding out for more money before she gives Alice up to Eichel.'

'Her position was as an infiltrator,' Kurt said. 'She could be doing the same job here, and I don't believe she would have turned you over. She knows about the camps-'

'What do any of you know about the camps?' Gus swung around suddenly, catching Eli off balance so that he dropped the gun.

For a second, all eyes were on the weapon. Alice got to it first, but a shattering pain came upon her as a stomping boot crushed her hand. Gus grabbed the gun. She stood to find him pointing it at Kurt.

'Everything that happened to you was by choice,' he charged.

'Do you know what I did? I dared to have "relations with a racial superior" – my own girlfriend! And do you know what they did to me?' He ripped off his shirt, revealing welts of scarred skin across his torso. He pulled at the wounds, his face creasing with pain, the weapon still trained on Kurt. 'You will pay for this.'

Before she knew what she was doing, Alice had positioned herself in front of Kurt.

'Get out of the way,' Gus said slowly.

'Do as he says,' Kurt said softly.

Alice didn't move, but instead turned to Eli. He stood motionless, his face again unreadable.

'Eli, this isn't you. Don't let him do this,' she begged. 'This isn't what you stand for!'

The gun was so close, she could smell the metal mixed with a sawdust scent. She closed her eyes and prepared to die. When she opened them again, Eli was talking softly and putting the gun away. Gus was pacing on the other side of the room, Malik following, trying to calm him.

'Alice, I'm sorry that I'm going to have to ask you this,' he said. 'I've been thinking it over, and I believe that you're not working with Eichel.' He took a deep breath. 'But I'm going to have to request that you get close to him again.'

CHAPTER TWENTY
The Boy and the Tortures of the Past

29th May 1939

'You can't do it.'

He heard the chair scraping across the dusty floor as she tried to move away from him, and recoiled at the sharp intake of breath that followed when her bandaged hands pressed down on the arm rests. In the end, she sunk back down so that he could barely see her face. The tension added to the oppressive atmosphere in the room, which had become hotter despite them being alone now, with only Freddie as a solitary guard outside the door, under strict instructions that nobody went in and nobody went out. Footsteps rumbled like rolling thunder all around them, but Eli was confident that this part of the ship would be too difficult to for their enemies to access. The burning oil and steam were almost unbearable. Kurt's throat felt as though it was closing over, with a drying treacle taste moving towards his stomach.

'This will relieve the pain,' Eli had told Kurt, handing over some powder and a flask of water. 'Here, you can read the label if you don't trust me, and I'll sip the water first.' He raised the flask to his lips and gulped the water down. 'I'll leave it here for when you're ready.'

Eli then bandaged Alice's swollen hand while Kurt drank the powdered water. It tasted chalky, but had relieved the worst of the pain at least.

'What do I need to do?' Alice had asked quietly once they were patched up.

They were going to use her as a pawn in their dangerous game of survival, and Eli thought that by treating her injuries he could somehow compensate her for the risk. Kurt wanted to shake him.

'First of all, find out where his keys are,' Eli had said.

'They're on a chain around his neck.'

Kurt saw her flinch when she said that. He'd felt sick to his stomach.

'You'll have to – get very close, and then use these,' Eli was looking away as he spoke, and had then reached once more into the medical bag, opening his hand to reveal a small bottle of pills. 'These will put him out cold for a few hours. If another crew member finds him, they'll just assume that he's drunk. It shouldn't be too much trouble to persuade him to keep your liaison… discreet.' He seemed to be grasping for words. 'The thing is… you only have two chances… if he doesn't drink the liquid one, you will… have to… kiss a capsule into this mouth.'

'No!' Kurt's voice had been filled with range. 'You can't expect her to do that.'

Eli cleared his throat and looked down at the floor as he spoke. 'It should be easy enough to place it into your mouth discreetly, and then transfer it quickly – well, forcefully – so that he has to swallow it.'

'That might not even work,' Kurt had felt his face turn red with fury. 'He could just as easily spit it out. Why would you risk that?' He'd then turned to Alice. 'I don't want you to do it. There has to be another way,' he'd said, before facing Eli again. 'Why can't you just attack him? Use the gun!'

Eli had dismissed the idea with a shake of his head. 'It can't look like there is any foul play. We can't attract attention to ourselves.'

'I've made my choice,' Alice then said, without looking at either of them. 'I'll do it.'

'Then we will go and make our plans.' Eli had looked at her for a moment before standing up and heading for the exit, followed by Malik.

Gus had hovered nearby for a moment, leaning down close to them. 'Your only other way out of here is to take all of those pills yourself. That's your choice.'

Malik pulled him away, and seconds later the door slammed shut.

'It must be killing you that you care about me,' Alice was speaking now, calling him back into the present. Her words were barely more than a whisper. 'Now that you know I'm a half-breed. I saw your face when you heard.'

Kurt felt every muscle in his body stiffen. Not so long ago, there would have been a truth to what she'd said, but he cared so much for her – and for Greta, despite what she was doing – that he hardly thought of them as Jews at all now. The only remaining question was would he have got as close to Alice as he had done if he'd known this from the start? He didn't want to have to find an answer with everything weighing so heavily on his mind; and besides, would any of it matter if the ship ended up being sent back to Germany? If that happened, they would all find themselves trapped in the same dark dungeons of horror, if not a camp.

'Why did you stand up for me?' she asked.

'I knew Greta was lying,' he said. 'Back in Berlin, she convinced our group that a member called Christopher was the one betraying us, when in fact he wasn't.'

Alice got up from the chair and walked around to face him. In the dim light, the rusty blood soaked into the bottom of her dress looked like nothing more than paint; but the pain on her face, the scratches and stains on her skin, seeping through the bandages on her arms, darkening the material, those were unmistakable. 'I thank you for believing in me,' she said. 'But I have to ask you this… how do you feel about me being a Jew?'

'You should have told me.' He couldn't meet her gaze.

'Would it have made a difference?'

'I… I care about you.'

He still couldn't look at her. It was one thing helping Eli, talking to him, mixing with the swing kid Jews, but almost having a relationship with a Jewess was something else altogether. With Greta, nothing had ever gone beyond just dancing. It was a flirtation that he had always been wary of allowing to develop further.

'You wouldn't have got close to me if you'd known,' she finally said.

He couldn't answer. He knew it was wrong, that his feelings were the result of a years of being bombarded with a hatred that had got under his skin and become part of him. The look she gave him implied that she understood. After all, she had been brought up to hate him, too.

'Why are you defending Greta?' she asked.

'Because I've seen Greta be driven to this before. It isn't who she really is – or at least who she was. She's become almost dehumanised. She... the SS men made her do things. It changed her,' he explained. 'And the danger you'll be in, you could... you could... I can't let anyone else die.'

'Alfons,' she said softly. 'You called out his name during your fever dreams. It was the name that you called out the most. What happened?'

The smell of blood, sweat and unwashed skin was all around them, but it was a nausea brought on by reliving the memory that brought the bile to his mouth.

'Alfons had never hurt anyone,' he said, his words coming slowly, stiffly. His mouth worked through the pain, fighting the waves of sickness that were washing over him, and the tightness gripping his throat. He saw Alice looking at him with confusion, her brow furrowed. It was better than the glimpses of hatred, and even fear, that he'd seen in her throughout this conversation. There was no need to lie now.

'Peter, my Hitler Youth leader, made Alfons and me fight each other. I... I punched Alfons. He gave me the signal to do it, but then-' All the awful images were boxed into his mind, and the space was getting fuller. He needed to open up and release the regrets – the awful, horrible secrets he carried around every day. 'Alfons got up and threw himself on top of Peter, and then all hell broke loose.'

He thought of his friend, who was usually so calm and gentle, raining down blows on their HJ leader, and then what had happened next. The other boys waded in, held Alfons arms open, and with one punch Peter knocked him to the floor. The noise it made when his head bounced off the edge of the pavement still replayed in Kurt's mind. It was a sickening crack, and the blood started to pour out almost immediately – a carpet of red leading up to Peter, who stood back, breathing heavily, but with a triumphant grin on his face. Kurt also saw himself in that moment, standing in shock, unmoving, still poised for the fight he was being made to have with his friend.

'I... I tried to save him,' he said. 'We went to a hospital, but Peter was there too. I could see in his eyes that he wanted us both dead. I knew that he'd followed us, waiting for an opportunity. I screamed at him that Alfons was in there, but he set fire to the place anyway.'

'He murdered Alfons,' Alice murmured. 'And then what did you do?'

'I went to kill Peter.'

'But you didn't do it,' she said slowly. 'Because you couldn't.'

'One of the last things Alfons said to me was not to be like them.'

He could feel himself choking up, a hard-lump forming in his chest. He couldn't explain how, despite the situation around him, when Greta had held up that photo, all he'd wanted to do was take it, keep it as a memento of that friendship.

'I couldn't do it,' he said. 'But then Peter tried to push me, and we both fell. Walter and Heinz, the leaders of the resistance I joined, decided it would be better if everyone thought that I had meant to kill him, but that was before the Gestapo started a manhunt for me. Then we saw that having me work for Heinz and his group boosted morale. I became a symbol of resistance. Everyone wanted to protect me, and more people joined the cause. If the ship goes back Germany, they'll put me on trial and guillotine me for Peter's attempted murder, and... and Alfons's death as well. That will be if I'm lucky. I could spend time in a cell or a camp first.'

'Do you wish that you had killed Peter?' she asked, her bruised face lit up by the low lights of the room.

'No. Yes. Sometimes,' he admitted.

'Where is Heinz now?'

'We had a party. Our secret locations were always being leaked, but there was something different about this. Your… Franz was there. When I first saw Greta on the ship, she told me that Heinz had survived the attack and was recovering in hospital. I'd do anything to go back and get him out.'

He paused and tried to sit up in a more comfortable position, but everything hurt. 'Tell me more about Franz,' he said, his tone harsher than intended.

She jolted back as though he had slapped her. 'I can tell you this now, as we are so many miles away from Germany, and you won't believe me anyway.' She swallowed. 'But he used to help the resistance group I was in.'

'What resistance group was this?'

'It was run by some of my father's old work colleagues. They did small but valuable acts, forging papers to get people out. I delivered them. I had the right look, and no one immediately recognised me as the daughter of Albert Sommer. It was still dangerous, though, and eventually my luck ran out, so they decided I would be better off helping them from America, where we have a contact. Also, they had promised my father that they would keep me alive. That wasn't going to happen if I stayed in Germany.'

'Did Franz betray you and give the Gestapo those photos?'

'Maybe. He might have got an offer that he couldn't refuse, but after all that he did for me, I don't think it would have been him. Not to mention that being seen in a photo with someone like me wouldn't be good for his position.'

The sadness transformed her face, softening its strong angles.

She looked more vulnerable than he had ever seen her before. He wanted to take her into his arms, warm her thin body, rub away the dark shadows under her eyes.

'You don't need to do this with Eichel,' he said. 'Eli should understand that.'

'Eli is a good person,' she said. 'He's just in an impossible position. I do believe him when he says he's keeping us here for our own protection.'

He waited for her to look up. 'But I don't think he's right to make you trap Eichel,' he said, the hot air from the engines burning against his skin.

'I have to do it.'

'Why?'

'Because I'm no better than Greta otherwise. I can't have any more blood on my hands.'

'What happened to Greta's brother wasn't your fault.'

Alice shook her head. 'I tracked him down, Kurt,' she said. 'I led them to him.'

'But you didn't mean to,' he said, taking hold of her hand.

Alice leaned in so close to him that he could feel her breath in his ear. Her voice was so faint that he had to strain to hear.

'Not at first, no,' she said. 'But I... I needed enough money to escape with Edie, and turning him in would have paid for both of us, so I went along with what Max said his contacts wanted. He told me not to tell Franz – said we couldn't trust him – but when it came down to it, I couldn't do it. I wouldn't take them to the meeting place. They arrested Max and they tortured me, but I held off until the time had passed for Greta's brother to leave the café. Then, I thought that they were going to kill me, but... they did something much worse. Franz showed up soon after it... it happened... and took me away, made sure I was looked after until my wounds healed, and then put me on a train to Hamburg to reach this ship.' She took off her shoes and her torn stockings. 'They didn't inflict any damage that could be easily seen, because they thought that if I took them to the café, Isaac would notice if I had a bruised and bloody face.'

He looked down and saw that all of her toenails were missing, and each foot was scarred by the slashes of a whip across the lower sides.

'My feet don't hurt anymore,' she said, tracing his stare. 'They never really did after the... the other thing. Later, when Franz told me that they'd caught Isaac anyway, largely thanks to the papers I'd had, I knew I'd got what I deserved.'

'What did they do?' he asked. He reached for her shaking hands and laced his finger between hers.

'They sterilised me.'

He felt the weight of her body collapse into his, and he held her tightly against him.

CHAPTER TWENTY-ONE

The Girl and the Weight of the Guilt

Some hours later, Eli returned, closing the heavy door behind him. He was carrying a tray loaded with china cups and dishes. The smell of coffee and yeasty bread permeated the room, fighting against the tar and oil. Alice was exhausted from crying, but still felt a yearning for food that she hadn't thought possible before the rich aromas entered the room.

'I thought you might need something to eat and drink,' Eli said, almost apologetically, setting the tray down on the floor and stepping back.

Alice considered asking how he'd got away with carrying all of that through the ship – as though he was taking afternoon tea down to the rats – and how he'd avoided Josiah and the others, but the lump in her throat caused by her confession to Kurt wouldn't allow her to speak.

'Berger got these for me,' Eli explained. 'Please, have a drink at least,' he added, when neither of them made a move towards his offering.

Aware of Kurt's eyes on her, but also conscious of the dryness in her mouth, Alice picked up one of the cups with trembling hands. She managed to force down some of the lukewarm liquid. It eased the pain in her throat slightly. Eli was also watching her. His dark eyes looked softer than they had been earlier, illuminated by the low lighting of the room.

She'd asked Kurt not to tell anyone what had happened to her. In the hours that followed their conversation, she'd stayed locked in his arms. They hadn't said anything else to each other, but his embrace and the light kiss that he gave her told her that it was okay. It was difficult not to relive what had happened, but she had done her best to close her eyes and concentrate on the comforting warmth of his body.

Franz had been so angry when he found out what they'd done to her that he'd punched a wall outside the hospital. Then he'd turned on her, asking her why she hadn't just told them where the meeting place with Isaac was. As she limped to his car, she'd seen his face fall, his eyes mist over. He proclaimed that he was getting her out of Germany for good. She was to go on the train to Hamburg the following week, after he'd bribed a doctor to see her.

She had lain in that grey-walled hospital for a week before Franz had found out where she was. Each day she became more certain that one of the men who'd dragged her to the hospital from the prison cell would come back. The one saving grace, Franz had said, was that they hadn't realised she was Albert Sommer's daughter, as the false papers she'd been carrying had held up to scrutiny.

She had to get back to the present. The need to get to the business of the mission was creating a churning in her stomach.

'Has Greta told Eichel who I am?' she asked.

The coffee spilled out over her cup and pooled into the cracks on her cut hands, where the bandages didn't quite cover. She bit down on her lip until she tasted a burst of metallic blood against her tongue.

'We don't think so,' Eli answered.

'What can he do even if he does know?' Kurt said, defiance in his voice. 'Kidnap us and smuggle us back to Germany?'

'There is a lot of support for the Nazis in places like Cuba,' Eli said.

Alice felt a chill descend over her. What was the point of fleeing from an enemy whose reach stretched out across the world?

'But we aren't going there now,' Alice interrupted. 'I overheard the crew saying that we are headed for Miami.'

'So, you do know,' Eli said sombrely.

'Know what?' Kurt said.

'That there is hardly a chance we'll get off this ship. Cuba has flat-out refused to take any of us. Our Visas are no longer valid, if they ever were to begin with.'

'But Miami?' Alice's heart lifted again, as it had when she had first heard the crew's plan. 'America will take us, surely?'

Eli shook his head. 'They won't let us off there.'

'Why not?' Alice put the cup back down on the tray.

'Roosevelt isn't exactly on the side of immigrants,' Eli replied steadily. 'Or Jews.'

'So where are we going?' Kurt asked.

Alice hadn't thought it was possible for his face to look any paler, or for his body to crumple any further into defeat.

'No one knows yet,' Eli said.

'How do you know that any of this is true?' Kurt sounded angry – accusatory, even. 'Your friend in the crew? Isn't he enough for you? Why do you need to drag Alice into this, too?'

'If we don't prove that you are both innocent, it won't be the Nazis that we'll need to worry about,' Eli said. 'Josiah and the others are getting closer. We can't hide you down here forever. Gus has pretended to defect to their group, and both Malik and Freddie are rotating between guarding you and staying with Berger, under his protection.'

'Why do you care what happens us?' Kurt pressed him. 'And why can't you just use this Berger character to get whatever it is that you need?'

'I believe that Eichel has information which could harm all of us, and it's impossible for Berger to get close to him because he doesn't trust any of the crewmen.' Eli paused and looked at the floor, taking a deep breath before turning to Alice.

'Eichel definitely doesn't know who I am?' she asked. 'He still thinks I'm Anna Gerber?'

Eli avoided her gaze. 'It seems he thought that Alice Sommer had been taken off the ship before it left Hamburg,' he said. 'That was the intelligence all the gestapo informers were given. Greta was telling the truth about having an outside source.'

A girl had been taken off the ship. The words cut through her like a knife. 'There was another girl taken instead of me?' she whispered. 'Who was she?'

'I tried to find out,' Eli said earnestly.

'Did she look like me?' Alice demanded. 'Could she have been mistaken for me?'

Neither of them answered.

'Everything I do puts people in danger,' she cried. She knew that there would always be a weight of guilt around her neck, she'd known that for years, but she hadn't been prepared for it to keep getting heavier.

'You can see that she isn't in the right frame of mind for this mission,' Kurt shouted at Eli. 'Don't do it.' He turned to Alice, taking hold of her hand.

'I have to, Kurt,' she said quietly. 'I have to.'

'I won't let you!' he roared, smashing one of the china cups on the floor, and then quickly grabbing a jagged piece that Alice could see was large enough to use as a weapon.

Kurt lunged at Eli, but Alice blocked his path, causing him to tumble down onto the floor as he shifted to avoid crashing into her. He got up quickly, throwing a punch at Eli that caught his face.

The door burst open, and Freddie and Malik hurried in.

'Tie him up,' Eli said, regretfully throwing out one hand as he turned to face Alice, and using the other to attempt to block the flow of blood from his nose. 'Are you ready?' he asked.

She nodded.

Clare Coombes

CHAPTER TWENTY-TWO

The Boy learns that Trust needs to be Earned

30th May 1939

Kurt gave a final kick out at the shattered pieces of china on the floor. His foot slipped on the spilt coffee, causing his back to crash loudly into the pipes he was bound to; bone crunching against metal. He turned, the ropes twisting uncomfortably into his flesh, so that his head rested on the cold copper. The cooling sensation offered some small relief to his aching body.

The door opened slowly, and he could just make out Eli's face in the darkness. The dried blood around his nose was evident in the shallow lighting, and he was carrying a metal flask that could have easily served as a makeshift weapon.

Kurt braced himself for the retributive attack that was sure to come, but Eli simply sat down, crossed his legs and looked at him as though he had something important to ask, a favour even. His face held the same apprehensive gaze that it had the night of the Azores. Panic still swelled through Kurt as he realised that this meant Alice could be alone with Eichel, with no one reliable to step in if she got into real trouble. He doubted that Malik or Gus would care enough to put themselves in danger as long as it meant having evidence to condemn Greta and save their own skins.

'I thought you were going to stay close to Alice,' Kurt said.

'We took her to the crew quarters, but Eichel isn't there yet,' Eli answered calmly. 'Malik is guarding the door. They're going to come for me when everything is in place. Do you want some water?'

He unscrewed the cap and held out the flask, close enough so that Kurt could anticipate the much-needed liquid touching his mouth and pouring down his throat, but his pride prevailed.

'I'd rather you were looking after her,' he said, ignoring his desperate thirst.

'You know that she was part of the Berlin underground,' Eli said. 'That she is trained for things like this.'

Kurt felt like he'd received a blow to the stomach. 'Things like this,' he repeated, imagining Alice receiving regular packages of lipstick and nylon stockings, and the sins that she would have been expected to commit in order to gain information.

'Kurt, she is a girl of great honour,' Eli said. 'But she has to act differently than she wants to at times, to survive. As we all do. We won't let anything happen to her.'

'I don't trust Gus.'

'Neither do I in his present state of mind,' Eli acknowledged, and then paused. 'But there are other people that we can depend on, and maybe we should learn to trust each other, too.'

Eli took something out of his pocket and unwrapped it. The smell of fresh bread ripped through Kurt's senses.

'You need to eat,' Eli said. 'Hang on while I untie you.'

'Untie me?'

'So that you can eat. I trust you, remember?'

He waited while Eli undid the knots of stiff rope, and then rubbed his sore wrists with relief before taking the bread and flask of water. The dip and ripple of the ship was affecting his stomach, and he was glad to weigh it down with a bit of food. Eli's use of the word 'trust' stuck in Kurt's throat, despite the cooling water. He was too exhausted to fight his way out regardless, and could sense that Eli knew this. Someone was probably guarding the door, too, but he had nothing to lose at this point, and decided to say what was on his mind.

'You and Gus are going to hand me over to the Gestapo, as a trade for safe passage off the ship,' Kurt had been waiting to say this since the moment they'd first offered him protection in exchange for his cooperation. 'And Alice, what about her? You want Eichel's papers to negotiate your own terms, don't you?'

'That was the plan at first, yes,' Eli looked away momentarily, but then turned back suddenly, fixing his eyes on Kurt's. There was a long pause while the machinery around them throbbed with its own tension. Eli scratched at the floor with his fingers, head down as though considering something. 'What I'm about to say to you is important, and I want you to listen carefully,' he said, his eyes blazing, tone urgent. 'I want you to know that people will do anything to survive.'

'I know,' Kurt said quietly, finding that he couldn't meet Eli's intense glare.

'No, you don't,' his voice was becoming angrier. The usual soft intonation was gone, and a deep rage was coming through. 'You see, it's not only people like me who'll do anything to try and live. Everyone, all people, will do anything to survive. Despite all that you've seen, there is still something inside you insisting that we're vermin, and that we'll destroy anyone and anything just to live, isn't there?' He let the question hang in the air. 'Even though you're in love with Alice and she is part you and part us, you still believe that Jews are vermin, don't you?'

Kurt wasn't sure how to answer. The walls of the room seemed to be closing in on them, creating a claustrophobic atmosphere that he couldn't avoid. The burning oil was twisting like coils of poison air in his lungs. Love. He didn't know he could feel such an emotion. It wasn't something that had been encouraged throughout his childhood, at least not when he was apart from his father and mother. At school, at Hitler Youth, with his friends – Alfons excepted – it was all about hate. He thought of those men who called themselves the great protectors of the German people, and what they had done to Alice; how they'd invaded her body, took something away from her. He knew that it was the very people he'd looked up to that had made her suffering possible: his teachers, his leaders, Goebbels, Hitler.

'I did consider handing you over to the Gestapo, to make sure I could survive,' Eli admitted. 'But deep down, I knew I never would. That's why I've been trying to find alternatives, and why I want Alice to give me the papers. I don't want Greta hurt, either. Gus probably would if it was up to him, but that's his character, borne out of his terrible experiences in the camps, not the overall genetic make-up of our people. What would you do to save yourself, your friends, your family?' He slumped back, the speech seeming to take everything out of him. 'I know it's not your fault,' he said, calmer now, defeated almost. 'I've seen it in your face, though, and I still see it now. I felt it in that first reluctant handshake, in the way you move around us.'

'I... respect you,' Kurt said, content that it was true.

'But you're wary of me, aren't you? It's hard for you to be around us. I know what everyone has told you. Your teachers say that we are like vipers in the grass, that we'll strike at any moment – and then when we get forced into situations where we have to strike, by those same people who told you that we would, it seems like what you've learned was right all along.' His voice rose against the pulsing sound of the engines. Muscles twitched in his jaw, as though fighting to suppress a long-held fury.

Kurt raised his hands in surrender, and, recognising this as a gesture of peace, Eli began taking deep breaths to calm himself. The rapid twitching along his jawline slowed to a halt.

'I started to learn otherwise long before I boarded this ship. Things happened-' Kurt started to explain, but trailed off as a pain in his chest caused his voice to shake with emotion. Too many things had happened, and it was hard to admit that, despite it all, his prejudice against the Jews was so deeply ingrained that it was almost an intrinsic part of him now. 'I am trying,' he eventually managed to say.

'Were your parents Nazis?' Eli asked, without any detectable malice.

'My mother didn't take any interest in politics, but she did believe that Hitler brought us some hope, at least to begin with. She was glad we had something to do again, and she thought we looked smart in our Hitler Youth uniforms. When I was little, she worried all the time about money and what options we'd have, especially after my father's butcher shop stopped making enough,' he paused. 'With my father it was a different story, you see.'

'Did he join the party early?'

'He never joined the party. They put him in a camp.'

Eli's eyes widened. 'For not joining the party?'

'For lots of things,' Kurt replied, thinking back over all the hushed arguments between his parents, the looks between them whenever him and Amon were in the room, his mother trying to calm Fraulein Furst from the apartment below when she said that their father had taken custom from the Mahler's, an old Jewish couple who mostly stayed locked in their home, curtains drawn.

That wasn't what had made him angry with his father, however; it was the first time he'd worn his Hitler Youth uniform that had done it. He didn't look proud, as Kurt expected. Instead, he merely shook his head and then left the room. Kurt's excitement had crumbled into a ball of disappointment, which later turned to rage. He had wanted to hurt his father, really hurt him. The memory of those feelings shamed him now.

'He made comments against Hitler and the party,' he went on. 'And continued to serve Jewish customers. They finally got him when they tracked these un-German activities to our home with a credible witness.'

'Witness? Did a neighbour turn him in?'

'No... my younger brother did.'

The machines hissed as Eli froze, his hand hovering over a shape he'd been making with the dust in the ground. 'I'm sorry,' his voice thickened. His eyes had calmed into deep pools.

'One day he'll realise what he did,' Kurt said. The words choked in his throat. He knew that the Nazis had got Amon so young that he had no chance of ever becoming anything but one of them. His personality was the party. His emotions could only be stirred by a rally or a speech. Alfons had tried to warn Kurt about it, encouraging him to take Amon under his wing and protect him, but he didn't really see the problem – not until the night his father was taken away.

He'd come home to find the apartment in chaos. Chairs were overturned and washing strewn on the floor, and in the midst of it all his mother sat crying at the table. 'It must have been Fraulein Furst,' she wailed. 'Oh, why couldn't he just keep quiet?'

He found Amon sitting in his room, turning a wooden toy train that his father had made him over and over in his hands. Kurt said next to him and put an arm around his shoulder. The little boy was shaking.

'Father was being tricked by the Mahlers,' Amon said, his voice breaking. 'I had to help.'

'What?' Kurt's blood turned to ice in his veins.

'My group leader told us that Jews are the enemy,' he said, wiping his nose with his sleeve. 'The root of all our problems, and that without them, Germany would be strong again, and people like Papa would have their businesses back to the way that they used to be.'

Kurt stood up and paced the room.

'He said I was doing the right thing,' Amon sniffed. 'They all did.'

'What did you do?'

'I wrote down some of the things Papa was saying and showed my leaders, so that we could help him.' He tried to raise his face in defiance, but the tears rolled down his cheeks.

'Where is the book?' Kurt said, trying to keep his voice level.

Amon pointed to the dressing cabinet, and Kurt opened the top drawer and pocketed the little black book that was issued to everyone in the Hitler Youth for the purpose of reporting un-German words and actions.

'Don't speak a word of this to Mutti,' he said. He grabbed Amon's chin between his hands, pressing the skin into hard creases. 'Promise me that you won't!'

Amon nodded as he burst into full sobs. Their mother rushed in then, wrapping her arms around her son's body and hugging him against her.

Kurt stormed from the room, and then left the apartment and went downstairs to the back exit, which opened into a narrow back alley with houses tightly packed behind it. Shame crept over him now, as he remembered how his initial reaction had been to blame the Mahlers. He stared at their apartment, picturing them sat inside. He picked up a stone and threw it at the window, and waited, fists clenched, for someone to come out. No one even came to the window, though.

Looking back, he realised how scared they must have been, and how his father would have been a saviour to them, just by allowing them into his shop, and offering to help with odd jobs like fixing their regularly broken windows, or painting over obscenities scrawled across their door. He often wondered what he would have done if someone had come out to meet him that day.

Kurt jammed the heels of his hands into his eyes in a vain attempt at stemming the flow of tears.

'I too wish that I could talk to my father again, and my mother,' Eli's words broke through the screeching of engines.

Kurt couldn't help being surprised. Eli had always seemed like such an enigma. A leader, but also a loner. It was strange to hear him talk about family. Kurt had never imagined that he would be able to empathise with these people. Hitler wanted the Jews to get out of Germany, and he had never understood why they didn't just leave; but now that he was part of their world, finding death and danger at every turn, being treated as less than human by the very people who told him he was part of the 'Master Race', he felt their sense of entrapment in the face of such few options.

'Where are they now?' he asked.

'My mother and father died at the Polish border,' Eli said. There was heaviness in his voice – a fatigue from the years of battling for survival. 'My father fought for the Fatherland in the last war. He has military medals, issued by Germany. But he died without honour, in a country his grandfather had left to find a better life.'

The 'returning' of Jews with Polish descent had been no secret. Kurt had once cheered the idea of it at a rally. 'But what about their homes here? Their jobs, their lives? Should we send Hitler back to Austria, then?' Alfons had muttered. Kurt had elbowed him a warning, in case anyone else should hear such treasonous talk.

There was a hard rap at the door. Eli stood up, his eyes sharp again.

'Let me come with you,' Kurt pleaded, but Eli was already walking towards the door. 'I thought you trusted me?' he tried again. His head throbbed as the machines around him pounded, and his vision was starting to blur with the fumes from the hot oil.

'I do, but you don't trust me yet,' Eli replied, smiling sadly. 'You might have earned mine, but I still need to gain yours.'

The door opened and then slammed shut behind the departing Eli. Kurt collapsed against the cold metal pipes and closed his eyes, knowing that, for now at least, there was nothing he could do for Alice or himself.

CHAPTER TWENTY-THREE

The Girl and the Red Lipstick

1st June 1939

'Are you clear over what needs to be done?' Eli asked, touching her arm gently, avoiding the maze of scratches on her skin.

They were in a room that Berger had taken them to. There was a mirror – broken, but still useable – that Alice had resisted looking in yet. 'Drug him, get the keys to his room and the safe and retrieve the documents,' she rattled off the plan in a flat tone.

'He's put the safe in his locker now,' Eli added. 'It's in the crew quarters, which makes things easier in terms of time.'

If Eichel did manage to take advantage of her, she knew that it would hurt beyond anything she'd ever felt before, but then what difference would it make? She was nothing inside. A void.

'Then you need to bring them to me,' Eli instructed. 'We can show everyone the information, and then slip everything back before he wakes up.'

'But what will happen to Greta if it does say she is the spy?' Alice asked, her words a rush, her mind struggling to keep up. 'Josiah and the others will kill her. And what will happen to her brother if she doesn't give anything to the Gestapo?'

'We'll have to deal with that when we come to it,' Eli said. 'I still have the gun, remember.'

'Don't let her die.'

'I don't want anyone to die.'

They regarded each other. Alice found that the Eli she liked and respected had almost completely resurfaced.

'You need to get ready,' he said, turning away.

'Ready?' Thin beads of moisture were forming on her face.

Eli picked up a large parcel. 'We have these for you.'

A tube fell out and rolled across the metal floor. Alice stopped it with her foot and picked it up, pulling the top off and twisting to reveal a thick red lipstick. She lifted out the next item, nylon stockings. Eli shifted his feet, kicking at the cold ground.

'I will be close by while you're with Eichel,' he said. His face was close to hers. She could see creases of worry, lines of doubt, and a film of sweat that wasn't just a result of the intense heat. 'We know that Eichel will be alone, as he'll be sent down to fetch something for the captain. He will find you there, still seeking safety, same as before. Say you had to leave his room because you heard people knocking on cabin doors further down the ship and you felt scared.'

'A damsel in distress,' she murmured, taking a bag from him.

He smiled weakly. 'I'll be just around the corner, so let me know when you're… ready.'

She waited until he was out of sight and the small area was hers alone. She was surrounded by dark walls, pipes, dim lights and the sucking and glugging of the ship's insides, but it was a relief to be outside the fug of the engine room. She removed the bandages from her hands and used the water left in a bucket on the floor to clean herself. The icy water was cleansing, although it sharpened the throbbing of her cuts.

The cracked mirror presented her with two versions of herself. She wanted to capture the existing image, to somehow keep the tired, worn and damaged Alice, and hold it up against the powdered and lipsticked Anna she was about to become. Anna, who ran illegal errands across Berlin under the nose of the Nazis; a sweet smile and 'doll-like' figure that the soldiers and secret police really craved above the pony-tailed BDM girls, in their shapeless blouses and pinafores, with hair plaited like children's.

The bag also contained a red dress, soft and expensive, smelling of a thick perfume that took Alice back to the vanilla tones of her mother's favourite scent. Emotion engulfed her with such force that it became hard to breathe, and then she made the mistake of thinking of her papa and Edie. She had flashing images of Edie crying and begging her not to leave, and her father's face lined with worry as he headed out the door that last time she saw him. The grief was so physical at times, it wrenched her apart. It was like a pull in her stomach, much worse than the operation. It was an invisible string stretching all the way back to Germany, sneaking under the barbed wire fences that held her papa, and navigating through the cracks in the stone walls of the convent that concealed Edie.

With quivering fingers, she first took off the jumper that Eli had given her, and then her mother's dress, which she folded up neatly in the hope that the rips could be repaired. The new red dress turned out to be as practical as it was glamourous, with carefully concealed pockets for her to slip the pills into.

She didn't mean to start crying. The sobs surprised her, heavy and raking, as though her body was emptying itself of the tears she'd managed to hold back until now. She thought about the girl who was taken off the ship. What had they done to her? She thought of the doctors who she'd believed were there to help her when she entered the room; but they were more interested in potential research material than patients who they saw as social degenerates anyway.

When she had calmed down she noticed the other items in the package, including gloves that had lambskin lining, soft on her skin. They were bright and colourful, an evergreen shade that matched the hat she also found. The shoes were white, the lipstick redder than red. A luscious full mouth would help to draw Eichel in. Her hand slipped as she shuddered at the thought of him, and she had to redraw the wonky pencil across her eyebrows, pushing the tip just that little bit too hard so that it caused a pinch of pain. She then teased her hair into curls. Rubbing Vaseline into her hands, she patted it onto her lips to add a gloss. The powder compact held a foundation darker than her normal skin; it felt dry, good enough to cover the cuts and bruises slightly, but not too much – they would be needed for the story she would tell him. She ran a finger across her cheek, searching for the smoothness that had been there before the attack, but feeling only callouses. She rolled on the stockings, and then poured lotion into her hands, smoothing it onto her legs and running over the flaking skin around the cuts.

Tears threatened to spill out again and spoil her powdered visage, but she forced herself to concentrate. She wanted something, needed something, to get her angry, to make her feel the injustice and the urge to fight that had fuelled her through missions back in

Berlin. The memory of being forced onto the operating table was so traumatising that she couldn't feel anything but sadness, though; so she focussed on Kurt instead.

There was a different kind of wariness about him, and it was one that she recognised. It had happened with the neighbours, the girls in school and her teachers after they found out that she was a half-breed, a non-Aryan. She was impure, unclean, dangerous. A rat that would do anything to survive. He was struggling with it, and although she believed that he genuinely cared for her, she knew that these beliefs were deeply ingrained.

She finished reapplying powder where her tears had streaked, and rubbed some of the lipsticks into her cheeks. She practised a smile, the red shade gleaming against her pale skin. The reflection didn't look like her any more. She was ready.

Eli was waiting at the door.

'We managed to get this,' he said, handing her a photograph.

She looked at it with surprise. 'How?'

'Gus managed to swipe it. You may need it.'

The dark and dusty passages that they passed through to get to the crew quarters seemed to leave a residue on Alice's skin. It was like fragments of the ship had settled on her face, which was already hot and glowing with nerves, threatening to destroy the veil she had just constructed. Eli took her hand before he left her, and kissed it lightly after unlocking the door.

'I'll be here the whole time,' he said.

Berger was waiting for them on the other side, keys in hand.

'I'm sorry you have to do this, Fraulein,' he said, eyes on the ground. 'But he won't drink with any of the crew. He doesn't trust us.' He coughed and cleared his throat. 'He always has a handkerchief in his pocket that he's very precious about. You'd think that bloody Hitler himself had given it to him. Anyway, if you need to distract him, find a way to drop it, and hopefully his eyes will be off you for a few moments.'

'Berger has set it up so that Eichel thinks he's waiting for an important contact to arrive,' Eli said.

'I have contacts with radio signals, too,' Berger explained.

'That fits in with the story that I am a spy like him,' she said. 'But what if someone disturbs us?

'It's all hands on deck at the moment,' Berger assured her.

'Why?' she asked.

'Passengers trying to get off the ship… a couple of suicide attempts,' he said.

'Attempts?'

'Try not to worry about that now,' Eli jumped in. 'Are you ready?'

She nodded, and waited as they moved a safe distance away before using Berger's key to open the door. He was going to lock them in. Eli was going to lock and guard the other door. Any crewmen who wanted to use the quarters were to be told the area was under temporary quarantine.

Inside, the room had the same stale, greasy odour as last time. It was poorly lit again, but not so badly that she couldn't see another article from Der Stürmer pinned up on the noticeboard. This one was an article about Jews as 'perpetrators of sex crimes for their own gain', complete with a shadowy cartoon image of a hook-nosed man seducing an innocent Aryan, her race emphasised by the pale contrast of her outline. Alice looked away and rubbed her lips together, trying to keep her hands steady on a small table laden with over-spilling ashtrays.

Eichel was sitting at one of the tables, his wide frame casting a long shadow. 'Fraulein Gerber,' his tone was officious, emotionless.

'Why did you leave my room the other day?'

She didn't answer, and instead stepped further into the buzzing light of the room, so that she was right underneath it. She held out her damaged arm.

'My God, what happened to you?' he asked, standing up and leading her to a chair. As she went to sit down, he reached forward and moved his fingers across a bruise on her face that was barely concealed by the strategically scarce powder. She twined her fingers together so that he wouldn't notice them shaking.

'I was attacked,' she replied meekly. 'I had to leave your cabin as I heard them coming for me, baying for blood. I have been in hiding below deck since, waiting for the right time to come to you. I ne- I need your protection.'

His arm wrapped around her like a heavy coat. She took the chance to feel at the edge of his pockets for the handkerchief, and managed to pull it out and throw it under the table. He pulled out a chair and instructed her to sit down, before running a hand through his dark hair.

'I have been looking for you, Fraulein Gerber,' he said. 'I radioed my contacts in Berlin about your position on the ship. I wanted to pass on the message, to let them know you were in safe hands with me.'

And to gain some leverage within his party ranking, of course, she thought.

He didn't sit, but instead paced in a semi-circle to the side of her chair. To the other side of her was a wall. She was trapped.

'My contact seemed surprised that someone fitting your description was on board,' he said. 'Apparently, a blonde female spy was pulled off at the last minute in Hamburg, as they already had another girl on here to do the job – a Jew, who would better integrate.'

The girl who was taken off the ship. She almost breathed a sigh of relief, knowing that it hadn't been someone condemned to an uncertain fate because of her, but at the same time the revelation had put her in danger. Eichel was playing with her, she realised. He knew who Greta was.

He turned to face her, moving so close that she couldn't help but look deep into his eyes. They were the colour of cognac, a stripped back, almost glazed brown. His breath was a musky mix of whiskey and cigar smoke. His hand gripped the side of the table.

'I'm not really a spy,' she said.

He sat up, a triumphant grin on his face.

With shaking fingers, she took the photo from inside her dress and used it to put some distance between them.

'What is this?' His small eyes scrunched up as he tried to decipher what he was looking at. Moving away from Alice, he held the photo directly under a bare bulb.

'We were childhood sweethearts,' Alice said, when she saw the realisation dawning on his face. 'He wants to keep me a secret, so his enemies can't track me down.' Everybody in Berlin knew what Franz looked like. He was a major success story of the Berlin Gestapo. 'I was threatened in Berlin, and the safest option was to smuggle me out of the country. Only a trusted few people know who I am, and now you're one of them... you remind me of him,' she added a playful tone to her voice, somewhat seductive, but not too much so. 'You're both strong men – power men.' Her heart was beating so fast that she thought her rib cage would surely burst open with the pressure.

He handed back the photograph, and she made sure that their fingers brushed as she received it. He looked at her intently, his brow furrowed in confusion. Self-consciousness crawled across her skin, and it took everything she had to summon a tone of coy flirtatiousness again while maintaining her story.

'It was mainly Jews plotting against me,' she said. 'So, I had to hide out on a ship filled with them, to make sure I was safe. Franz said that I could return when they were... dealt with.' The words made her feel sick. 'But some of them must have found out who I was, and a group of them attacked me. The only reason they didn't kill me was so they could use me to blackmail Franz.'

'These savages will get what's coming to them soon,' he said. 'And then you can return home.'

She nodded her agreement, but he wasn't look at her. It was then that she saw fear in him, hidden behind the granite jaw and broad shoulders. He was as scared of Franz as everyone else was. The soft rattle and groan of the docked ship continued around them, but Alice felt a quietness descend upon the room, turning it into a closed-off bubble of tension. Eli or Malik would be outside if anything went wrong, emboldening her to try a new tactic to shock Eichel out of his terror. In a way, it would be easier.

She burst into tears; full sobs that wracked her body and caused him to leap to her side.

'Franz would hate to see me like this,' she struggled to say.

'Is there anything I can do?' he asked.

She made herself shake, as though involuntary.

'You had a terrible shock,' he was whispering to her, patting her carefully with his hand. 'How about a drink to calm you down?'

She sniffed and nodded, and then watched as he strode across the room, his heavy steps booming on the floorboards, and grabbed a bottle of cognac and two glasses. As he poured the drinks, she asked for a clean handkerchief. He felt in his pockets, and she could see that the mention of Franz, her tears and the fact that he couldn't find the handkerchief in its usual place had flustered him. Impatience jutted out in his stiffened jaw.

'I think it dropped out of your pocket,' she said, pointing to where she had thrown it.

Tutting with annoyance, he got down on his hands and knees and reached under the heavy wooden table. She used the opportunity to take out the sleeping draft and pour it into his drink, swilling it gently. He stood up victorious, and shook the tissue before reluctantly handing it over. Her heart felt like it had lifted to her throat as he raised the glass to his lips, only to then set it down again without taking a sip.

'I am carrying out important work for the party on this ship,' he said. 'The Abwehr network have shown great faith in me.' His chest puffed out with self-importance at the mention of what she knew to be an operation on American intelligence. 'Perhaps you could let Franz know about the risks I am taking by helping you, as it could compromise my own mission?' he suggested. 'Maybe you could use my radio to contact him?'

He was still testing her.

He didn't pick up his glass again. She felt for the capsules in her pocket, smooth to her touch. As he regarded her, his gaze slow and steady, she imagined what would happen if she couldn't transfer the capsule quickly enough. The top of the chain around his neck was visible from the angle he was sitting at. She held her breath as he picked up the cognac again and finally took a long drink. It didn't take much time at all before the drug kicked in, as Eli had promised would be the case. Eichel was soon snoring in his chair.

Alice crept over to the sleeping giant, the glass still resting in his hand. She removed it, placing it on the table, and reached for the chain. The scent of cheap cologne and cigarettes clogged her nostrils.

Her stomach recoiled as she breathed him in. Once she held the key in her hand, she decided on a new plan of action. She wouldn't alert Malik or Eli, or whoever was waiting outside. Instead, she would slip through to the locker room herself, and see what information she could find.

The room was stiff with stale air. She tried not to breathe in too deeply as she searched for Eichel's locker. It was already open, clothes and belonging strewn on the floor. She looked around, stunned, expecting an attack. The files were on the floor. She picked them up, flicking through them quickly, shock sharpening the words on the pages, the names on the pages, even in the dim light.

A hand on her arm. A voice from the darkness. 'Are you going to tell them?'

The light switched on and hissed above them. It was Greta. She was shaking.

CHAPTER TWENTY-FOUR

The Boy and the Drawings

2nd June 1939

'We've left Havana for good.'

Malik's words, although not wholly unexpected, made Kurt lose his breath. He'd heard the rumbling of rumours but it was different to hear it confirmed.

Gus paced the room, muttering to himself in what Kurt took to be Hebrew. Eventually he stormed out, slamming the door behind him.

'He thinks we're going back to Germany,' Malik explained.

Kurt swallowed his own panic at that idea. He'd already asked several times why Alice was taking so long. The thought of her at the mercy of a monster like Eichel was consuming him.

Malik was still talking about the action of the ship. 'At the moment, we're circling the coast of Cuba. Maybe America will take us-'

He was cut off as the door burst open again and Alice stumbled in, falling to the ground with a thud. Kurt tried to get up and help her.

'It's okay,' Alice put her arms out in a surrender pose and stood up. 'Eli, please, you have to listen.'

Before Eli could respond, a second figure was thrown into the room, followed by Gus, who was carrying an iron bar, and Berger, trailing behind looking uncertain. The second person was Greta. Her eyes were cast towards the floor, and her normally animated features were dull.

'What's going on?' Kurt demanded.

'This so-called ally of yours was only leading Greta the Gestapo Catcher straight to us,' Gus spat the words out.

'She isn't a catcher,' Alice said, still gasping for breath after her fall. 'She has been blackmailed. I have the documents to prove it, and also to show how we are all in terrible danger because of Eichel.'

'Who was working with him, then?' Eli asked.

'No one,' Alice replied.

Kurt saw her lock eyes with the silent Greta. A strange look passed between them. Alice looked like she was reassuring Greta with a thin smile before making a gentle pull on her woollen cardigan. They both moved further into the room, and it was then that Kurt picked up on the smell of burning, as though they had both recently been around a fire that had stuck to their clothes and skin.

'We are all on his list,' Alice said. 'Including Greta.'

'What list?'

'Enemies of the Reich,' she answered. 'To be arrested when the ship docks back in Germany. Goebbels's orders.'

No one said anything for a few moments. The idea of going back, and the Gestapo waiting for them all, including him, brought on such a terror that Kurt was considering how easy it would be for them all to jump off the ship close to a port – any port – and risk swimming to shore – any shore – other than Germany's.

'I can't go back,' Gus muttered. 'I can't go back.' Unsteady on his feet, the protruding bones of his shoulders shook as he paced in front of Greta and Alice, still clutching the iron bar. The whites of his eyes were threaded with veins.

'It has to be someone from our side giving them information,' Malik said, but he sounded uncertain. He took off his glasses and wiped his eyes. His visible exhaustion was shared by the entire group.

'Let me see the papers, Alice,' Eli said, with a wary glance at Greta. She produced a few papers from down the front of her dress.

Eli held out his hand, but Gus snatched the documents from her, dropping the pipe with a clang that echoed throughout the room. He turned the pages around, his eyes narrowing as he read out names. Eli tried to wrest them from him, but Gus pushed him back.

'Most of us are mentioned here,' Gus said as he scanned the papers. 'With descriptions of what we look like, and even sketches, if you could believe that. Pretty good drawings, actually. Eli Lewisham – Polish parents, Zionist sympathies, looks like a typical Jew. He hasn't got your nose quite in proportion to your face, though. Alice Sommer – looks Aryan, father is, trap and bring immediately to contact boarding in Cuba, to bring back under special custody. Kurt Hertz – so they used your real surname - well he's definitely an ex Nazi-boy, but they want to make an example of him most of all. Attempted murder of Peter Fischer, murder of Alfons Lehmann. That's what happens when you mix with Jews, apparently. You start killing people. He's even put a note about the scars on your hand.'

When Gus had mentioned the drawings, Kurt saw Greta glance at him from under her thick eyelashes. He looked at Alice, who shook her head ever so slightly.

'They're handwritten by Eichel,' Alice said. 'But there's an official letter in there about reporting back to the Propaganda Office in Berlin.'

'Me, Aryan relations. He's made me look like a skull with no skin,' Gus spat out that one, and moved a hand towards the wounds on his chest. 'Malik, you have too many "German" friends, and you encourage listening to "un-German" music, you massive degenerate you. Also, you engaged in black market deals. Is that true? Of course it is, a man's got to eat. Stop wearing your glasses and he'll have to do a new drawing of you,' he laughed, but it sounded forced and no one joined in. 'Greta, you're here, too. Your crime is helping your brothers with their resistance activities – everything from printing out anti-Nazi leaflets to trying to set up a Jewish army. The drawing of you is very rushed. He's blurred half your features,' he paused. The rattle and spark of the engines was the only sound in the room. 'Other random names on here, but no mention of a catcher. There should be a document on who is working with the Gestapo.'

Everyone's eyes were back on Greta.

'If we're all such big shots on this wanted list, why haven't they arrested us already?' Malik was trying to maintain his usual cool demeanour, but the fear was evident in his constant fidgeting. He'd finished cleaning his glasses, and now the fingers on his left hand were mashing at tobacco leaves while cigarette papers were being rolled ad nauseam in his right.

'Why let us on the ship at all?' Kurt asked.

'Can't you see?' Alice addressed the room. They all turned to look at her, and even Greta lifted her head slightly. 'The ship was never meant to dock at Havana. We were always returning to Germany, and once there, Goebbels could make a big show of arresting us, using our status as "criminals" as the reason why no other country would accept us. That would allow them to justify treating us as their enemies. Eichel was getting regular radio contact, receiving information and then reporting back who we were, our descriptions. He was even going to get a camera from Cuba and start taking photos of us all, under the pretence of it being for our new Visas. The films were to be developed there, and then posted back to Germany ahead of our return.'

'But I saw her talking to Eichel.' Gus pointed at Greta. 'He mentioned a deal!'

'Greta would hardly be on the list if she was the catcher, would she?' Alice said.

'I approached him about getting my brother out... the one I thought Alice had led the police to,' Greta said, stumbling over her words a little. 'I'd already tried it in Berlin, and... in exchange for some favours and a ticket for the ship, an SS man gave me Alice's papers and that photo. He said they'd been given to them by a resistance member who was a double agent. I was to keep a close eye on her, and make sure that none of the other passengers helped her escape.'

'You tried your best to fulfil that part of the bargain,' Kurt reminded her.

'I was angry when I thought she'd killed him,' Greta acknowledged. 'But when I saw Eichel's file, I knew that my brother... he had... he had... been picked up and killed after we got on the ship. There was a note that the half-Jew they had in custody wouldn't co-operate following her arrest.' She stopped and looked awkwardly at Alice, who had placed a protective hand over her own stomach.

At that moment, Kurt wanted nothing more than to hug Alice; to tell her it was okay, and that no one would ever make her relive that trauma again. He guessed that her and Greta had burned the part about what they did to Alice, amongst other things.

Greta closed her eyes, as though she didn't want to see the words she was speaking, and continued. 'Look through the file and you'll find that Isaac... that my brother... is already dead. They killed him two days after we set sail.'

As Greta spoke, Kurt watched Alice. There was a fury in her face that he had never seen in her before. A defiance; a defence of something beyond what she was telling them.

'It does make sense,' Eli said, his voice calm and measured again, and his hands no longer troubling his hair. 'We're the young ones – the ones who could cause the Nazis the most trouble. So, it's better not to let us into another country, where we could speak out against them and inspire others to join in the fight.'

'There is one entry that is different from the rest,' Gus said. His voice sounded heavy, and then he slammed a fist into the page he was holding up and started to laugh. It was a deep but hollow sound, like choked anger. 'You'll never guess who the real Nazi is!'

Eli took the paper from Gus as he sunk to the floor, the unhappy chuckle continuing as he put his head in his hands.

'Josiah,' Eli whispered.

A hush came over the room.

'It can't be,' Malik said, shaking his head. 'He's an out and out Jew, and he's not clever enough to keep up a lie like that.'

'He's not the catcher,' Gus said. 'But his father is one of Himmler's closest advisors.'

'Then it must be Josiah working against us,' Malik surmised. 'Who else would it be? He has never even admitted to being so much as a Mischling.'

Kurt saw Alice flinch at the word.

'You need to read the file properly,' Greta said, her voice low. Seeing Eli looking at her again, she met his gaze. 'Read it properly,' she repeated.

'It says his father wants him dead,' Eli said. 'Looks like Eichel has been tasked with killing him before he gets back to Germany. It's to be made to look like a suicide.'

'Someone needs to go and get him,' Alice said.

'Oh, that is just as suicidal as the ship heading back to the Reich,' Gus spluttered. 'We might as well just radio his papa now, and ask for an escort straight to Dachau.'

'We only need to say his father's name, and he'll surrender without any trouble,' Eli countered. 'He won't want anyone else to know. If they find out that the ship is heading back to Germany, they'll use him as a scapegoat if they find out who he really is.'

'How do we get to him?' Kurt had to ask. 'He's always surrounded by his "guards".' He wanted to be free of the floating prison he'd been confined to, and to prove himself useful once again.

'I'll get Berger to tell him that he's been summoned to the purser's office,' Eli said. He's the youth representative of some pointless passenger committee they have, so he'll have no reason to be suspicious.'

'What happens when Eichel wakes up?' Alice asked.

Although she sounded steady and focused, Kurt saw the worry cross her face,

'If there is no catcher, we should just kill him,' Gus said.

'We should,' Greta murmured.

Upon hearing this, Kurt felt compelled to study Greta for a moment. There was something not quite right about this newfound meekness of hers.

'That isn't going to help us,' Eli sighed. 'Let's go and get Josiah.'

Kurt stood up and started walking towards the door, but felt a heavy pull on his shoulder.

'Not you,' Gus said. 'Or her.' He pointed at Alice.

Before Kurt could begin to protest, Eli nodded in agreement. 'It's too risky,' he said. 'We need Josiah to explain to his mob that you are innocent before either of you can be seen publicly again.'

'Don't mention his father yet,' Kurt said, wanting to assert some authority over the situation. 'Tell him you have us both held captive and need his help. If you mention what we know too early, who knows what he will do. It sounds like people out there are desperate.' He pointed at the metal ceiling above. He only wished that he could poke a hole in it and finally let in some air into what felt like his coffin.

The others took this in.

'I agree,' Eli confirmed.

'I have to… I need to… go to the washroom,' Greta stumbled over her words, but the request was granted. Eli gave Malik a nod to take her to the makeshift bathroom in the dark corner of the corridor outside.

'Handcuff her,' Gus called after them.

Eli gave him a look as though he found the idea ludicrous.

They all left the room, leaving Alice and Kurt behind. When the door closed, and the key turned in the lock, Alice sat down and leaned against the wall, her eyes closed. Kurt watched her take a few short, steadying breaths, trying to calm herself without taking in too much of the stale air that surrounded them.

'You burned Greta's other file, didn't you?' Kurt said. 'She is the catcher, isn't she?' He was aware that his tone sounded harsh, resentful, but he didn't like the idea of more secrets, and especially not dangerous ones like this. 'Why are you protecting her?'

Alice let out a long exhale and stood up, walking towards him. 'She's suffered enough.'

'I know, but what is the truth?' he asked. 'I know Greta is a brilliant caricaturist. I saw her work in Berlin. Those drawings of us are her work, aren't they?'

She nodded. 'Eichel didn't write the notes, either. It was Greta spying on us, drawing us, adding in descriptions to the basic information that Eichel had been given. She was the one who was going to hand us over back in Germany, and then she and her brother would be allowed to leave on a ship. But then she broke into Eichel's locker and found the document he'd hidden, stating that her brother was already dead.'

'Why did she break into his locker?'

'She saw him with me, and thought their deal had been broken.'

'Why did you decide not to give her up?'

'Because she's already lost everyone.'

They were both silent for a moment.

'I gave her time to add in notes on herself and a sketch,' she added. He could tell she was still holding something back by the way her hands hovered over her neck, as though pulling an imaginary chain. 'She'd kept mine and yours back, to use against Eichel if she needed to. We added those in with the others. That's why he wasn't sure who we were. She never showed him the photos that were given to her in Berlin. It wasn't Franz who supplied them, but that doesn't mean he wasn't involved.'

'Did Greta betray Heinz and Walter?' he could still picture Walter's face as the truncheon came down on his head, his features contorting with pain. He replayed Heinz's last words, telling him to run and save himself.

'I don't know,' she admitted. 'You know how the Gestapo use people – put them in impossible situations, turn them against those closest to them.' She stopped suddenly. He thought she was going to say more, but then, unexpectedly, she took his hand. Alice's skin was smooth against his callous palm, which she gripped gently. He was thinking about Amon, about how he had been turned against their father.

They sat quietly for a few moments, the engines whirring, taking them away from the country where they thought they would be free of all of this; where Gestapo files didn't matter, and there was no need to constantly watch your back, but perhaps such a place could never exist for them. A scent of lemon soap drifted from her, and he became more aware of the sour odour of the room, and how he itched for a wash. He wanted to be clean in all ways; from the mark of being a killer, a traitor to both sides and a liar. He thought about his parents, wondered what they were doing at that moment; if his father was still surviving in the camp, if his mother was still surviving everyday life, and if Amon was turning even colder and less child-like with each Hitler Youth meeting, each parade and each day at school. In a few short months, and particularly during his time on the ship, he had slowly come to see that what he'd been taught was nonsense. Holding Alice's hand now, feeling the warmth and pulse of her blood pumping through it, he knew that they were the same. Just two people trying to survive, on a ship that the whole world was watching. There was always an audience.

She took her hand away. 'Kurt, I have to give you this, and I'm very sorry,' she took a document out of the front of her dress, and passed him a match. 'I wish I could give you a moment on your own, but I didn't know if you'd want the others to know or not. It is up to you if you want to tell them.' She dropped her voice to a deep whisper. 'Try to remember that, like with Greta, it really isn't his fault.'

Kurt took the paper, holding it at a distance as though it might burn him. The name was clear, in bold in the middle of the page, as was the announcement of death, and the name of the person who had given Paul Hertz up to authorities for a second time for UnGerman activities: Amon Hertz.

The room seemed to close in on him, and he had to place a hand against the cold steel wall to steady himself. He could see Alice, her brow furrowed with concern, watching him, uncertain of what to do until she suddenly moved forward and put her arms around him. His papa, a person he now knew to be braver than anyone else, was dead. He sank into her, his whole body collapsing in on itself. It was only when felt the dampness on her jumper that he realised he was crying.

CHAPTER TWENTY-FIVE

The Girl and the Hunger for Identity

3rd June 1939

Kurt's suffering eclipsed any pain she felt from knowing that Franz must have betrayed her. He was the only person who knew that she was on this ship. He must have found the papers under the floorboards and given them in, although it didn't make sense that he would give in the photo of them both in their younger days, too. Greta didn't have any answers to this. She'd just been following orders, given to her by the men who had kept her last brother in a cell. The way she described the men made them sound like a mass of grey, angry faces in dark prisons. Alice knew that now wasn't the time to question her further.

'You were tortured for my brother?' Greta had whispered. 'It says here that they only knew it was you after you escaped, after they-' she stopped, and her eyes filled with tears. 'Oh.'

'We can burn that one, too,' Alice had said, taking the medical document from her.

There was a small part of her which had hoped that by destroying the evidence, she could somehow erase the event from history. Now, as she held Kurt, crumpled and defeated, all his brave optimism gone, she knew that the suffering was everywhere. Everyone on the ship had been touched by some type of evil.

It was the early hours of the morning before they finally heard heavy footsteps and raised voices competing with the hiss and clanking of the engines.

Josiah strode in, his thick mop of hair only slightly dishevelled, and his mouth sucking on an unlit cigarette, as though he'd come of his own accord. But his shirt and waistcoat were ruffled, and Gus, who came in behind him, had the beginnings of a black eye. Josiah wrinkled his nose up at the smell which Alice had long since become accustomed to.

'Have you two been hiding down here all this time?' he laughed. 'There I was, doing my passenger committee duties after listening to some fool from the Jewish Organisation in Cuba tell us how he was going to pray for us – "sisters and brothers, do not give up hope. Be strong!" He said we won't land in Germany. "The world is watching you," he told us. He got no applause. He may even pray for you, Nazi boy.' Josiah turned his attention on Kurt. 'He was an American, this Milton Goldsmith, but he stood on the platform with a police officer and Cuban official.'

He paused, and despite his cocky stance and casual tone, Alice could sense the underlying fear in his words.

'People are crying all the time,' he went on. 'Their relatives, who were bobbing along on the launches next to us, have been made to leave – even the ones who'd paid to come and see the drama, and the press who supposedly feel sorry for us. Everyone on the bridge was either silent or sobbing as Havana slowly receded. Then I see the boat with those refugee workers, and that Milton. The other guy who came on with them was a German official, and he gave a Nazi salute as they were leaving. I think that tells us all we need to know about those who are trying to "help" us.'

Nobody said anything. The fight seemed to have left the room. Alice felt exhausted. Every bone ached. It was hard to keep her eyes open. She looked over at Kurt. He'd retreated into himself, his face a taut mask of pain. She picked up the faint smell of bread and fish competing with the baked metal of the room. Eli had put down a picnic basket by the door.

'Those are the latest affairs of the ship,' Josiah concluded. 'So, since you've decided to see sense and follow my leadership, shall we decide what to do about the two spies? Couldn't bring yourselves to kill them? Hand me the gun and I'll do it.' He gestured to Eli, who took a step back.

'You sound just like your father, Josiah,' Gus said. 'He's keen on killing Jews, isn't he?'

The cigarette fell from Josiah's mouth to the floor, and the colour drained from his face. Eli tried to go to him, but Gus blocked his path and pushed him away.

'Unless you want everyone to know who your father is, including all of those who have been in a camp, I would keep quiet,' Gus continued, his voice rising with a rage that coloured his pale, drawn features. 'Isn't that why you have a first-class ticket? He's also had your mother removed from Germany, you know. She's in Britain, isn't she? Not good for him to have his chequered past exposed for all to see, is it? Even if you did come along before all the inter-race relationship laws.'

Eli finally pushed Gus away from the centre of the room and took his place.

'Is that my file?' Josiah asked. He looked defeated, smaller even. 'May I see it?'

Eli instructed Kurt to hold Josiah's arms while he held the document in front of him. At first, Alice thought that Kurt was going to refuse – his face was still blank from the shock that only she knew about – but he obeyed Eli in a way that must have been a remnant of his Hitler Youth days. A blind and unquestioning response to orders.

'I didn't want to leave Germany,' Josiah said. 'I wanted him to give me a new identity. Instead, he gave me this.' He touched the scar on his face.

'You wanted to join the SS!' Gus shouted from the corner of the room. 'That's what is in your file, you traitor!'

Eli signalled for Kurt to let go of Josiah, who let out a roar of anger and kicked at the wall. Eli placed a hand on him, calmly leading him to the floor, where he sat, head in hands. Alice knew that everyone in the room could relate to having their identity pulled apart, no matter how they felt about Josiah.

'You might be a Jew from your heart to your head,' she heard Josiah quietly telling Eli. 'But at least you know what you are.'

'Josiah, you need to listen to us,' Eli said. 'There is no catcher. It was a Gestapo agent named Eichel. You need to call off your mob. We must work together. The ship is going back to Germany, as was always intended to be the case. We're all in danger now.'

'What happened to the "wholesale resettlement of Jews"?' Josiah said flatly. 'That is how they speak of us – how my father speaks of us. I thought he wanted me out of the country, not dead.' He indicated towards the basket of food that Eli had brought with him. 'We only have twelve days' supplies left.'

Alice's insides tensed. The idea of being hungry again terrified her. The ship was becoming a floating prison, and the possibility that they would soon be at the mercy of the Gestapo was also tugging on her nerves. 'Eichel will wake up soon,' she said. 'Or someone will discover him. We have to get the documents back in his locker. We've wasted enough time.'

She asked herself why she was doing this. To atone for her sins, because she understood the desperation of someone like Greta? She knew well enough the survival instinct that kicks when a loved one's safety is threatened. How could she judge someone else for doing everything possible to help their family?

'Where are Malik and Greta?' Eli asked, looking around as though he expected them to emerge from some part of the small room.

'We haven't seen them,' Alice replied. 'We thought he must have decided to guard her in another room after locking us in here.'

'She'll have given him the slip,' Kurt said.

As though summoned by his words, there came a frantic banging at the door. It was Malik, and he was shouting to be let in. He entered, breathless, panting, distraught. 'She's gone,' he rasped. 'And she has the gun.'

'I know where she will be,' Alice said without hesitating. She hoped that they wouldn't be too late.

CHAPTER TWENTY-SIX

The Boy and the Body

3rd June 1939

Kurt hadn't been in the crew's quarters before. He took in the damp and sweat with his first breath, and then his eyes were drawn to the copies of the Der Sturmer, with its crude warnings about the 'Jewish problem' and grotesque cartoon drawings. He couldn't believe that he had once swallowed the bile that such publications spewed out. Amon had devoured them too, quoting articles and angrily scrubbing anti-Nazi graffiti from a newspaper stand near to his Hitler Jungend centre. This was all done behind their father's back, of course. He had been fiercely critical of the paper.

Kurt pushed away thoughts of his father. He was going to have to live completely in the present to get through what was in front of him. He wiped his brow with the back of his sleeve. The body was in the corner of the room, rolled up in old carpet. There was a bitter taste in his throat, and his stomach heaved. There was a thick ammonia scent where Berger had already started the clean-up, warm and humid.

Greta had been sitting in one of the chairs, blood speckled across her face and arms, as though someone had playfully flicked paint at her. Berger, who had found her standing over Eichel's corpse, had locked up the rooms and told any crew members who tried to get in that it was under quarantine, as the Gestapo agent had taken ill. They didn't have long before the ship's doctor would get wind of this and demand to be allowed in. A cushion had covered the noise. The final bullet from the gun was still rolling across the floor when they had descended on the scene.

'What should we do?' Malik asked. His face was ashen, although Kurt guessed that, like the rest of them, this wasn't his first time seeing a dead body.

Growing up in Nazi Germany, murder was hard to avoid, regardless of which side you were on. It happened on the streets, in homes, in jails, in parks. It was normal – just another part of an upbringing twisted by Hitler's madness. That wasn't the only reason why Kurt felt numb, though.

'Let's own up to it,' Gus suggested. 'Say that we were all involved. A foreign jail would be better than a camp, and if war breaks out then it's just another dead German. A British jail would be my choice.'

'You think they would take us, even as prisoners?' Josiah laughed. 'You think they don't mistreat Jews there, too? They even have a Kindertransport quotas. I heard they choose the kids who look able to work, and put them on farms or use them as servants. My mother now works as a housemaid!'

Kurt watched Alice become pale under the dim hissing lights of the quarters. The Kindertransport was her sister's only remaining way out, he knew.

'We need to get moving,' Berger said, indicating towards the rolled-up carpet.

'The files,' Alice said, clutching the papers that sealed all their fates. 'They will probably break open and search his locker when he is discovered missing. He has a direct link to Berlin.'

'Alice, you put them back exactly where you found them,' Eli instructed. 'The rest of you, help me get this up on deck.'

'And what will we say if we're stopped?' Malik was speaking through chattering teeth, despite the thick heat. A metallic scent of blood seeped from the material that held Eichel. They were running out of time.

'There is so much uncertainty on the ship, everyone is distracted,' Berger said. 'I can say that the carpet needs to be disposed of as it's an infection risk, and I've gathered up some other things that need throwing out, too. We'll hide him in a lifeboat and then, at the right moment, launch it overboard with holes in so that it sinks. People will assume that he fled the ship in the lifeboat.'

'But why would anyone believe that?' Kurt asked.

'We're heading towards Florida,' Josiah nodded. 'They'll think that he left to join up with an American-Nazi spy network.'

American spy networks meant American sympathisers. It wasn't lost on Kurt how the influence of the Third Reich was inescapable.

They began to climb the fuggy tunnels of the ship. Alice returned and hovered uncertainly behind, looking as exhausted and drawn as Kurt felt. He wanted to reach out and touch her, and tell her that this had to be done, that it was them or Eichel. She was distracted, holding on to a still-stunned Greta, blood cleanly wiped from her face and hands, wearing clothes that must have belonged to one of the boys; a shirt and some slacks, which hung loosely from her thin frame.

The weight of the carpet and its contents required all of Kurt's physical and mental strength. He began to focus, calling on his HJ training. It was better than thinking. The task pushed his father and Amon's faces away. When they passed members of the crew, Berger explained that the carpet was toxic with germs. One or two of the crewmen made jokes about Jews finally earning their passage. When they reached the surface, Kurt blinked in the blinding light of the early morning. The sea was slate grey. The area of the deck that Berger had chosen was deserted. They kept a careful look out, whistling a signal when two crew members, patrolling the ships and threatening the passengers, were heading in their direction.

'Greta, Alice, distract them,' Josiah instructed.

Kurt could feel his blood boil at how quickly the son of an SS officer had taken control, and had immediately set about putting others at risk.

'That puts them in unnecessary danger,' Kurt said, making no effort to conceal the ice in his voice.

'The captain is worried about suicides and has his men out on patrol,' Eli explained. 'We will have to look out for them, too.'

'We need to take turns watching the lifeboat,' Berger said. 'There's a funeral tonight, for an old professor.'

'Suicide?' Malik ventured.

'They think so,' Berger replied, the strain in his face obvious.

'So much death already,' Greta whispered.

'But we can time it so that we launch this as they send his body overboard?' Eli asked.

Berger nodded.

Kurt concentrated on the hollow thumping of the waves against the ship.

'Someone's coming,' Gus hissed. They moved quickly to lift the creaking lifeboat, and rolled the carpet and the body underneath it.

It was one of the passenger-led patrols, and not the Gestapo agents who had now made themselves visible within the crew, but they rushed to separate before the men reached them nevertheless.

'A few suicides and they think everyone is going to be at it,' Josiah huffed as he walked away from Kurt. 'If we were going to do something we'd storm the ship, not kill ourselves.'

'That's enough,' Eli said, putting a stop to Josiah's ranting. 'Berger is doing the first shift on lifeboat watch. It'll be too conspicuous if we all hang around here. You may as well all go and get some rest. They'll be opening the washrooms soon.'

'Greta needs to sleep off the shock,' Alice said. 'She can stay in my room.'

Kurt wanted so much to lower his battered body into a bath, and feel the softness of warm water against his skin. His head was pounding, and even though he was finally free of the engine room, his ears still rang with the shrieking of distressed metal. However, rather than relaxing, he found himself following the girls and then settling down on the floor outside the room, leaning his back against the hard wall. He closed his eyes for a moment, grateful that he was accustomed to dozing in awkward positions, and was now such a light sleeper that the smallest sound had him on high alert. Alice might have been prepared to trust Greta, but Kurt still had too many unanswered questions.

After an hour or so, these questions became overwhelming. He knocked softly on the door.

Alice answered, eyes wide. 'What's happened?' she said. 'Are we in danger?'

'I want to speak to Greta,' he told her. 'I need to ask her. I have to know.'

'She really isn't up to it,' Alice said, attempting to close the door behind her.

'Please,' he implored, easing past her. 'I have to know.'

She moved to walk in after him, but he requested that she leave them alone. She hesitated at first, but then relented and stepped back out onto the corridor.

Greta was sitting on the bed, clasping and unclasping her hands. Her eyes were ringed with purple, and her lips looked blood-red against a face that had lost its usual olive complexion to a mask of pale misery.

'You're going to ask me about the dance,' she said. A single tear rolled down her cheek. She didn't wipe it away. 'They promised me Ralph... my eldest brother.'

'But Heinz, Walter, all of them,' he said. 'They were doing so much good. They were-'

'I thought they'd be okay – that they'd just get off with a warning. Heinz had his connections, as did Walter. You know that.' Greta spoke in an uncertain tone, but kept her eyes on him, some of the fight coming back. She was pulling at her hair in a way that looked painful. 'They're not Jews for a start. I knew that would give them a chance.'

He considered this. 'That's not fair,' he concluded. 'Look what they did to Heinz the first time they got hold of him for not obeying them.'

He noticed that she was shaking uncontrollably, and holding clumps of her own hair in her hand. She shut her eyes tightly. A moon-like face and mousy hair. He was hungry and thirsty, and his arms and legs ached. Egg shell skin. The light was fizzing in the room. He stiffened to attention. His heart was racing.

'And Alice?' he said quietly, looking away.

'Alice was for Isaac,' she said. 'They wanted me to get on the ship and find her, as they didn't know which identity she was currently under.'

'Why did you say it was Franz who betrayed your father, when you told me it was a neighbour?'

'You don't know what it's like for everyone to hate you, do you? At school, I was top of the class in German, but then suddenly the teacher started failing me. My best friend looked the other way when we passed one another. I was no longer allowed to ice-skate in the park when the lakes froze. It was only my brothers that made me feel safe, but then one by one, they took them away.'

'You let Christopher be cast out to save yourself!'

'I chose him because his Nazi boyfriend was always going to help him out, and it was too dangerous him being linked to us when he was always sneaking off to meet him. I... wasn't going to give you in,' she finished. 'I told you not to come to that dance.'

'But Heinz!' Kurt shouted. 'They put him in hospital. Or did you lie about that, too?'

'You have a brother, don't you? What would you have done in my position?' she yelled back, openly crying in a way that he had never witnessed during the time he'd spent with her in Germany. It was remorse, devastation, hopelessness, all combined in gut-wrenching sobs. 'I know I'm a monster. I know that's in me. It's part of me now, and I can't change that. It's what they're always saying about us anyway, isn't it? It's in me. But they're all dead, all of them. I've lost all of my brothers. I don't even know who I am anymore.'

She started hitting herself in the head. Kurt managed to hold her hands down and she collapsed into his arms, wailing. He thought about how the Nazis had made monsters of all of them in one way or another.

'I know,' he found himself holding her, trying to take some of the pain away. 'I know.'

Alice rushed in, and looked at him reproachfully as he transferred Greta over to her outstretched arms. He left the room stunned, and almost collided with Eli, who was pacing the corridor. He placed a hand on Kurt's arm.

'What you have to understand is,' Eli hesitated, his dark eyes looking right into Kurt's. 'Greta is what they turned her into. Some of us, some of you, they turned into Hitler Youth… some believed enough to betray their own families… and for that we can only blame those who indoctrinated them.'

Kurt found that he couldn't speak.

'Some of us came to realise that we must be Jewish and not much else,' Eli continued. 'And within this, some of us became proud, but most, over time, believed what everyone was saying about what it meant to be Jewish. Rats, vermin, non-German. Rats, vermin, non-German. Day after day, for six years. Getting spat on in the street, beaten up for sitting on the wrong bench, being arrested for entering a park. Trying to get reason and help from your teachers, the police, old friends, "real" Germans, but everyone just says you deserve it. Rats, vermin, non-German. You are no longer part of anything, and what you want most of all is to be accepted. Greta and Josiah are self-hating Jews, indoctrinated against themselves by the Nazis.'

'She still gave up her friends to them,' Kurt said, but he couldn't look up at Eli.

'And what would you have done to save your family?' Eli asked. 'What would you still do?'

They were interrupted by vibrations throughout the ship. The engines were starting up.

'We're turning,' Eli explained.

'Why?'

Footsteps came pounding along the corridor. Malik spun around the corner, catching his breath, beads of sweat on his hatless forehead. 'A notice had been put up by the Captain, saying that we're sailing close to the American shore, and negotiations are taking place!'

'And yet they're singing Nazi songs in the nightclub, loud enough for everyone to hear,' Gus said, appearing from around the same corner. He was holding one of Josiah's makeshift batons. 'They're celebrating the fact that America won't accept us. They seem to think it's a done deal that we're going back to Germany.'

'Why have you got that weapon?' Eli said, barely suppressing the anger in his voice.

'Josiah's suggestion,' he answered, facing up to Eli with a cockiness that Kurt hadn't seen before. 'The Gestapo men are still patrolling, when they're not singing.'

'Josiah has called a group meeting,' Malik informed them, dropping his head and not meeting Eli's stare. 'After the Professor's funeral. After we've got rid of the... the lifeboat's contents.'

CHAPTER TWENTY-SEVEN

The Girl and the City of Blinding Lights

4th June 1939

The ship awoke in a state of excitement. Passengers were running along the corridors, calling out about seeing the bright lights of Miami, and how America would be their saviour. Alice could hear it all alongside the tossing and turning and cries of despair from Greta, who was sleeping fitfully in the bed opposite.

During the long night, Alice had placed a reassuring hand on her brow whenever the terrors got too much. 'You're okay,' she'd repeated. 'You'll be okay.'

Occasionally, Greta had briefly opened her eyes and whispered, 'They're all dead, aren't they? Isaac, Ralph, Felix?' This usually gave way to another bout of feverish dreaming before Alice could answer her.

If Alice felt anything approaching guilt over what had happened to Eichel, it was buried deep beneath all the other horrors. She guessed it was the same for Greta. At one stage during the night, Greta was calm, wide awake, and that was when Alice had asked for her help. Greta nodded and took the pencil and paper, working quickly before enveloping herself back in the covers once again. Afterwards, looking at the drawing, Alice felt her insides run cold, as though the blood had frozen in her veins.

She glanced over and saw that the girl finally seemed at peace, and decided that she needed to take the opportunity to leave the confines of the cabin for a while; the compressed air was overwhelming her senses. She dressed quickly. Her aching arms and legs called for a warm bath, but a quick wash in the sink with cold water would have to do.

Kurt was dozing against the wall outside. His head snapped up when Alice stepped out through the door. Eli was sitting on the other side, his long legs stretched out across the corridor. He smiled at Alice, and offered her a cup of coffee. He didn't attempt to give any instructions or ask any questions. Eli always knew the right time to leave things alone, just by reading someone's facial expression. The coffee was fragrant and smoky as she put it to her lips, sipping gratefully. Kurt also took some and followed her onto the deck. They didn't speak.

The deck was sun-warmed, and in any other circumstances, she would have enjoyed it. Some of the other passengers were leaning over the rails, as though trying to get as close to Miami as possible. Alice didn't want to look at the city's blinding lights. Instead, she focussed on the deep sea fishing yachts, until she noticed that the passengers on them were taking photos. She turned her face away. It wasn't just the press, but ordinary people, too. They were now a tourist attraction. A US Coast Guard cutter, a much larger ship, was moving towards the fishing fleets. Its crew were waving. She didn't wave back. Kurt was a comforting shadow at her side.

'I went too far with Greta,' he admitted.

'You had to know,' Alice replied. 'I had a question to ask her, too.'

She thought of the sketch. The tall, well-built man, the thin face, the high Slavic cheekbones. 'It definitely wasn't Franz who betrayed me,' she said.

'Who was it?' Kurt asked, speaking softly.

'It was Max,' her voice was hollow, the shock draining it of tone. 'He was my father's friend, like an uncle to me.' Her hand went to her mouth, as though to stem the flow of words.

'How do you know?'

'I asked who had been feeding information to the Gestapo, if it wasn't Franz,' she said. 'Greta drew him from memory.'

'But why would he betray you? Why-'

'Why not just hand me over and force my father to work for them?' She had to take a few sharp breaths to gather herself. 'Money? Power, maybe? I think he knew that the ship was always meant to come back to Germany, making it look like he had tried to save me, and avoiding suspicion from the others. And all the while, he's selling more people that he's been entrusted with helping.' She took a deep breath. 'I need to warn the rest of my resistance group, but I have no way of contacting them.'

She saw him pause, his mouth ready to form a new question before a feeling of uncertainty held him back.

'Max never knew where Edie was hidden,' she said, guessing at what he was about to ask. 'He dropped us off miles away. The map would have made no sense to him. If nothing else, it's more than likely that my sister is safe. I'm glad she didn't get on this ship.'

CHAPTER TWENTY-EIGHT

The Boy, a Burial at Sea and a possible Mutiny

Monday 5th June 1939

The plan was in place for Eichel's body to be thrown overboard. As they waited, Kurt asked Alice for the real story of her and Franz – the one she wasn't telling – and why she couldn't bring herself to believe that he could have been the traitor. The lack of sleep had left bruises beneath her eyes, but he guessed that she was the same as him, running on a frisson of panic and adrenaline that wouldn't allow her to rest.

She didn't answer at first, and he didn't push her. They sat on the softly furnished chairs, watching people as they seemed to sleep-walk past, moods set constantly to anxious; the everyday actions of walking, eating and surviving conducted via autopilot. The whispers and the rumours floated past, talking of reporters who were on their side and others that stood against them. They listened to gossip about the captain looking aged, stooped and tired, and how even he was starting to lose hope. There was a growing belief that the ship had been marked for something back in Germany – as an example, or some kind of test. After all, the British ship, the Orduna, had sailed into Havana, dropped everyone off and sailed back out again without issue.

Eventually, Alice leaned in close to him and started talking. 'Franz might think that he hates Jews,' she said. 'But he didn't hate my mother. He blamed himself for her death. He promised her that he would look after me.'

'What happened?' he said.

Alice tapped at the ship's railings to try and steady her trembling fingers. 'It was a couple of years ago. They said it was a car crash, but they – the police, the Gestapo, the SS – had been tracking Mama for weeks.' She lowered her voice as a few passengers walked close by.

'It was to get back at my father,' she said. 'He wouldn't divorce her, and he spoke out against the Party and in defence of Jewish academics. We didn't want her to go out anymore, but he was late home one night and we knew that there had been a disturbance at the university, so she went to look for him.' She paused for a moment. 'Franz joined the Gestapo to try and protect her, but he couldn't stop them. He became so powerful, so feared, and still he couldn't do anything.'

Kurt leaned forward and placed a hand on hers.

'A witness said that they ran her off the road, but of course nothing could be proved,' she said. There was a spark of anger mixed in with her sadness.

Grief for his father, for his own loss, pulled down like a weight in his stomach. It felt like a punch. Alice's eyes were blurred with tears, and he could feel water pricking at the back of his own eyes.

'We will survive this,' he said. 'And we'll take revenge for everyone they've taken from us.'

'But what does revenge get us?' Her blue eyes stared intently into his. 'What did it do for Greta?'

'There you both are,' an exasperated voice broke into their conversation. It was Malik. 'Come on, it's almost time.' He gestured for them to get up and follow him.

As they walked through the ship, an orange dusk peaked through the windows along the way. They passed the noticeboard, where telegrams had been posted, pleading for President Roosevelt and his wife to let them into America. The orchestra was playing *Freut euch des Lebens* (Be Happy you're Alive) to an empty social hall.

'They certainly know how to cheer people up,' Malik muttered. 'Did you know that they were trying to bury that professor with a Nazi flag? Apparently, it's the tradition now, but the captain wouldn't allow it.'

They kept going until they reached the engine bunkers. Inside, an argument was taking place between low voices.

'We're not storming the ship,' Eli hissed at Gus. 'It isn't the answer.'

'If they're planning on taking us back to Germany, what choice do we have?' Gus said, his chin raised and his fist clenched.

'Tell Josiah that we will attend this meeting,' Eli said through gritted teeth. 'And we will listen to all suggestions.'

'He's expecting you anyway,' Gus shrugged before walking off, still swinging a baton.

Malik paused, unsure of which way to turn, before ducking his head in apology and running along behind Gus.

Eli's eyes were blazing. 'As though we haven't got enough problems.'

'Josiah wants to storm the ship?' Kurt asked.

'We'll have to handle that later,' Eli said. 'Let me explain what will need to be done tonight.'

'Where's Greta?' Kurt scanned the room for her.

'Resting,' Eli said. 'Freddie is guarding her cabin. This would be too much for her right now.'

There was a light tap at the door. Kurt jumped at the sound, but it was only Berger, announcing that everything was in place. The plan was to wait until night fell, and then time it so that the carpeted corpse and lifeboat – which, in addition to the thick rug and sink holes, had also been fitted with sandbags – hit the water at the same time as the professor. They would have to set up a chain of people to send signals of the funeral's progress.

The darkness was dense and sooty, and the fog, which had appeared as evening began to draw in, became an expedient velvet blanket to hide the deed beneath. They could hear the professor's funeral starting on the far deck, where a small crowd had gathered. As they passed on the other side, Kurt heard the words, Remember God, that we are of dust. A series of small thuds followed.

'They're sprinkling handfuls of sand over the shroud,' Alice explained as they reached the meeting point.

Berger had rigged the lighting so that it wouldn't work in the area around the lifeboat, and Eli had positioned guards at multiple points along the deck. This included Josiah, who Kurt prayed wouldn't do anything stupid.

Berger had already cut at the lifeboat ropes and hoisted it up with the help of several others. There was a small gap in the ship's railings, meant for emergency evacuations, where the body could be rolled out and the lifeboat lifted over it. Eli, Kurt and Malik carried the body between them. Another group led by Berger took the lifeboat. The metallic smell of blood got at Kurt, but overcoming the heaviness of the now hours-dead Eichel took all his concentration.

The engines stopped and a signal came from the last look-out, a sharp whistle. A dull splash on one side of the ship, almost immediately followed by another, and a blast of the horn, hiding the lifeboat drop. He went to find Alice, who had been positioned close to the edge of the funeral. He could see tears running down her cheeks, lit up by the ship's dim lighting. She was attempting to wipe them away, but they kept flowing.

'It had to be done,' Kurt said gently. 'We would all have been blamed for his death-'

'It's not him,' Alice indicated Eichel with a sudden rage. 'It's this – all of this.' She gestured to where the service for the professor had taken place. 'I saw the professor wearing a Kirah before he was covered. It's a black ribbon placed over the heart, demonstrating anger in the face of loss. These customs and traditions that my mama grew up with, they could all be gone soon.'

Eli's voice came from behind them. 'They won't win,' he said determinedly, putting a hand on Alice's shoulder.

Eli started quietly praying in Hebrew, and Kurt noted how he could now listen without recoiling, as he had done at the start of the voyage. He knew it was ridiculous to be jealous, but hearing Alice saying snatches of it along with Eli made him feel insecure. It was a form of intimacy that he couldn't be part of. It occurred to him that everything he had ever known, or could have wanted to know, was being destroyed, too. His teenage years had been stolen by Hitler, and what did he now have left to preserve? He was German, apparently, but he didn't even know what that meant anymore. In his early years it had meant suffering, a lack of food and a loss of pride in the shadow of a lost war. It then became about what he used to think was strength, but really was just violence. There was more food, but also a lot more death to go with it.

'We'd better go,' Eli interrupted Kurt's wandering thoughts.

Alice was wiping her eyes.

The meeting, he remembered. The plan to storm the ship.

They headed in the direction of Josiah's first-class cabin. Malik and Freddie formed part of the guard at the door and averted their eyes from Eli. Their shoes scuffed against the floor, old and worn leather, in pitiful attempts at stomping like SS guards. Kurt felt an involuntary shudder ripple through him.

The other young passengers were still giving them a wide berth, even though Josiah had announced to everyone that they were innocent, and that the Gestapo spy had been 'silenced'. Eli had assured them that everyone believed this, but Kurt knew Alice was feeling just as uneasy as he was. Eli walked ahead, gesturing for them both to follow.

'Eli wants us to stay with him,' Kurt said quietly.

'Why?' Alice asked.

'To try and prevent Josiah from starting a mutiny,' he said, seeing her eyes widen. 'He needs our help. I told him that no one here would listen to reason, and he agreed.'

'So what are we supposed to do?' The hesitancy in her voice made it clear that she knew something dangerous had been suggested. He would have to tell her the main thrust of the plan.

'Berger is going to lock us all in the room and warn the captain,' Kurt said.

Alice's mouth moved to form a question, but then she simply

shook her head no instead. Eli was still urging them on, and they piled into the room with the others. Heidi was near the front, gazing at Josiah as he spoke. Her expression reminded Kurt of the way people looked at Hitler, as though a spell has been cast over them.

Josiah was holding court, standing on the same bed where Alice had been judged and condemned. He was sweating so much that he'd unbuttoned his waistcoat, but the wide room felt strangely chilled to Kurt, despite holding around thirty heaving bodies within its walls.

'Kurt and Alice have been proven innocent and are to be welcomed as friends,' Josiah said. 'This has been discussed, and the committee have voted on this. They are… heroes of the cause, and should be treated as such by all. Greta is still recovering after being attacked by the Gestapo crewman, who incidentally has now fled the ship in a stolen lifeboat.'

A burst of anger worked through the crowd. The story was convincing, and Josiah had told it well. He waited for the crowd to calm down again before continuing. 'One of the suicide attempts led to a man being taken to a Cuban hospital before the ship left Havana, and they wouldn't even let his wife disembark to go and visit him. I think this confirms that they won't let anyone off unless there are extreme circumstances.' He paused and surveyed his audience. 'Well, I say that we create such extreme circumstances ourselves, and get off the ship together.'

A cheer rose up from the crowd.

'We will all leave the ship, or no one will,' Gus called from across the room, the baton waving above his head.

Kurt was keeping a close eye on him and his weapon.

'That's the plan, Gus,' Josiah held his hands up.

'What are we going to do, then?' another boy shouted.

'Seize control of the ship,' Josiah replied, a smile spreading across his face as he spoke.

There was a collective hush, and then suddenly, Alice was talking, shouting at Josiah.

'You'll destroy all sympathy for us,' she said. 'Remember, the world is watching. We don't want to show that we are the criminals that many of them think we are.'

'Oh yes, the world,' Josiah said sarcastically. 'The audience. Our sympathetic friends, who would see us dragged back in Germany, where we would most certainly die... No, we storm the ship.'

There was a loud cheer from most of the others. A few were hesitant, but had a fixed fear on their faces that showed they would do it anyway. Going back to Germany was worse than any other option.

'And if we fail, which we probably will, the captain will be full speed ahead to Germany,' Alice rebuked them.

Kurt could feel her trembling beside him.

'What does she know?' Heidi said, her mouth curled in disgust as she pointed at Alice. 'She spent long enough pretending that she wasn't one of us, and now she expects us to trust her? A mischling?'

If Josiah was panicked by Heidi's words, it didn't show on his face. He remained calm and collected, with an arrogance to his smile.

'Everyone here is in the same situation,' he reminded them all. 'Even the ex-HJ Kurt. He is an enemy of the Reich too, because he stood up to them.'

The crowd started to grumble and shift. A feeling of agitated tension came over the room.

'I've already told you that he was framed,' Josiah spoke sternly in response.

'But none of us have seen these files you talk of,' someone shouted, inspiring a fresh rumble of discontent.

'We had to destroy them,' Josiah insisted. 'Why would I lie? Why would Eli lie? He saw them, too.'

Josiah appealed to Eli from across the room, who nodded and said yes in Hebrew. Everyone quietened down. Despite Josiah's rise in popularity, Eli still held trust, and in that, power.

'The Nazi-turned-hero doesn't seem too keen to help us now,' Freddie remarked.

'I agree,' Kurt said. He felt Alice stiffen next to him. Surely, she knew that he was just playing along with this bit of theatre? 'I say we storm the ship.' He raised his fist.

'You see,' Josiah said, turning to Kurt and Alice with his own fist raised, drinking in the accompanying shouts of encouragement. 'We storm the ship.'

'How are we going to do it?' came another shout.

Josiah nodded to Gus, who brought out a bag from the side of the bed. Kurt leaned over, curious at the smell of wood and the sound of heavy blocks banging together as Gus brought whatever their solution was to the front of the room. Kurt's heart sank when he saw that it was a pile of weapons – wooden sticks, like the one Gus had been carrying around as though it was a part of him.

A jangle of clashing voices came from outside, followed by the sound of running footsteps. Someone was hammering on nearby cabins and getting closer. The room stilled, the weapons forgotten. Kurt wondered how many others were reminded of the raids on their houses, of Gestapo and SS coming to take people away, with their heavy boots and heavier knocks. No one spoke. Heidi was shaking. Another girl started to cry. It took all of Kurt's efforts in those few moments to remind himself that the threat was gone. Eichel was dead, and he didn't have enough allies on this ship to do any damage. He reached for Alice's hand. Eli was one of the few who had the presence of mind to leap into action, and positioned himself against the door, as though he planned to use his own body as a shield. His eyes cast quickly over Kurt and Alice's joined hands as he turned around. Then, from outside, came the sound of cheering.

The door burst open, knocking Eli to the side, and a man stumbled in, still gripping the handle. Kurt recognised him as one of the leaders of the main passenger committee. He was greying at the temples, and like most of the adults on board, worry had worn more lines into his face than was normal for his age. His expression was jubilant, however. It made him look much younger.

'The Isle of Pines will take us,' he shouted, breathlessly. 'We are no longer wandering Jews.'

CHAPTER TWENTY-NINE

The Girl and a Thing of Two Halves

By seven o'clock that night, the decks were full of luggage again, as they had been when the ship had first approached Cuba. Alice almost tripped over a set of suitcases, but steadied herself just in time.

The shrieks and laughter and giggles of some of the passengers were in stark contrast to the more guarded happiness, hushed conversations and slow steps of others who didn't quite believe that they were safe yet. Food was short, there was no longer a menu to choose from, and all social intercourse between crew and passengers had been banned. The ship's orchestra played to a deserted dancefloor, and the cinema was always empty.

When the news first came, Alice had been convinced, as she could tell the whole room had been, that the SS were somehow storming the ship. She knew Kurt had felt it, too. The way he had grabbed her hand. The look from Eli. She didn't know what to make of any of it. Survival was all that mattered, and Kurt knew her secret; how she could never continue anyone's traditions, because the people who were trying to destroy them had also made sure that she could never have children.

Much like Alice's internal anguish, the veil of hopelessness that had been covering the ship had failed to lift altogether, despite the ongoing preparations to finally leave. It didn't help that no one knew anything about the place they were heading, or even where it was, not to mention the open wounds that still festered following their last experience of a so-called 'safe' port in Cuba.

'What is this island like?' she asked Eli, skirting around a battered leather carrier. Someone's whole life is in there, she thought, looking down at the suitcase.

'It was a penal colony, an island thirty-five miles wide. It will be safe. Those who want to can build a community, and others can move on with support,' he answered quietly, without looking away from the children's game he had joined in with.

'That's a tenth of the size of Berlin,' Kurt muttered. 'And I heard someone say it was owned by the French, who of course hate us.'

Alice wasn't sure when Kurt had started to refer to himself as 'us', as one of them, but it warmed her inside; gave her hope that maybe other fervent Nazis could learn to change, too. At the same time, though, she was acutely aware that even in his case, it had taken the death of a close friend, followed by an extended period of forced interaction with a group of Jews, to break through the multiple layers of conditioning.

'Think of Australia,' Eli's tone was light, but there was no accompanying smile. 'That was barren land and a penal colony, too.'

She could see he was brooding over something, and that all was not well. He had more insight than anyone into what was happening on the ship, which told her that there was an underlying reason for his subdued demeanour. What was he hiding?

Josiah and Gus had called off storming the ship, after the unanimous decision of all the others led by Eli, that they shouldn't create trouble when a place had agreed to accept them. Josiah had taken it well, whereas Gus had booted the bag of weapons and left the room, slamming the door, muttering about it all being just another trick.

Heidi scowled at Alice, as Eli motioned for her and Kurt to follow him to a lifeboat on the edge of the deck. He lifted up the cover to reveal the bag of weapons.

'I need help getting rid of them,' he said. 'We have to throw them overboard before Gus notices that I've taken them.'

'What if someone comes?' Alice asked.

'Heidi is keeping look out on one side, and Leah is watching the other,' he explained.

It seemed that most of the group had given up their devotion to Josiah, and were back to supporting Eli. Kurt started pulling the weapons out of the bag and hurling them overboard. The noises of the moving ship disguised the splashes.

As Alice went to take another one out to tip over the side, she caught her hand on a nail which ripped through her skin. The pain caused her to gasp, and she tried to cover the wound with her other hand, but the blood was already seeping out and dropping onto the deck. She almost lost her balance, but Kurt caught her before she fell.

'Alice, are you-' he stopped, noticing the expanding thick red line across her palm. 'Right, use this as a bandage.' He took out a clean serviette he had started using as a handkerchief – many of the boys did this, as an attempt at acting gentlemanly – and carefully wrapped it around her hand. 'It's not as bad as it looks. I'll clean it and then cover it up properly with the kit I have in my cabin.'

'What happened?' Eli asked, looking back from the railings. He hurried over and practically pushed Kurt of the way. 'You don't want it to get infected,' he said. 'I'll get my medical kit.'

'No, it's fine – just a simple cut,' Kurt subtly nudged Eli aside. 'We had to deal with injuries like this all the time at camps.'

'Camps obviously has a very different meaning to you, Nazi bastard,' Leah muttered from her look-out point.

For once, Eli didn't reprimand her. He seemed to be enjoying the look of horror on Kurt's face.

'I'm sorry I… didn't mean-' Kurt stammered.

Even with the throbbing in her palm, Alice knew that Eli was being unfair to Kurt, and that the tension was rising. 'I'm not helpless. I can sort this out myself,' she said, walking off to find the ship's doctor. She'd only got a few paces down the deck when she heard footsteps running after her. It was Kurt.

'I shouldn't have used the word camps,' he said, pushing his fringe back with awkward hands.

'Eli shouldn't have been like that with you,' she replied. 'And Leah, well, you know what she's like when it comes to us.'

He shrugged. 'I can accept that I'll be a scapegoat at times. I was a Nazi bastard once, even if it does feels like that was a different life now,' he trailed off as he caught sight of the blood dripping through Alice's makeshift bandage onto the floor. 'We need to get you cleaned up.'

They walked to his cabin. It was small inside, but clean and tidy, with a scent that seemed like chalk mixed with oil. As they both sat down on the bed, the first flush of embarrassment came over her. They had already spent plenty of time together, of course, between their respective illnesses, and the week hiding down in the engine room. This felt different, though. It was more intimate, sitting on a bed in the tiny private cabin, almost crushed together as he inspected her hand. He turned it lightly and gently, and she felt a rush of blood to her head that had nothing to do with what was seeping from the cut. She couldn't think of anything to say, and it seemed that neither could he. She hardly noticed the pinching pain of the antiseptic, or the uncomfortable pull of the fresh bandage across her skin. Once he was finished, they sat in still silence.

'I'm glad you're here, actually,' he eventually said, a flush creeping up his neck as he became unusually flustered. 'I have something to show you.'

He went into the small wardrobe and pulled out a couple of items. It was her mother's dress, made into two smaller pieces, a scarf and a skirt. The splashes of blue intersected with newer black material.

She broke out in goose pimples, despite the smothering heat in the room.

Kurt was staring at the floor, shifting nervously on the bed. 'I hope it's okay,' he said, his face colouring slightly. 'I had to use two different fabrics.'

'It's perfect,' she managed to say. 'A thing of two halves, just like me.'

'You're not a half of anything,' he corrected. 'You're all of it. You're everything.'

It was impossible to say who had instigated the kiss. All she knew was that it was one of the most intense moments of her life. The slow, steady, respectful way he held her, the warmth of his hands on her shoulders, felt through layers of clothing, as though he was touching her skin. When they finally both pulled away, it was like waking from a deep dream.

'What about what happened to me? What they did to me means I could never be a proper... I can never have... I'm nothing-' she couldn't bring herself to say it. They had taken from her two of the things that she wanted most in life: her mother, and her chance of becoming a mother herself.

'You're everything,' he repeated. 'We will always have each other.'

The pressure in her chest eased as she relaxed into the feel of his mouth on hers, the sense that they were sharing a breath. She kissed him back, on the mouth. He kissed the curve of her neck. The tension melted from her body. His touch sent shivers to her toes. He embraced her, pressing his cheek against hers.

Without speaking, she lay in his arms on the bed, the reassuring beat of his heart against her ear. She wanted the feeling to last as long as it could, but even as she felt herself drift off to sleep, she somehow knew that it would only be for one night.

CHAPTER THIRTY

The Boy and the Bad News

Wednesday 7th June 1939

They woke to the sound of loudspeakers. The voice was muffled by the cabin walls, but not enough to disguise what was clearly bad news.

Alice immediately retreated back into the coiled anxiety that had become her default state. 'We're returning to Europe, aren't we?' she said. 'I heard him say Europe, which means Germany, doesn't it?'

He had never seen her so panicked. He found it hard to get any words out. His head was spinning. Smoothing down her clothing, Alice headed for the door. He did the same and followed her. Outside, the ship had descended into chaos once again.

'What happened to the Isle of Pines?' someone down the corridor was shouting.

'Even an island no one has heard of doesn't want us,' came the reply, but the attempt at humour was too closely surrounded by fear, and the voice soon shook itself into worry.

They followed the other passengers towards the social hall.

'The German radio has been celebrating the announcement that no one else will take us "shabby Jews",' Josiah's voice rang from behind them. 'We're now pinning our hopes on Great Britain.'

'We've got to find Eli,' Alice said.

Kurt took that like a slap to the face. Even though it made sense to try and find Eli, who always had more information and was, once again, top of the pecking order in the minds of the young passengers, he'd seen the way Alice looked at him from time to time, and something deep within him ached whenever he witnessed it. Their kiss, although happening only hours ago, was already lost in the strange, hyperbolic time warp that the ship seemed to float in. It could have been a lifetime ago, if it even happened at all.

Josiah clapped a hand on his shoulder as they watched Alice skirt through the crowd. 'She'll never settle with you, Nazi boy. Even though she's a mongrel like me, she's going to choose the side that needs to be preserved, in case Hitler destroys us all. You wouldn't get it. You're not one of us.'

The old Kurt would have corrected this by telling the smug-faced son of an SS soldier how she had slept in his cabin last night, but he couldn't; just as he hadn't been able to do any more than kiss her. Anything further would have felt intrusive, wrong and rushed. He shrugged Josiah's weight off and followed Alice, not caring about the mocking laughter behind him. Catching up with her, he tried to hold her hand, but she shook him off. When she turned around, he saw tears glistening her eyes.

'We've been judged by everyone, and still no one wants us,' she said.

'I know,' he said, feeling every bit of the pain and desperation of Alice and the other passengers around him.

They walked around to the other side of the deck. Eli had his hands resting on Gus's shoulders, their heads bent close, a discussion taking place. As he edged nearer, following Alice's lead, he could hear Gus talking, low and angry, monotone and repetitive.

'I told you it was a trick,' Gus was repeating over and over, oblivious to Eli's words of comfort and reassurances that they would make plans, that it wasn't a trick and that they weren't going back, and no one would get him.

'Where are my weapons?' Gus said, becoming frantic. 'We need to take over this ship.' He threw Eli off him and turned around wild-eyed and chalk-pale. 'Where are my weapons?'

'They threw them away, Gus!' Josiah's booming voice called from behind.

Gus' whole body seemed to crumple at that, from his face down to his stick-thin shins. Then, so suddenly that Kurt wasn't quite sure it had even happened, he disappeared overboard. The splash as he hit the water was met by another one seconds later. Alice had dived, too. Before he had time to process what was happening, his surroundings became blurred as he ran and jumped after her.

The water hit him like a pane of glass. He swallowed a lot of it after his awkward attempt at a dive, making it even harder to work his way back up to the surface in the murky surf. His lungs sucked in air greedily as he finally made it to the top. Scanning the area, all he could see was the St Louis pulling away, passengers hanging over the side while someone tried to lower a lifeboat. That was when he spotted Alice, breaking the surface and struggling with Gus, who was trying to wriggle free from her rescue hold, and dragging them both down as a result. He could feel the current, created and strengthened by the ship's momentum, tugging on his arms and legs as he began a desperate front crawl towards them. His energy was almost completely sapped by the time he reached Alice. Between the two of them, they held onto Gus, who no longer had any fight in him, but was threatening to sink at any point. Alice's eyes were heavy, and her head was dipping lower. Kurt wanted to take more of the weight, but exhaustion was starting to overwhelm him.

A silhouette of a lifeboat appeared in the distance.

'Please hurry, please hurry,' Alice was whispering to herself.

Something had shifted in the current, and they were now having to swim against it just to stay still. Kurt's teeth were chattering violently. Everything was blue from the sky to the sea, but the sea was winning.

Eventually, the lifeboat reached them. Together with Alice, he pushed a weakly protesting Gus towards the boat, into the waiting arms of Eli and Malik. Alice started to climb over the boat and held out a hand to him, but he couldn't reach it, and it was then that he felt himself slide under the waves, and everything went from blue to black.

'Please, please wake up.'

Alice's voice was distant, as though she was talking to him through a tunnel. He opened his eyes briefly, and he could see the outline of her features. Water was dripping from her face onto his, and he became aware of the sodden weight of his clothes and the salt starting to solidify in the sun. A surge of something caught in his throat, and then he was coughing violently, bringing up water until he could finally see Alice clearly, her face lined with concern, and Eli not far behind her.

'Give him space,' Josiah was shouting. 'Move away!' He was also dripping wet.

A crowd had gathered on the deck, which seemed to be filled as much with water as it was with people. Kurt could feel his body slowly shaking off the ocean's attack.

'It's okay, I'm fine,' he said, sitting up, only for dizziness to almost strike him back down again. 'Where's Gus?'

'With the doctor,' Eli said. 'Under lock and key.'

Alice enveloped him in a hug that took away whatever breath he had managed to regain.

'She released him. 'Greta jumped in, too. On the other side, when no one was watching.'

He spluttered water and gulped in more air. 'Did anyone go in after her?'

'Josiah did.' Alice pressed her lips together into a hard line. 'She's with the doctor, too... she's not in a good way.'

'Josiah jumped in to save Greta?' Kurt couldn't help but blurt out.

'I'm not all bad,' Josiah said, shrugging his soaking shoulders. 'The whole bloody ship is watching us now, though. There'll be no chance to take it over. I could push you all overboard for this... but since you're all alive, I am billing that girl for my suit when we find a country that'll take us, and failing that, I'm billing you, Hertz.' With that, he stomped off across the deck.

Something about him has changed, Kurt thought, noting how his swagger no longer seemed laden with menace.

Heidi and Leah stepped into the space left by Josiah. They were carrying bundles of towels. Heidi was wringing her hands and tapping her worn brown shoes in one of the puddles. Leah, still beautiful despite an anguished frown, bit down on her lip.

'We're glad you're both okay,' Heidi finally said.

'And thanks for rescuing Gus,' Leah added. 'Let us know if you… if you need anything else.' They dropped the clean and warm towels into Alice and Kurt's hands and departed.

'It took us almost drowning for them to trust us again,' muttered Alice, as she folded the towel around herself.

'We all say things we don't mean when we're scared,' Eli said, and, appearing to note their reactions to this, took a step back and melted away into the crowd, as though he had never been there. He instantly became the centre of the children and young people again, as they gathered around him, asking for news, looking for reassurance. It was typical Eli, and Kurt had to smile.

Alice was looking down at her hands. 'Will you forgive Greta?'

'Yes,' he replied immediately, and he meant it. He knew that Greta would always punish herself, because she knew better than anyone that what she had done was wrong. Suddenly, his brother came to mind. Amon didn't know better, and at his age, while in the hands of the Nazis, he couldn't know that what he did was wrong. That was the difference. Who would be there to save Amon from them? From himself? And, even if he was somehow rescued, how would he ever forgive himself? For the first time, Kurt processed the fact that his father was dead.

'One of the lifeboats is missing,' he heard a crewman say.

'So is that swine Eichel,' another muttered. 'We'll have to tell the captain. Looks like he's definitely jumped ship.'

They shared a smile when the men had passed.

'One less worry,' she whispered.

'One less worry,' he repeated. He knew that she would also be mulling this over inside – that it was another death, and therefore shouldn't sit well with her. He could tell as much from the strained nature of her smile. It was the same for him.

'I'm going to go and check on Greta,' she said, standing up. 'But first I must get changed.'

'I'll meet you back at the social hall,' he said, intending to go and find fresh clothes himself, but then noticing that Eli was beckoning him over.

'I'm sorry too, about the camp comment,' Eli said. 'I shouldn't have... it's just...' For once, he seemed lost for words. 'It's just... you and Alice.'

If the conversation had happened a day earlier, Kurt would have said there was no him and Alice, but he didn't want to lie. Eli stuck out his hand and Kurt accepted it. There was no malice on either side, and in that moment, looking at the other boy, Kurt knew that there never would be.

'I won't go back to Germany,' they heard people saying over and over across the deck.

'I have to go back,' Kurt said quietly.

'Me too,' Eli replied.

CHAPTER THIRTY-ONE

The Girl and the New Plan

Thursday 8th June 1939

Alice headed to the social hall. There was chanting, and it was getting louder and clearer as she got closer.

'We must not die... we will not return... we must not die...'

It sent shivers down her spine. After spending a sleepless night watching over Greta, who was conscious but mostly incoherent, apart from the chilling screams that followed her calling out her brothers' names.

Eli had slipped into the cabin at some point after he'd checked on Gus, who he said was faring a lot better, albeit dulled and drugged by the strong medication prescribed to him by the doctor. He had started to pray, and Alice had felt compelled to join in, with tears rolling down her cheeks as she remembered her mother and thought of Edie. Her sister should be safe, she knew, but for how long?

Eli had kept a respectful distance for the majority of the time he was in the room, but at the conclusion of the prayers he'd come over and hugged Alice softly, before leaving and closing the door gently behind him. It had felt like a goodbye of sorts. Although Kurt would never have spoken of it, she flushed to think that Eli knew about her spending the night in his cabin. Nothing had happened beyond the kiss, but she knew what it would have looked like to the others.

Entering the social hall, she spotted Eli hanging back on the periphery. A man in a brown suit was talking too fast and sweating profusely up on the stage, where the band usually played.

'What's happening?' she asked.

'The useful man from the useful refugee place is apologising and saying that he'll pray for us,' Josiah snorted. 'This ship is just a messenger service for the Nazis.' He turned to Alice. 'You in?'

'On what?' Kurt's voice came from behind them.

Josiah sighed and gestured for them all to step outside onto the deserted deck. The sun was a molten orb in the first harsh taste of daylight. Alice shielded her eyes with her hands.

'If you two would stop spending all your time locked in a cabin together, you might keep up to date,' Josiah playfully reprimanded them.

Alice refused to let Josiah get the reaction he wanted. She maintained eye contact until he looked away. Kurt was shifting awkwardly next to her. Eli told Josiah to shut up and get on with it.

'It was that Miststück Eichel who gave me the idea, or rather his dead body did,' Josiah paused, and Eli knocked his shoulder, causing him to stumble. 'Okay, okay, well it goes like this. We might not be taking over the ship anymore, but we are going to get off it.'

Visions of lines of passengers jumping overboard flooded her mind. It was like she could taste the salt water in her mouth again, the weight of Gus in her arms. His voice saying let me die, but his body saying otherwise. Everything in his movements had screamed horror. The children among them would never make it.

'No,' Alice said.

'It's decided,' Josiah answered.

'You're on board with this plan?' Alice asked Eli.

'I don't see any other choice,' he replied. 'He hasn't explained the key part. We're using the lifeboats. We're going to wait until the ship is as close to England as possible, and then release them.'

'The captain? The crew? What will they do?' Kurt said, taking the words out of Alice's mouth. 'And how many passengers have agreed to this?'

'A number of us will hold the captain's men off as long as possible,' Josiah said. 'And we are going to spread the word to as many people as we can,' he paused. 'That last part was Eli's idea. I'd sooner keep it to just our group.'

'We can't put the children at that kind of risk,' Alice needed them to understand this. 'We're still days away from Europe. Britain might yet take us.' She wanted to try and delay these plans, but her words came out as though she didn't believe them herself, which she didn't. Not after everything that had happened.

'They're not going to take in more refugees from a country they're about to fight,' Josiah said.

The others nodded, even Eli.

'But we'll die if we don't make it,' she said, looking around for support.

'What choice do we have?' Eli said quietly. He hated the plan, that much was obvious, but there was something else agitating him. His knuckles had turned white under the stress of his grip on the railings.

Josiah, bored now, knowing that the attention was no longer on him, went back into the social hall, muttering. 'We've been on here for bloody ages anyway. Isn't anyone else sick of doing nothing but wait for someone to save us?'

'Want me to go after him?' Kurt asked, seeming to sense that Eli had other things on his mind.

Eli nodded, thanking him with a thin smile.

'What's wrong?' Alice asked him once they were alone.

'I got a letter from that plane drop too, but it only came through last night,' he said. 'The circuit group I was a part of has been blown apart. I need to go back. There is someone… there are people depending on me.' He was leaning far over the railings now, as though trying to edge himself closer to land.

'Why are you going ahead with Josiah's plan, then?'

'I think the best way back to Germany is through England. I can hardly just walk off the ship at Hamburg and expect not to be taken straight to a camp, can I?'

'Please don't go back, Eli.' She put a hand on his arm. He looked down at it for a second, and she could see the emotion welling in his dark eyes.

'I have to, Alice,' he said softly. 'I have to.'

The next couple of days were a blur of planning; seeking out passengers that they could trust, and crew members who wanted to leave too, and getting the message out about the lifeboat launch for what felt like a pilgrimage to England. Alice tried to spend as much time away from the deck as possible, leaving the planning of the mechanics of the lifeboat launches to the rest of them. It took a while, but she eventually managed to arrange some time alone with Kurt. They sat in the lounge near the social hall, drinking coffee that he had somehow foraged from the ship's dwindling supplies.

'Eli wants to go back to Germany via England,' she said, the weakened caffeine still a comfort, as well as a burning inside that gave her a much-needed lift. 'We have to change his mind.'

'I'm going back, too,' Kurt said firmly, unexpectedly, and then continued quickly before Alice could reply. 'Heinz and the others – I have to try and help, to get more people out. I left him to die at that party. The look on his face when the soldiers were bursting in.' He took a breath. 'And I have to try with Amon – try and turn him around. Most of all, I want to tell Alfons's family what really happened, what Peter did. There is so much that I need to go back and do.'

'Kurt, they will find you-'

'Eli has contacts. I can go submarine again, change my appearance and have false papers.'

'And what will Eli do? His face is so well known and, well, so…'

'Jewish?' Kurt finished her sentence with a wry smile.

'You can say that word without flinching now?' she joked.

'He will stay out of sight.' He paused. 'Why don't you come with us?'

For a moment, she was tempted. But she could be more useful in a country where she knew the language. 'I'm going to stay in England when our lifeboat lands there,' she said. 'I'll offer my services as a translator. I'll put myself forward for training in any capacity – the army, the air force, anything.' As she spoke, she realised that she had never felt braver or more afraid in her life. Kurt took her hand and nodded. She squeezed it back.

They sat in silence for a few moments. Passengers were hurrying past with jewellery, clothes and cameras that they were pawning to raise money to send telegrams to Prime Minister Neville Chamberlain, and other high-profile British political figures, in the hope of gaining asylum. The Nazi crew members, who everyone knew were linked to the Gestapo, were patrolling the decks, sneering at the men, women and even the children, and issuing threats that Dachau and other concentration camps were waiting for them. Other crewmen were different, though, leaving fruit in the cots for the young ones, and hurrying after those who needed help.

At dinner, there was an address from the captain. No one was expecting good news, so when it did arrive in the form of his slow, measured words, we are not going back to Germany, it took everyone a few minutes to react. Then, all of a sudden, the questions poured out in an un-co-ordinated symphony. Who is going to take us? Did Britain say yes? Or did France? Don't be stupid, why would the French take us? But mostly people were celebrating. The captain left the room as the ship's purser reassured everyone that there would be an update soon. The relief of not going back to Germany washed over Alice in waves of happiness. It didn't matter who took them. There was no need to risk their lives launching lifeboats to England. They were safe.

Alice turned to find Kurt leaning against the door, smiling. She ran and jumped into his arms, not caring who saw or what they thought. He spun her around and they both laughed, before they were joined by Malik, Leah and most of the others, even Josiah, who joined them as they cheered and the group hug became a half dance and someone got out a violin. There was no sign of Eli.

Alice had to step outside into the cool air as the music and dancing got more raucous. Kurt was busy talking to Malik about his plans to find a paper who would report the story of this ship properly. Eli was there, looking out to sea once again.

'There's someone in particular that he is going back to Germany for, you know,' Josiah said smugly, gesturing towards Eli. 'And he will find a way back there. That should make your choice easier, if you haven't already made a decision.' He nodded back at the room, in the direction of Kurt.

Alice didn't know what to say, but when she turned around Josiah had already melted back into the crowd in the social hall.

She went to see Greta and smiled along with her at the news. She was recovering so much better than expected, but the medication to dull her anxiety had also dulled her intelligence. She grasped Alice's hands in a child-like grip and said, 'So, we will soon be free.'

By Monday, there were rumours that Belgium, Britain, Holland and France had all agreed to take the passengers, and on Wednesday this was confirmed.

'I can operate a resistance unit from Belgium,' Eli said. 'I have contacts who have already set up there, and are maintaining contact with those still undercover in Germany. They can help us get forged identity papers across the border and get communications in and out without me needing to go back into the country myself.'

Alice felt a weight lift off her chest. 'You're going back for someone?' she had to ask.

'For a lot of people,' he replied. 'As many as I can help.'

She didn't press him, or reveal that Josiah had mentioned a 'someone'. It was none of her business.

'Thank goodness people are washing their clothes again,' he said, with a smile that was more like the Eli she had first met – the positive one – as the smell of fresh linen and lemon balm soap seeped into the salt air of the deck, while people ran about them preparing their luggage.

'I'm going to find out if Belgium will take me too,' Alice said, standing up to leave. 'I want to work with you.'

'Alice!' he called after her. 'I just want to warn you… it isn't too friendly in there.'

'It's fine. I've had years of being rejected,' she tried to joke.

He walked up to her, took her by the shoulders and kissed her cheeks.

'We'd love to have you with us. Present a good argument,' he said. 'Tell them you have relatives in America who will be sending for you soon, so that they think you'll only be in their country for a short time.'

Alice felt tears break in her eyes. She forced them back. No matter how many years she had lived with hate in Germany, it was no easier watching it spreading across the rest of the world.

She was still trying to maintain the lightness that Eli's kiss had given her when she entered the social hall, where the portrait of Hitler watched over people pleading for countries to take them.

'Hey.' Kurt was at her side.

'Did you get into Belgium?' she asked.

There were rumours that a Nazi youth organisation had got out a message ahead of their docking at Antwerp: We too want to help the Jews. If they call at our offices, each will receive gratis a length of rope and a long nail. They planned to target the men and older boys from the ship. Her thoughts must have been betrayed by her face.

'I think this voyage has proved that it's dangerous for us everywhere,' Kurt said. 'Is England still your first choice?'

'No,' she said, and found her voice wobbling. 'I'm going to go with you and Eli. There's a lot I can help with.'

'It will be very dangerous, Alice-'

'You will need a fast runner,' she replied.

He smiled and put his arm around her, and she leaned into him, his scent reassuring.

Once inside, however, the Belgium official told her they were full and refused to enter into further conversation with her. Instead, she was moved across to try England, where a man in a suit listened to her intently, deciding her fate as she moved between speaking English and German. Rubbing his chin, he muttered something about her possibly proving useful in the coming months. She was accepted with a stamp and a stern look.

'Come on,' Kurt said, holding out his hand and walking them both away from the cacophony of crying and celebrations; the begging and the bargaining of those yet to find acceptance.

They waited outside until the officials left, and listened as the band set up for the farewell party. As a melody produced itself in the form of a gentle Glen Miller track, a mournful Moonlight Serenade, Alice could see that Kurt was close to tears.

'You know I had to choose Belgium,' he said. 'My French is good, which is the main language in the region where Eli has support, so I can really help people there – a lot of people. I could sneak across the border, getting messages to Heinz. I will come over to England as soon as I can. It is better for you to go there anyway. You speak the language, you can do so much from there.'

She wanted to tell him that it was okay to be scared, that her heart was racing too, because what was a thin strip of sea between her and Hitler? And for him, what was a border to the bullying SS? Instead, she took his hand and, pulling him up, said, 'Shall we dance?'

Wrapped up tightly in his arms, she felt emboldened enough to kiss him first. It was as soft as the first time, but also tinged with sadness. When they broke apart, he traced his fingers along her arm, like he was drawing a map. She rested her head on his shoulder, swaying in time with the ship.

'One day, when this is all over and the world is normal again, we'll go back to Hamburg station,' he said. 'We'll be just like any other couple ready to take a trip across our country.'

'And we'll be able to look back when we're saying goodbye,' she said. 'And it won't feel like the last time.'

Inside, she was swallowing tears, and as they danced cheek to cheek, she could feel the tension in his face as he fought them back, too. They waltzed slowly across the ship.

The call from the captain came too soon. The passengers destined for Belgium were to disembark at Antwerp Harbour. Eli had used bribes to get Gus and Malik off with him. Josiah insisted on carrying on to England, keen to see his mother. Greta was to go there, too.

Alice embraced Eli, and he whispered, 'One day, we will all meet back in a free Germany'. There was friendship and love in his words and touch.

She turned to Kurt, and the others moved away to give them space. 'It has been-'

He cut her off with a hug that warmed her whole body. She buried her face in his sleeve, and bit her lip so that she wouldn't cry. She closed her eyes, and they were back at the train station, holding onto one another again, providing temporary comfort in that desperate time.

'My name is Kurt Hertz,' he'd whispered in her ear.

'I'm Alice Sommer,' she'd replied.

'Goodbye, Alice,' he'd said, picking up his battered suitcase. 'I wish you the best of luck.'

Just as the gangplank was being drawn up, he looked back and smiled.

Epilogue

02 August 1939

My dearest Kurt,

I have some good news since my last letter. Edie is booked on a Kinder-transport for 4th September. I am beside myself waiting to hear that she has made it. I have been assured that she is safe and in trusted hands.

Life here is a mix of relief and tension. We are still housed together with the children, and are well provided for by various charitable organisations. I can't get any information on Josiah – tell Eli how sorry I am not to have an update. One minute he was kissing the ground in Southampton, and the next he was being hauled off to an 'alien camp' up north with the other men.

I'm still no closer to getting over to Belgium. Money is tight, and sur-veillance on us even tighter. Why don't people realise that the Nazis are our enemy too, and that we want Germany back from them?

Whenever we go into the town to purchase food, we are advised not to speak or act in a 'German' way. If we slip up, which we often do, it can get nasty.

In a way, it's nice to be called German again, even if they mean it as an insult, and often follow it with the word 'bitch'. Greta takes it harder, but she is growing in strength, mentally and physically, each day.

Please be careful on your journeys. I worry about you.

Yours,

Alice

05 September 1939

My dearest Alice,

Since Britain have finally declared war on Germany, the borders have been harder to get through. But my work is now more important than ever. We hope to get out of Belgium before they invade here, and there is much talk of that. More and more families are coming to us for help. There are too many people to save and not enough time. We want to get as many people out as we can before we leave.

Heinz and Walter are safe, for now. I have to help them before the net closes, and it's closing in fast.

It is too dangerous here. Stay put, and I'll be with you in England soon.

German civilians are never told about attempts on Hitler's life, but it does happen. More of us can make it happen.

If they censor my letter for being German, all they will read is that I hate Hitler.

Yours,

Kurt

Telegram 9 SEPTEMBER 1939.
KURT TRAPPED IN GERMANY. STOP.
WAITING FOR NEWS. ELI.

The War Office - London
10 September 1939

The clear winter sun reflected off Alice's handlebars as she cycled through the wide roads. The grand houses were gradually giving way to smaller apartments, the blue sky shrinking as the city closed in. She stopped at the trapezium-shaped building, with its four distinctive domes. Leaving her bicycle outside, she took the steps with a deep breath.

'What can I do for you, miss?' The man looked up with interest as Alice walked towards his desk, her heels clipping on the marble floor. He was wearing an army uniform, and the smell of boot polish clouded his aftershave, which was of cloves and lime.

She adjusted the scarf on her neck, pale fingers pressing at the blue flowers stitched into the black fabric.

She spoke in clear, crisp German, emphasising her Berliner roots.

'I have to go back to Germany,' she said.

Stay in touch with

Clare Coombes

For updates, including the release of other books in this series, write to **clarecoombeswriter@gmail.com** to join Clare's mailing list, or visit: **www.clare-coombes.com** Twitter: **coombes_clare**

Clare Coombes lives in Liverpool, UK, where she spends her time writing, reading, researching and editing, tap dancing – and looking after a toddler. She is one half of the Liverpool Editing Company, a publishing consultancy group designed to guide authors through each step of the publishing process. Her commended short stories and novel extracts feature in a number of publications, competitions and journals. Her debut novel, Definitions, was published in 2015 by Bennion Kearney to acclaimed Amazon reviews.

Her wide-ranging non-fiction portfolio comprises everything from art to astrophysics, and her work has been published in a variety of national media outlets, receiving award nominations such as Science News' 'Breakthrough Story of the Year'. She has judged fiction competitions, taught on Creative Writing postgraduate modules and given talks in schools and at high-profile events on writing as a career.

Author's Note

In her author's note for Between Shades of Grey, a book that tells the story of the deportation and genocide of Baltic people during World War Two, Ruta Sepetys has a simple request: 'Please research it. Tell someone.'

This request has stayed with me.

We Are of Dust is based on a true story, one that I researched and decided to retell. The S.S St Louis was a real ship. Although my characters are fictional, they each represent many stories left untold.

By early 1939, the Nazis had closed most of Germany's borders, and many countries had imposed quotas limiting the number of Jewish refugees they would allow in.

On 13 May 1939, more than 900 Jews fled Germany aboard this luxury cruise liner, the S.S St Louis. They hoped to reach Cuba and then travel to the US, but were turned away at Havana. The captain then steered the St Louis towards the Florida coast, but the US authorities also refused it the right to dock, despite direct appeals to President Franklin Roosevelt. Many thought that he too was worried about the potential flood of migrants it could inspire. Canada refused appeals for help too.

In the end, the ship's passengers did not have to go back to Nazi Germany. Instead, Belgium, France, Holland and the UK agreed to take the refugees. But the American Jewish Joint Distribution Committee (JDC) posted a cash guarantee of $500,000 – or $8 million (£4.7m) in today's money – as part of an agreement to cover any associated costs.

So, why am I telling this story? Haven't we heard enough about the Nazis?

I have to tell it because the Nazis are still here.

As Michael Rosen's states in his poem, 'Fascism: I sometimes fear...', they don't arrive in fancy dress worn by 'grotesques and monsters'. Instead, they come in the guise of protecting or saving a country and its people. They come behind the construction of cages for children in Texas; they come in the dire conditions of the refugee camps in Calais; they come in the failed Dubs scheme to accept unaccompanied child refugees into the UK; they were watching as one thousand people drowned in the Mediterranean trying to reach Europe in the first six months of 2018. They think throughout all of this: It's okay, as that is them and this is us. They come to convince us of that, too.

Rosen's poem also makes the point that fascism can arrive as your friend, restoring honour, giving you a job, telling you how great you are – the same empty platitudes that had warped Kurt's adolescence.

I wanted to bring both sides of Nazi Germany together, from those who have been indoctrinated into it, like Kurt; those have turned away from it, as we find with Heinz and Walter's group; to those who have been forced out of it, like Alice and Eli; and how small pockets of resistance existed within children and young people, despite the world around them and everything they have been brought up to believe.

We Are of Dust brings to light how young people manage situations that are out of their control, and the way that love can always be present.

Fascism, I will always fear. But I also know that humanity, love and the will to resist and fight for justice is in all of us. And that is what fascism should always fear.

Q and A with St Louis passenger and Holocaust survivor Herbert Karliner

"What we don't learn will happen again." Herbert Karliner

St Louis passenger Herbert Karliner was 12 when he boarded the ship. He had watched as his family grocery store was destroyed on Kristallnacht and his father was imprisoned in a concentration camp, leading them to flee Germany when he was released. Herbert's parents and sisters, along with two hundred other passengers from the St. Louis, were murdered by the Nazis.

"What we don't learn will happen again. It's essential to retell these stories so that no generation has to go through what we went through. I lost my family for no reason."

What was it like growing up Jewish in Nazi Germany?

At first, it was small things. I wasn't allowed to play on the soccer team anymore. I wanted to join the Hitler Youth because I thought it sounded exciting, but my father told me I couldn't because I was Jewish. I soon saw what they thought of me. They would push me off the pavements and make me walk in the gutter when they past. The violence built up. We were sledging once, and a boy punched my little sister in the face. I hit him back, and that night the Gestapo came for my father and imprisoned him for the night. Then Kristallnacht came. They destroyed our family grocery shop and our home. I remember the synagogue burning. I never went back to school after those attacks, and my parents made plans to leave.

What was life like on the ship?

We had a wonderful trip. We had movies, we had dancing. The food was delicious. I had never seen the Ocean before. I thought it was beautiful. My brother, sisters and me, we were all excited, but my parents were sad. Captain Schröder was a good man. On the ship, we were treated with respect and had rights. We weren't used to that. The captain even took the portrait of Hitler down during the Sabbath Friday night services. However, once the ship started back toward Germany, we got very panicky. Nobody wanted us. Captain Schröder, promised us he would scuttle the ship in British waters rather than return them to Germany, but eventually other countries agreed to take us in.

What happened after the ship?

My family went to France, but we didn't have any money. The Nazis had taken everything and had even charged a tax on anything we sold back in Germany. My parents and sisters were given an apartment in Mirabaud, and my brother and I were in a Children's Welfare Organisation home. I worked in a bakery, and then, when the children's homes were no longer safe, worked on farms under a false identity, and lived in the woods until liberation. I'd had no schooling since I was 12, and I had to learn French – my survival depended on it.

How did you survive?

I feel that I was lucky. I had friends hiding under false names who didn't make it. I watched people get arrested by the Gestapo. One day, a wagon turned up at the children's home. I didn't get on because it was two weeks until my 16th birthday, and there were only taking away those over that age. None of them returned. I later found out that my parents and sisters had died at Auschwitz. I still think about them all the time.

Why did you choose to live in Miami?

It took me nearly a decade to get here after the war, but I promised myself when I was 12-years-old that when I can make it, I'm going to come back and live here. I have only been back to where I lived before the St Louis once. Peiskretscham is now part of Poland. I left after an hour. It was too much. Every morning, I get up and look around Miami and think of how lucky I am to be here.

Acknowledgements

I am indebted to so many amazing people who helped me to write and produce this book. My fantastic editor and business partner Matthew McKeown, of course. There is no one more skilled at developing a plot, revealing key historical details and pointing out a rogue semi-colon. I also want to credit Lee Philpotts of Bodhi Design for the beautiful cover and formatting.

My writing group, Hilary Alexander, Nicola Copeland, Shirley Razbully and Angela Pearsall, who once again believed in a book of mine from the first page and guided me through it. We are a team, and I am always grateful.

The legendary historian, Professor Frank McDonough from Liverpool John Moores University's History Department, for his expert guidance, documents and talks; giving me a real sense of the world I was getting into.

Mike Morris and Writing on the Wall for their continued support and the incredible work they do in helping writers from all backgrounds to get published.

Herbert and Vera Karliner for sharing their stories of survival and hope, and their campaigns for justice and awareness.

Robert Krakow Director of the The SS St. Louis Legacy Project whose mission is to promote greater awareness and dialogue on issues of human rights, immigration and refugee policy.

Philomene Uwamaliya, who fled Rwanda with her family after the genocide in 1994, and has worked tirelessly in support of advancing the rights and well-being of asylum seekers and refugees ever since.

My parents and grandparents for their sense of social justice and standing up for what is right.

And, as always, to my husband and daughter.

Clare Coombes

33198177R00170

Printed in Poland
by Amazon Fulfillment
Poland Sp. z o.o., Wrocław